"*The Ocean Above Me* is an intense and pow____ ____ ____
way and then finding it again in the unlikeliest of places. I found it
moving, thought-provoking, and gripping in equal measure."

—Ian McGuire, *New York Times* bestselling author of
The North Water

"Longtime war journalist Kevin Sites crafts an edge-of-your-seat story
that is part *MacGyver* and part *Perfect Storm* with well-developed and
introspective characters. *The Ocean Above Me* mines the survival skills
Sites honed in real-life war zones with a gripping plot and prose that
hums with humanity."

—Beth Macy, *New York Times* bestselling author of
Dopesick and *Raising Lazarus*

"Kevin Sites's long career in journalism taught him to listen closely to
cries and whispers. He has crafted an epic tale of a man whose life
turns inward. Out of suffering emerges the strongest soul. This story
twists and turns so fast it's like trying to read a book with a four-year-
old flipping the pages. You won't put it down until it's done."

—Bob Dotson, *New York Times* bestselling author of
Make It Memorable

"An unforgettable story of guilt and survival that is also a nail-biting
thriller. . . . Sites has crafted a profound exploration of a war correspondent's dark secret and the toll that holding onto it has taken in his life.
The plot is ingenious and the hero's path to redemption is both stirring
and unique."

—Peter Maass, Los Angeles Times Book Prize–winning author of
Love Thy Neighbor: A Story of War

"Absolutely riveting. Sites grabs you by the throat and pulls you under in chapter one and, you won't resurface until long after this story ends. A profound, heart-pounding journey to the edge of life and death, filled with unique characters who leap off the page. I can't stop thinking about it."
—Richard Murphy, author of
Confessions of a Contractor

"Kevin Sites has produced a richly suspenseful page-turner filled with believable characters and a plot that keeps you hanging on until the very end. The submerged story line speaks gracefully to the lingering trauma and scars from wars long forgotten except by those who were there. Only an accomplished war correspondent like Sites could produce a thriller so unique and genuinely authentic. Once you start reading this book, it's hard to put it down."
—Keith B. Richburg, author of
Out of America: A Black Man Confronts Africa

"Sites's first work of fiction is more terrifying and claustrophobic than his years of reporting from wars. Set in a small space the novel ranges far and wide in the mind of the protagonist. A read in one sitting journey that you will not put down."
—Robert Young Pelton, author of
The World's Most Dangerous Places and *Licensed to Kill*

"Propulsive. . . . Sites intersperses Landon's underwater struggle with the journalist's articles and his interactions with the crew in the days leading up to the storm. These . . . make for engaging character portraits. . . . Landon's commitment to finding a way to the surface will keep readers turning the pages."
—*Publishers Weekly*

"The novel dresses an action thriller's survival story in literary filigree . . . the suspense is sustained to the end."
—*Kirkus Reviews*

THE OCEAN ABOVE ME

ALSO BY KEVIN SITES

Swimming with Warlords:
A Dozen-Year Journey Across
the Afghan War

The Things They Cannot Say:
Stories Soldiers Won't Tell You About
What They've Seen, Done or
Failed to Do in War

In the Hot Zone: One Man, One Year,
Twenty Wars

THE OCEAN ABOVE ME

A NOVEL

KEVIN SITES

HARPER ● PERENNIAL

NEW YORK ● LONDON ● TORONTO ● SYDNEY ● NEW DELHI ● AUCKLAND

HARPER ● PERENNIAL

FIRST HARPER PERENNIAL EDITION PUBLISHED 2024.

Designed by Bonni Leon-Berman

Library of Congress Cataloging-in-Publication Data has been applied for.

ISBN 978-0-06-327829-5 (pbk.)

$PrintCode

For Anita

DEATH BY WATER

Phlebas the Phoenician, a fortnight dead,

Forgot the cry of gulls, and the deep sea swell

And the profit and loss.

A current under sea

Picked his bones in whispers. As he rose and fell

He passed the stages of his age and youth

Entering the whirlpool.

Gentile or Jew

O you who turn the wheel and look to windward,

Consider Phlebas, who was once handsome and tall as you.

—T. S. ELIOT, *THE WASTE LAND*

PART ONE

NIGHT

We live as we dream—alone.

—Joseph Conrad, *Heart of Darkness*

CHAPTER 1

STORM

Philomena rose on the swell of an early-winter sea. A humble, cupped-hand offering to angry gods, 110 gross tons lifted like a 110-pound ballerina. The mid-Atlantic water turning gunmetal gray as it stretched and then clipped into windblown froth. Her outrigger arms, shaken loose from their bindings, struck hard against the deck, hammer to gong, sending a bass current resonating through the ship. At the helm Captain Clarita Esteban allowed herself to glance back, momentarily, wary of the next monster that would crash across the bow. In the loose flapping of the outriggers she saw the skeletal wings of a flightless, heavy-bottomed bird. All velocity, no lift.

"Shrimping 101, Junior," she shouted above the noise of the storm. "Secure the damn outriggers."

She shook her head in disgust, but knew it was no time to school her crew. Junior, the deckhand, ducked away among the five others gathered in the wheelhouse, all dressed in boots and rain slickers, summoned in the middle of the night by the unexpected ferocity of the storm.

They struggled to keep their footing when the arms soared skyward again, slapping against each other as the water disappeared beneath the ship after a moment of zero gravity at the wave's crest. *Philomena*'s bulk, unstoppable on the downward stroke, displaced its weight and more on splashdown, sucking in torrents over the gunwales before washing back out again on the next lift.

"And where the hell's the reporter?" Esteban demanded, once confident they'd all stuck their last dismount without injury.

LUKAS LANDON HAD slept through stormy prelude, woken only now by his nausea. The hot lavender tea the cook had given him, mixed with a teaspoon of a peculiar white powder, had indeed helped him sleep. Too well, it seemed. He climbed down from his top bunk, slothlike, timing his movements with the ship's rise and fall. Pushing himself against the back wall, in a lean-to squat he threaded one leg through his jeans, then the other. He was wearing a mil-spec T-shirt the color of cocoa powder, bought from the mall-size post exchange in Bagram, his thick, green wool sweater pulled over it. The sweater was an ugly pragmatic thing of ropy Celtic weave, a gift from Vanessa, handed to him blank-faced on their last Christmas together. Even in his fuzzy state, Landon noticed that the two bunks below his were empty. Junior and Chuy were above deck already, no doubt, tying things down, battening the hatches or whatever it was deckhands did in rough seas.

Landon looked at his feet and made a tactical decision to peel off the dirty socks he'd worn to bed. Bare feet, he figured, were better for gripping *Philomena*'s lower deck as she pitched and rolled. Plus, if he had to swim tonight, he'd rather his feet be unencumbered by socks or shoes. He shuddered at the thought, considered another almost as scary: the possibility of his MacBook Air falling to the floor and getting smashed to pieces. He reached to the top of his bunk, found it inside his sleeping bag, and stuffed it back into the waterproof black polypropylene shoulder bag where it normally lived on the ship when he wasn't abusing its keyboard. Then he rolled his sleeping bag around it like a burrito and stuffed it all into his duffel bag. He was about to pinch the bag's loops together and clip it shut when he remembered his smartphone. He might need it to grab photos of the crew in action topside. He dug his hand deep into the duffel, retrieving it with just a few sweeps of his hand. He'd double-wrapped it with resealable sandwich bags before they left Port Royal, just in case of a night like this.

He slid the bagged smartphone into the back pocket of his jeans, closed up his duffel again, and rehung it on the bunk's footrail, content that the expensive gear inside was safely insulated from harm. His insides were a different story. His stomach was becoming queasier by the second. Before climbing up to the deck he'd first need to make a pit stop to expel the ornery remnants of what little he'd eaten earlier that evening. It had been choppy when he finally went to bed past midnight after filing his last dispatch, but nothing like this. Landon's innards sloshed from side to side.

The marine toilet was a dark mole hole tucked into the curve of *Philomena*'s bow at the bottom of the ship. To reach it Landon would have to descend a small staircase that led from the closet-size staterooms. While he hated the idea of going deeper into the guts of the ship, better to purge in private, he thought, than embarrass himself in front of the captain and crew. Once done, it would be another short trip up the double-stacked tower with the galley at its base and wheelhouse at its crown.

The distance to the head was a diagonal downward journey of just eight feet. So why did he feel like one of the Flying Wallendas about to cross a tightrope hundreds of feet in the air between skyscrapers? When the sea leveled out, he took a breath and went. He reached the handle of the head's oval metal door in two steps and a shuffle. But as he pushed in against it, he felt a new dread in his stomach. *Philomena* being scooped into the air yet again. Reproach for himself when he realized his feet were too close together. Regret when they were both swept out from under him. He had only a fraction of a second to tuck his chin and brace with his forearms. His body rotated, pig on a spit, exposing his back to the steel jut of steps, and a sudden torque of the ship hammered his spine against them. Even with the discordant storm sounds echoing in that space, Landon could hear the crunchy snap of his number-six rib, and with it an oscillating short-circuit of pain and shock. He would've dwelt there, but he sensed *Philomena* beginning to rise yet again. He scrambled to his knees, pushed open the door to the head, and shut himself inside. This drop was more forgiving than the last, with the ship caught in the slough of a following wave, a gap long enough for him to register the ripping pain in his back and his nausea reaching its peak.

He crab-scrabbled to the lidless bowl of the marine toilet and emptied his guts in a deep, hollowing retch. While that cleared his useless ballast, the muscle contraction around his broken rib ignited a stabbing pain so fierce his eyes watered, forcing him to check the panicked intake of his breath to avoid repeating the torture in reverse. Instead he drew air in wisps, short, shallow, cautiously. He wiped his mouth with the back of his right hand, releasing it from its death squeeze around the rim, adrenaline, fear, and pain still surging across his synapses.

"The glory that was Greece," he whimpered, "and the grandeur that was Rome." Repeated the mantra until it calmed him, but also, unintentionally, distracted himself from the ship's next rising cycle. When it reached its apex, the hangman's trapdoor opened. The downward force folded Landon's left arm. His unsupported weight dropped in a half-meter free fall, his face leading the charge, slamming into the back of the bowl. A flash-bang grenade of white exploded inside his head, then petered out in an ephemera of gray mist and stars. He ran his tongue against his uppers, found both incisors relocated as enamel arrows pointed toward his tonsils. Landon wondered if the next battering would simply finish him off. Oh, that would be merciful. He could see now how people in life-or-death situations decided to just give up. It was manifestly easier to choose less suffering than more. In the lull, he swallowed the blood accumulating in his mouth. It tasted of iron, salt, and defeat. Would he choke on his own teeth with the next gulp of blood? The thought still inchoate, he reached up with his right hand and wiggled them free of their sockets. New pain surged through his septum, but then a moment of pride as he looked at the bloody Chiclets he'd delivered. Pitiful as it was, he upended the cycle of doom by taking action, tucking the teeth into the front pocket of his jeans while his tongue now probed the bloody gap. Maybe a dentist could replant them after it was all over. But that consideration was wiped away by *Philome-na*'s latest ascent.

Landon rolled onto his right side and uncoiled his six-foot frame, pressing his bare feet against the toilet base and his back against the metal curve of the wall. With the tight wedge and his right shoulder to the ground, he hoped his body mass would muffle the shock wave before it reached his broken left rib. He had a million digital magazine descriptions, and he'd read in some lad mag a similar tip on the right body position to survive a sudden elevator drop. Probably nonsense, but he clung to the concept nonetheless. It was that or wait for the ship and the sea to finish him off, a fate he was still fighting against, at least for now. Historically, his optimism had been weak. Any dark prognosis consumed him, rolled him over quickly, conclusively, repeatedly.

The drop never came. At least not the way he expected. He braced, waited for the climb to slow and for the inevitable elevator plunge. But at the peak, the trawler seemed to hover for a moment, and the rumble of the engine went silent, its vibrations still. He felt the hot flash of a new fear. *Philomena* had lost power. Landon raised his head, spat out the stream of blood that had been pooling in his mouth, and returned to his defensive crouch. Then came a massive slam against the ship's starboard flank. The wave's energy raced through the hull, concussing through his back and the contours of his body. His feet slipped as *Philomena* tipped low to port. He pushed harder against the base of the toilet bowl, exerted so much force he'd thought he might displace it from the rivets that held it fast. As the ship's port side swung back up, now dipping to starboard like the low end of a cradle, he relaxed slightly.

Anticipating the next cycle, Landon pushed with his feet again as the boat rocked hard, back to port. But it would make no difference. A bulldozer of water pushed *Philomena* into her portside momentum and did what seemed impossible; it flipped the ship keel up. The momentum pinned his body to the highest point in the room, as if at the top of a roller-coaster loop. But just as quickly as it had spun, the ship's spiraling keel came to a stop. The inverted wheelhouse had found friction like a surfer's hand raking the inside of a wave. With the centrifugal force suddenly cut off, Landon plunged, left side down. This time the pain had color and texture, a searing campfire of orange cracking through every nerve ending. And then . . . nothing. The overloaded machine of Landon's brain shut down.

GIVEN THE CHOICE, he might've preferred that to experiencing what came next. With no forward thrust, the nearly three-ton weight of *Philomena*'s Caterpillar D343 diesel engine became an enormous anchor at the ship's midline. The imbalance of the weight and position dipped the tapered edge of the starboard gunwales like a knife into the surface of the water. The angle of the slice drove the ship downward with such force that it was entirely submerged in seconds. Giant bubbles of air burped out toward the highest point of every opening. The high, shrill whip of the forty-five-knot Force 9 winds that had buffeted it just seconds before vanished. Seawater squeezed through every crevice in the ship's deck, flooding forward from stern to bow. First filled was Philomena's freezer-plate hold, with a six-hundred-box capacity but only two-thirds full of white shrimp. Next the water climbed to the engine room, rising at a steep angle toward the bow and the ship's head, where Landon lay unconscious. With its firehose pressure, the sea penetrated nearly every hollow cavity, purging it of air and creating a cacophony of sounds, the screaks and clicks of metal and wood pushed to near-failure points. Then *Philomena* shuddered. Was finally silent, before it began its fluttering descent to the sandy bottom below.

CHAPTER 2

BITTER SEAS

Sunday, December 16, 2018
Four days before the storm

First in a Globe-Democrat series on South Carolina's beleaguered commercial shrimping industry.

Our features editor Lukas Landon is filing dispatches all this week while aboard the trawler Philomena as her captain and crew make one last run in an attempt to stay solvent at the end of a brutal season.

IMAGE DESCRIPTION: Globe-Democrat reporter Lukas Landon (carrying a duffel bag) requests permission to come aboard the trawler Philomena, docked in Port Royal, South Carolina.

(Globe-Democrat print and digital editions, published 12-16-18.)

BITTER SEAS
Reporter's Notebook: *Going to Sea*
—*Lukas Landon*

Like over 50 million other Americans, I baited a hook and tossed a line in the water a few times last year. But I've never done it commercially or spent any time on a commercial fishing vessel. That changed at the end of this month, when Clarita Esteban, captain of the shrimping trawler Philomena, agreed to let me onboard the ship to document the lives of herself and her crew as they complete their final run of 2018. Full disclosure: it wasn't easy to convince Captain Esteban or my own bosses to agree to the series. With staff cutbacks, my editors were hard-pressed to allow me to report on a single story topic for a full week. But ultimately they understood the integral role shrimping has played in the Lowcountry and the importance of exploring its uncertain future.

As for Clarita Esteban, she's a decorated U.S. Army veteran with multiple deployments to both Iraq and Afghanistan, but a relatively new shrimping captain. Her success or failure and that of her crew now becomes part of the public domain. She bought Philomena only last May, taking a big gamble on an industry that many believe is already in its death throes due to dwindling shrimp populations and competition from Asian seafood farms. Captain Esteban doesn't like the spotlight, and told me as much. But she has allowed me aboard so that you, as the Globe-Democrat audience, can begin to understand both the joys and struggles of the modern seafaring life. This is a time when our excesses have stripped our oceans perilously bare, raising questions about the wisdom and sustainability of commercial fishing overall. While fishing mechanics have changed little in thousands of years and fishing is still done with lines, hooks, nets and boats, all of those tools have become bigger and more efficient in draining the sea of its bounty without allowing the natural cycle of replenishment. Marine scientists fear that if we continue at the present rate, the oceans will be emptied of our main seafood sources as soon as 2050.

So it's through this perilous prism that we begin our adventure; that of a new captain starting over with a mixed crew, working an older boat in an ancient profession during a time of epic change. It's an adventure to be documented both in our paper's regular print version and in the rich media of the digital era, with text dispatches, still photographs, infographics and even audio and video clips posted to the Globe-Democrat website as frequently as I can transmit them over the next week at sea. Welcome aboard.

CHAPTER 3

COUNTDOWN CLOCK

Under the Sea: Day 1

It was the sound that roused him and toppled that first domino of pain. A grotesque squeak and groan of insistent torque; metal being twisted against riveted seams. Disoriented, eyes still closed, Landon felt an aching pressure building in his eardrums. He pinched his nostrils shut and blew out. The Valsalva maneuver, an impressive name for an inelegant method to equalize the pressure of the air trapped inside the cavities in his ears. Instantly he wished he hadn't; the action forced down his diaphragm and puffed out his rib cage like air through a paper noisemaker. He had forgotten the rib again, his hurt coming out as a piteous praycr. Pathetic and mournful. But there was no time to wallow. Other dominoes were falling. The Valsalva had created enough pressure to make his incisor sockets bleed again. He swallowed the blood to clear his mouth. Should've spit. He rose to his knees and vomited, the spasm reigniting the nerve ends of his broken rib. An endless agony feedback loop. He toppled forward like a man in flames, but with a strange soft landing. He vomited again while prone, his extended position reducing bone movement and its follow-on torment. It was then Landon realized he was immersed.

Reluctantly he raised his head and finally opened his eyes. What had he landed in? He was floating on what seemed to be a pool of blood. He pulled himself up, looked around the space more carefully, jogging his memory. He finally remembered that during the storm he'd taken shelter in the marine toilet. The red LED emergency light that had always glowed overhead was now beneath him, illuminating the rising pool of water.

Landon wrapped his arms around himself. He was empty as his adrenaline seeped away, perceiving for the first time the water's chill. With the sleeve of his sweater he wiped away strands of congealed snot, tears, and blood from his face. This was not how he'd imagined his end. He had reasonable expectations it would've been in Afghanistan or Iraq. Not like this—slowly and without dignity inside the crapper of a capsized ship, drowned by a rising pool of putrid water, filthy and stinking of shit, diesel fuel, and his own blood and vomit.

He should give in to this paralyzing self-pity. Who could blame him? His rib was broken, his teeth were smashed out, and he was trapped at the bottom of the sea. He wasn't certain about the last part, but the evidence was there; the constant clearing he needed to do with his ears meant he was below sea level. But how deep? It was likely *Philomena* had come to rest on the ocean floor. Otherwise there would be more movement, even in calm seas. The concept of being trapped in an air bubble in a sunken boat, a too-perfect limbo, created a terrifying cognitive dissonance. Was it really possible that when the ocean flipped *Philomena* like a metal pancake, his detour to the very bottom of the boat had put him in a kind of Goldilocks zone, a "just right" environment that now kept him alive? And if so, for how long? If *Philomena* was on the bottom, it couldn't be too deep. Landon knew from his research in the weeks before coming aboard that the continental shelf in the area extended for almost twenty-five miles. It wasn't like they went down in the Mariana Trench. Shrimp were bottom feeders, and that's where they were netted. If *Philomena* settled shallow enough, he might be able take in a deep breath from his bubble and swim to the surface.

Just imagining that gave him the willies. Thankfully, there was much more to determine first. He recalled one of those childish acronyms from his hostile environment news media training course, visualized the infographic of a traffic signal with colors and corresponding words: red = stop, yellow = think, and green = act. Simple enough. He stopped and focused only on his breathing, slowing down, calming himself. Took a few minutes before moving on to the second step, thinking, taking inventory of his environment. But that calm was interrupted by a violent leftward shift, as if the ship's tower superstructure or outer rail had collapsed under its weight. The movement thrust Landon against the wall. Instinctively he extended his elbow to steady himself and absorb the impact. Instead, he slammed his ulnar nerve, the unaptly named funny bone, against a ridge on its surface that set off shooting stars of stabbing and tingling that inflamed his left forearm, hand, and fingers. He shook the limb, howling murder and mayhem, but was drowned out by an even more terrifying sound: the piercing wail of metal folding in under weight and pressure. Fuck this place that didn't give you thirty seconds to register your latest trauma. At least he wouldn't become complacent, stew in the horrible wonder of it all. He thought of the yellow and green of the traffic signal. He needed to think, and then he needed to act.

Landon appreciated that science's own countdown clock was determining precisely how long he might last in this place. His mother had been a high school physics teacher, after all, though for him the hard sciences never came easy. Perhaps more fortuitously in his current circumstances, he'd trained in recreational scuba and dived frequently to offset the stress of reporting inside war zones. He had learned, for instance, that atmospheric pressure at sea level was a little less than 15 psi, or pounds per square inch, and was considered one atmosphere. Every thirty-three feet down was considered another atmosphere and added more pressure. At one hundred feet down there would be nearly 45 psi on whatever happened to be under it. Recreational divers breathing compressed air in scuba tanks routinely went to that depth or past it. But because of the combined water and atmospheric pressure on their bodies, nitrogen, which makes up the majority of breathable air, would accumulate in their body tissues. It needed to be released progressively with lessening pressure from a gradual ascent to the surface. Otherwise the nitrogen gas could bubble out all at once, similar to popping the top on a can of shaken soda. This painful and potentially deadly condition was formally known as decompression sickness, but casually as "the bends," because of what it did to a diver experiencing it.

Landon studied his surroundings. The space was claustrophobic, only slightly larger than a hallway coat closet. But because the air inside was underwater, it was compressed, the same way a small scuba tank could hold about an hour's worth of air with calm breathing. He couldn't recall the exact wording of Boyle's law, but he remembered the overall point: as the pressure on a gas increased, the volume of that gas decreased. In his case, if the volume of air in his bubble was a hundred cubic feet at sea level, based on Boyle's law it would shrink to a quarter of that at a hundred feet down. But while the volume became smaller, the oxygen would become denser. His bubble might not look like much, but the pressure of the surrounding water packed it with a high concentration of oxygen. How long that oxygen would last would be the critical factor in whether he should hunker down and wait for rescue or try to make it to the surface. Having options was good, but the clock was ticking. The longer he stayed in his bubble, the greater the nitrogen saturation of his tissues and the higher probability of getting bent if he made a break for the surface. And while his environment might be oxygen-dense at the moment, Landon was distressed by the thought that with every exhale he was poisoning it with carbon dioxide, the waste product of his own breathing.

At some point, there would be more CO_2 than O_2, and his breathing would become ineffective; he'd suffocate. There would be warning signs: shaky hands, dizziness, disorientation, maybe even hallucinations. Thankfully, none of that yet. But he was beginning to feel both cold and tired as his adrenaline continued to wash out. Standing hip deep in the water for much longer would lead to hypothermia. He needed to stay awake and find a way to get himself above the water. That was the physical priority. Tops on the mental side was to short-circuit the obsession of new fears that flooded over him.

What if the ship somehow righted itself underwater? The last sudden movement suggested it could. The inverted bow was currently a primitive diving bell, but a powerful surge could tip it upright, releasing a thousand silver spheres like iridescent jellyfish scurrying to the surface, extinguishing his life-giving bubble and leaving him to die. He wondered too how long the red LED light might last, submerged. Being trapped in total darkness at the bottom of the sea was not something he wanted to ponder. But his scattered thoughts were chimps in a boundary war, charging, screeching, banging against each other, all heedlessly retreating back to the event itself. It either defied all physical laws or obeyed them with exactness that a 110-ton ocean trawler could be picked up by the sea and dropped back down at such a sharp, precise angle that it would disappear as completely as if devoured by the water itself. *Philomena* hadn't so much sunk as vanished. And while he was here alive, trapped in the head, what had happened to Captain Esteban and the rest of the crew? Hard to imagine how anyone else might've survived.

The emptiness was about to overtake Landon when he leaned back against the door and felt a pinch on the small of his back. His smartphone. He pulled it up to get a closer look, resigned to finding it swimming in its plastic baggie like a carnival goldfish. Instead, the brightness of the screen in the dark room reduced the dilation of his pupils. It was still warm and glowing, activated by his touch. The double sandwich bags, meant only to repel the water, had fortunately been waterproof in the few inches and few minutes they'd been submerged. A lost soulmate—he brought it to his mouth and kissed the screen. The touch of his swollen lips reminded him that while he still had light, temporarily, he no longer had front teeth. While he'd hoped the phone would also tell him how long he'd been out, the screen read July 5, 2000, the time capacitor either damaged or reset in his fall enough to be wrong by eighteen years and five months. Hopefully everything else was still working.

Keeping the inner bag sealed, he pulled open the outer one and slid in a finger to activate the flashlight app on his touchscreen. It instantly came to life like a tiny floodlight. He panned around to get a better look at the space. The toilet bowl was now a stumpy porcelain stalactite, the small sink another, both growing out of the ceiling of his steel cave. And there was something else he hadn't noticed before: cupboards of some type. Latched oval doors on either side of the toilet, well above the waterline. He'd investigate that further, but the journalist in him felt compelled to report what had happened while his phone still had a significant charge. He wasn't sure who, if anyone, would ever see it, but this was his muscle memory as a reporter, an attempt to make sense of the trauma that had enveloped him and maybe even exert a modicum of control. Saying things out loud, he knew, would help shake him out of the woozy surrealism that dominated and paralyzed his brain. He also knew, if nothing else, that this could be his final testament.

He reached inside the outer baggie again, touched the small camera icon, flipped it to the selfie mode, touched record, and held it at bent arm's length. His image in the viewscreen surprised and disheartened him: the pummeled loser of a particularly vicious MMA fight, face swollen, bloodstains around his nose and mouth, hair wet and matted to his head. His hypertropia, a slight upward tilt of his right eye, was a genetic insult rather than injury, but it added to the effect. From below, the red LED gave a nuclear-bunker patina to the atmosphere. Had he been making a doomsday thriller, he couldn't have set it up any better. Landon felt the blood building up in his mouth again, and had no choice but to spit it out before he started.

"Sorry," he said, wiping with his sleeve and looking back up into the camera lens. The sound of his own voice caught him off guard, tremulous and feeble. The fragile timbre of someone who might be in his mid-eighties, not his mid-forties. He had a slight lisp now, no more top incisors for his tongue to push off against. He stopped, swallowed, readjusted the camera:

"This is Lukas Landon." He took a deep breath, resolved to project more, speak from his diaphragm. "I'm a reporter for the *Charleston Globe-Democrat*. I was on the shrimping boat *Philomena* out of Port Royal, South Carolina, when some weather came up overnight. It was rough when I went to bed, but nothing terrible on the radar, nothing anyone was really expecting." He paused, composed himself. "Captain Esteban decided we were going to make one last run before coming back to Port Royal. We were motoring farther southeast into deeper water. A better spot so the crew would be ready to fish at dawn." He halted. "But out of nowhere, the sea started boiling. It got so rough I decided to leave the bunkroom and go topside to see what was going on, but I had to use the head first. I thought it was going to be a quick stop, but that's when everything went sideways. I got tossed on my back, and then the waves," he trailed off, shook his head. "Their power, I've never felt anything like that in nature before." He broke off, looked around, started again. "I think we're actually underwater. Or at least I am. Not sure about the rest of the crew because I'm still trapped here, in the head." He looked behind him, positioned the camera to show the inverted toilet bowl.

"I'm pretty certain we're upside down because it wasn't like that when I first got here. Wish I knew more about Captain Esteban and the others. Maybe they were able to abandon ship before we flipped. Yeah, they were already topside," he said, trying to convince himself. "I'm sure they were wearing their PFDs. Captain Esteban would've sent out an SOS with *Phil*'s last known coordinates. I'm sure they all got picked up by some Coast Guard rescue boat and are wrapped in big fluffy towels and eating hot soup right now. Chuy's probably complaining about the food, Emmanuel is trying to dry the pages of his little black notebook, Junior's whittling something, Olveda's scratching out a new poem from what happened. And I'm certain that Lorenzo and the captain are helping the Coast Guard find where the ship went down." Landon took in a big breath, nodded. "And to find me. They wouldn't leave me down here. I mean, I wasn't part of the crew or anything, but I think they were okay with me. At least they wouldn't want this for me. Not to die here, like this. Alone."

His voice caught on the last word. He stopped, projected past it. "The situation is not good, but could be worse. This head is at the bow of the ship, and it captured an air bubble. Not a big one, as you can see." He panned the camera around again. "But better than nothing. The water level hasn't risen much in the last half hour or so. Just at my waist now."

He dipped the camera from his face to the water. He paused, spit blood again, then continued. "I haven't heard anyone talking or moving or anything—except the ship, that is. There's been some shifting or set-tling. Whatever you call it. I call it scary shit." Landon steadied himself within the camera image after noticing his hand shaking slightly. He stopped, closed his eyes, then back to the camera. "Honestly, I am pretty scared. I don't know what to do."

Landon's voice had begun to crack, and he felt himself filling with despair. He fought it back, tried to finish quickly before it could overtake him. "Man, this is not what I expected. Over the years, I wasn't really afraid of dying. But now, for some reason, when the opportunity has so perfectly presented itself—I don't want to die. Maybe that's the way it is. We're all so brave in our minds, ready to embrace it, go down like tough guys, but when we're face-to-face with the reaper, we crap our pants."

He let out a short snicker. "What I do know is that I want to live. I don't know why, I just do. Maybe because I'm just afraid to die." He pinched up his face, thinking of what to say next. "But if I don't get out, maybe this phone can be a record, you know, like an airplane's black box of what happened down here. My final report."

Landon was about to switch off the recording, but he stopped. "I wish I could send this to you now, so you could hear me, so you could send someone to help." He sighed. "But that's impossible. Can't even get four bars when I'm in downtown Charleston, sure as hell won't get any-thing from the ocean floor. Maybe I should've thought of that before now." He tilted the phone in his hand, looking down on it. "Used this for more than just work. Called my mom every once in a while, my sister . . . Vanessa. But that was me. That is me," he corrected. "Always other stuff to do." He shook his head, disgusted with himself. "Look at me now, at the bottom of the sea feeling all fragile and mortal, whining and sniveling for some kind of last-minute forgiveness or redemption."

He paused long enough to seem like he was done, but then looked up again. "That always works out well, doesn't it?" Sarcasm bitter in his voice. He pressed the red button and ended the recording. Then he brought up the stopwatch app on his phone and activated it; 00.01.62 it read, number fractions and seconds whizzing by. He resolved to let it keep running; the app used almost no power, he knew, having absent-mindedly left it on for days in the past. He didn't know how long he'd been down there, but at least now he could keep track of how long it would be.

CHAPTER 4

PHILOMENA

Sunday, December 16, 2018
Four days before the storm

Captain Esteban had invited Landon to watch from the wheelhouse as they set out from Port Royal to the open sea. She dressed in a threadbare olive-green M-65 military field jacket pulled over a white waffle-knit shirt and jeans. Her hair was a no-nonsense cut, shorn only about an inch from her scalp but still long enough to touch the collar of her coat. The captain scanned the horizon, hands at ten and two on the wheel as *Philomena* pushed back against the channel waters. She knew the simple crossing could be as unforgiving as any desert highway in Iraq. But the enemy here was human error: a collision, grounding, or some other disaster in which she might lose not only her ship but also the command and respect of her crew. Her time at war had taught her to stay calm amid chaos, to summon deep concentration almost effortlessly during challenging moments. This, she understood, was one of those moments—not just performing the task she'd done so many times before, but doing it while a reporter watched and recorded every move. But even the deep *whump, whump, whump* of a Marine CH-53E Super Stallion helicopter from Parris Island didn't trigger a wash of memory overload, didn't make her break with the present. She was here. Nowhere else.

LANDON WAS GRATEFUL for her initial silence. The rumble of the engine and rhythmic heaving of the ship's bow through the water was calming, hypnotic even. He regarded the moment, then composed some observations in a rectangular, spiral-bound reporter's notebook:

> Through a thick and pitted windscreen Captain Clarita Esteban clocks her surroundings, searching for danger, perhaps as she did behind the wheel of her wrecker in Iraq. But now the desert has become an ocean, one she hopes will sustain her in this second act of her life. The ship's glass through which Esteban sees this new beginning is so splattered with a diaphanous layer of recently dead winged insects that, in the orange glow of dusk, the sections appear as slabs of amber already holding all the memories of the world—with little space for even one more.

He read it over. Grinned, knowing it was too precious. Just another darling to kill in the midnight massacres of his editing. Caught up in his meanderings, Landon didn't see they had already cleared the channel and were now coming into open water. Captain Esteban brought the lumbering craft up to nine knots, near its maximum cruising speed. She broke the silence, more willing to engage now that the intensity of that early port-to-ocean passage was finished.

"You wanna know a little story about this ship?" she asked.

Landon thought about recording audio with his smartphone, but decided it was too early for that much tech. The captain had hardly been won over yet. A rapport built from gradual trust would be sturdier over the long run. He raised his pen and notepad instead. She nodded her assent.

"She used to be registered in Florida, not just a shrimper though. Commercial fishing. Went after 'bout anything that swims. Bought new in '76 by a guy named Miguel Bustamante, Cuban out of Miami. Fled like a lot of middle-class folks after the revolution. Hated Castro, because he and his family had to leave everything behind and start over. But after sixteen years scraping and saving, they went all in. This was a top-of-the-line high-speed girl at that time." Esteban chuckled. Landon took notes without breaking eye contact, a critical skill he'd learned on his first newspaper job, before ever leaving Ohio.

"When it came time to christen her," she continued, "well, that was easy. He chose *Philomena*. When they left Cuba, one of the few possessions his wife Flora took was a small statuette of Santa Philomena, one of the patron saints of lost causes."

Landon glanced above the starboard window, where a holy card with the image of Santa Philomena was taped. She was depicted as a kneeling young maiden in a stone-walled dungeon, crowned in roses and a golden halo. In one hand she held a lily, a sign of purity. In the other, the tools of her torture: an arrow, a flail, and an anchor.

"So it was sentimental?" Landon asked, still staring at the card. "Reminded them of home, the hardships they had to overcome?"

"You'd think. Turns out Santa Philomena was their mule."

Landon stopped writing. "Drugs?"

"Damn, Landon. You suck at guessing. Maybe just listen," she teased.

"Right after they reached the shores of Miami and got political asylum, Flora smashed that thing on the sidewalk and pulled out a big wad of Benjamins, a hundred or more. She'd been trading Cuban pesos for dollars as soon as ol' Fidel started to make some headway. Then—get this—she stuffed them up *Philomena*'s hollow ass. Ten thousand US dollars! It was a better stake than most smuggled out. That money got them started with a small boat, then a bigger one, and then, eventually"—she made a sweeping gesture with one hand—"something big enough to name, our girl here. They had a whole fleet of trawlers before they were done, apparently. Retired rich as Rockefellers."

Landon used the tip of his pen to scratch a mosquito bite, but he froze when *Philomena*'s Cat D343 engine belched loudly under their feet and she settled back momentarily into the wheat-brown water. He followed the captain's eyes as they darted to the temperature gauge to the left on the wheelhouse console. The gauge needle had spiked into the red, and for a beat it held there before dropping back into normal range. While the captain's face betrayed nothing, Landon picked up on her body language: a contraction of her shoulders, the tensing of her hands on the wheel until the brief incident played itself out. He caught himself before asking what in sea-sputter-fuck was that. He knew to file it away, save it for another time. This early he needed to be a welcome collaborator, not a muckraking ass-ripper pouncing on every wobble and warble in the operation.

"And how do you know all this?" he asked. "The provenance of a boat more than forty years old?"

Landon sensed Captain Esteban scan him warily. Perhaps she had done her own research on him. Discovered something that gave her pause?

"Now, that's the story I was fixing to tell you about," she said with enthusiasm.

"That wasn't the story?"

She shook her head. "Just the prologue. The story is that four years after buying her and making bank in the plentiful waters off South Florida, Bustamante took *Philomena* farther south, to Cuba."

Landon thought for a moment, then got it. "The Mariel boatlift?"

"Getting better at that guessing game, I see," she acknowledged with a tilt of her head. "Bustamante made five or six runs with *Philomena* between Mariel Harbor and Miami. Right at the beginning, before things got really crazy. Brought near a thousand Cubans back to Miami. The Phil was so overloaded with bodies, she almost sank a couple times in weather. Did it all for free, felt it was his duty."

"Again, how do you know all this?" Landon asked. She paused, shook out her legs, stiff from standing, and leaned back into the worn vinyl of the captain's chair.

"Because Enzo was one of them," she said, finally. Landon noted her affectionate abbreviation of the first mate's name. "Told you it was a story. He was just eight at the time, and he still remembers sitting on the bow as the Miami skyline came into view."

"So," Landon probed, "Lorenzo had a wave of nostalgia and sought out *Philomena* after all these years?"

Captain Esteban looked at her GPS readings, showing they were farther out to sea. "Nah. Enzo doesn't like to live in the past. It was just good timing. He'd had steady work on an even older trawler down in Miami, kept him crazy busy. Both he and Chuy. But the owner finally cashed out. So old he sold it for scrap. And I told you early on, I was having some trouble mounting a crew after I got title. Put some ads for an engineer/mate in some maritime papers up and down the coast. Surprised the heck out of me to get a call from Enzo. Twelve years on fishing boats and still willing to work with me. Said he'd bring along his younger cousin too, that he was a little shit, but worked hard and he'd keep him in line. Figured I'd be open to that since he'd also heard I was crewing up with some of my own too."

"All this because he knew you bought *Philomena*?" Landon asked.

"Some. Don't think that was all of it. You'll have to ask him yourself. But you'll need to do that later," she said. She pulled back on the throttle lever, cutting the engine to a crawl. "Time to catch some shrimp."

CHAPTER 5

HAMMOCK

Under the Sea: Day 1

When Landon finished the personal recording on his smartphone, he noticed that the water level had risen from his hips to his waist. His space was becoming smaller, his oxygen pocket depleting. He felt the squeeze of animal panic as the walls bent inward. He sucked air in deep gulps. He'd hyperventilate if he didn't slow down. Maybe pass out. His mantra wasn't working; nothing calmed him. Instead his head, like the room, was flooding—one with water, the other with a miasma of disturbing thoughts. One concerned the painting *Jonah and the Whale* by Pieter Lastman, a seventeenth-century Dutch master and teacher to Rembrandt, that he'd seen at a museum in Dusseldorf during one of his month-long breaks from reporting in Iraq. The painting depicted a sensational moment from Old Testament lore when reluctant prophet Jonah is disgorged from the belly of a whale after what must've been three wildly disconcerting days and nights there. Landon had been mesmerized by the work, staring at it until the museum closed. It featured a grotesque, baroque-looking sea creature vomiting a horrified Jonah, arms and legs akimbo. But an unusual detail connected the work to Landon. The artist had rendered Jonah's right eye locked upward, underscored by the white of his sclera. The artist had no doubt intended on capturing Jonah's surprise at God's bizarre plan to goad him into prophetdom by way of a whale's (incomplete) digestive cycle. But in doing so, Lastman had also mirrored Landon's own permanent countenance. Now Landon too found himself in the belly of a beast. So what did God want to coerce from him?

Real memories also flitted through his hippocampus, like that time in Karbala. It was late 2003. The US invasion of Iraq was over, and the occupation had begun. Landon, embedded with an army mechanized cavalry unit, had witnessed six US soldiers drown in the middle of a desert. Their heavily armored Bradley troop carrier had been threading a narrow path between two irrigation channels at night. The driver miscalculated, and the $3 million, thirty-ton vehicle slipped off the embankment and tumbled upside down into the water. The gunner and vehicle commander were crushed in the rollover, while the driver made it out through the front hatch. But the metal rear drop gate, where the infantry soldiers entered and exited, was wedged into the mud. Stagnant water filled the interior. It took twenty minutes to winch the Bradley out, wheels up. Landon had been in the same convoy farther back. After the rear hatch on the Bradley was blown, a soldier shone a flashlight inside. They were all still belted and inverted in the metal hollow of the troop carrier; two rows with three soldiers on each side, arms hanging below them as if they were trying to surrender, rivulets of muddy irrigation water running down their fingertips and dripping onto the vehicle's steel-plated ceiling. Their faces, Landon recalled, were pale but calm now that their war was over. They were all young, and Landon imagined them as high school students on summer vacation, riding the Mean Streak at the Cedar Point Amusement Park as he had, screaming and laughing with their hands in the air. That was where they should've been. Not dead in an irrigation ditch killed in accidental violence so overwhelming no one had been able to pop the quick-release buttons on their safety harnesses. But Landon felt the worst for the driver, who sat on the edge of the ditch, soaked and shivering, being examined by a medic who yelled for someone to get a blanket. How many times in the years ahead, he wondered, would that young soldier wish he had not given in to his survival instinct but stayed inside with his comrades? He was just a boy, robbed of the glory he had been promised, confused and shamed by his desire to stay alive. Collateral damage.

All this imagery of death, this endless fear feedback loop, was just Landon walking himself off another psychological cliff. It had to stop. Finally he ratcheted the nerve endings of his broken rib with a forced cough, and the pain changed the subject, bringing focus.

Now that he had his own attention back, he tried the mantra again. "The glory that was Greece, and the grandeur that was Rome. The glory that was Greece, and the grandeur that was Rome. The glory that was Greece, and the grandeur that was Rome." *There we go, that's better.* The repeated alliterative sentence from Poe's "To Helen" earwormed its way into his mind from his first reading in high school and was now and forever his audible talisman. Vanessa had tried to reroute him instead toward her mindful breathing techniques for yoga. But like most things she tried with Landon, she'd only been half successful. He kept his mantra, but relied on her method as a follow-on for particularly stressful situations. He used it now, trying to wrap his head around his new undersea reality. He breathed in through his nose and out through his mouth, counting to four each time. He continued until the only sound was the slight whistle of the intake through his deviated septum; the only sound that mattered here. With each breath he also gathered the humid stench of the place, like the bracing rot of a passing garbage truck. It smelled of excrement and desperation. His rib ached, and his gums throbbed in the hollow where his teeth had been. He tried to concentrate his mind on his breath, away from the pain, but it was insistent.

The glory that was Greece, and the grandeur that was Rome . . .

It took time, but he finally succeeded in pushing back against the tightening vise of panic. To stay calm, he needed to force himself to see the space in a way that might help him survive, the way Vanessa had looked at things. He imagined her telling him to see the head as a sanctuary instead of a tomb. There was always hopeful wisdom in her way of thinking, the teacher in her gently leading him down the right path. So why, he wondered, had he so consistently rejected it until now? That answer would have to wait. More important was what she would say if she were beside him now. She would reassure him in her calm, kind voice that the walls weren't closing in on him. They were keeping the water out and protecting his air supply. And no, he was not an unlucky fool trapped in an upside-down shitter. He was a fortunate survivor ensconced in his own personal diving bell.

He was playing mind games with himself, but it was essential. He knew this because not just Vanessa but also Viktor Frankl had told him as much. Purpose was the thin membrane that could keep you alive. In December 2004, after a three-month reporting deployment to Iraq in which he was still digesting his experiences in Ramadi and Fallujah, he wasn't ready to go home, even though he'd planned to rotate out for the Christmas holidays. Everything still felt raw, unprocessed. He wasn't sure how to explain it to himself, let alone Vanessa or his family and friends. In Dubai, last minute, he changed his flight destination from Atlanta to Tel Aviv.

It had been a gut-punch to Vanessa, who was mute with anger, laying the first rows of brick in the wall that one day neither of them would be able to surmount. Landon understood the pain he had seeded and countered it by stocking up. He bought a bottle of Maker's Mark and of Stolichnaya at the duty-free shop before boarding, and after he landed, a copy of Frankl's *Man's Search for Meaning* at Ben Gurion, probably the only airport bookstore in the world with that book on the shelves. Armed with his purchases, he took a taxi to the Crown Plaza on the beach and checked in with what some might consider mutually exclusive goals of minor enlightenment and major inebriation. Landon pursued an ambitious alcohol intake comprised of a thermos of vodka and tonic during the day at the beach and the Maker's at night on the balcony. Perhaps because of that, Frankl's documentation of his experiences in a World War II German concentration camp found deep emotional resonance in Landon. In him such things were not always welcome, but in that moment he was an eager pupil, desperate to decode the moral crises that beset him and quell his festering guilt.

Because Frankl was trained as a neurologist and psychiatrist, he, perhaps better than most, was able to devise a construct that helped make sense of the suffering perpetrated in the Nazi death camps. Landon remembered sitting up from his lounger on Hilton Beach, highlighting passages in the book in between slugs from his thermos and watching locals surf the nearby reef break. The book contained many profound thoughts, but the vodka had made nearly every printed word revelatory. By the time he was done, the thin volume was awash in yellow.

The thesis, however, was clear, simple, and insoluble: to survive the worst hardship and misery, you needed a purpose, a reason to live. To Frankl that purpose was love, the thought of seeing his wife again. Purpose wasn't Landon's problem. He'd always known his: telling others' stories. But he'd betrayed this purpose in Iraq, and blood had been shed. So now what was he to do? The answer wasn't in Frankl's footnotes or anywhere else.

His immediate purpose was to move out of the water, but how? Landon stood on the tips of his numb toes, reached to his left to slide back the door latch on one of the cupboards. He activated his phone's flashlight app and looked inside. The cupboard was the height and width of a steam radiator, with a single shelf. Tangled at the bottom were three orange life vests, old-fashioned horse-collars with white cotton straps. The foam was hard and crumbly inside the fabric, signs of dry rot. Still, Landon was encouraged. He could sit on them or wrap them around his water-logged legs for warmth. He piled them to one side and turned his head so he could reach farther back into the recesses of the bin. The twisting shifted the ends of his broken rib, forcing out of him a sorrowful whimper. He had to move more slowly, deliberately, knowing that a cough or sneeze could bring him to the point of tears. This time he held his body rigid as his fingers felt around, finally landing on a small, fibrous coil. He pulled it out. A bight of white nylon rope. Probably had been used to set a small marker buoy. Landon reached in one more time, swept the space, and found it empty. He switched his attention to the bin on the right, opened it, and found another two life preservers, same condition as the others. Again Landon swept the bottom of the cubby with his hands, his fingers brushing across something thick and coarse. He swept it forward into his eyeline, excited to see that it was a thick gray blanket. It was tied in a roll with a loop of twine, cowboy style. The blanket was quilted with heavy stitching similar to those used by moving companies to protect furniture during transport. By its weight, this one felt like it had something wound inside it. He unrolled the blanket, careful not to let the ends dip into the water, then pulled it from the darkness of the bin to get a closer look. It was a magazine wrapped around—he pulled it open—two tallboy cans of Cobra Malt Liquor. Still full! He was so thirsty it took all his willpower not to pop both open and guzzle them straight down. He shifted his gaze to the magazine, flattened the rolled edges of the smudged glossy stock. The masthead read "Jizz" in bold black lettering, and the cover photo featured the kind of second-string pole talent that populated some of the seedier titty bars in the outer boroughs of the Lowcountry. Landon didn't think they even made magazines like this anymore, what with the internet handling all the heavy lifting in the self-gratification arena. Some connoisseurs still liked their porn analogue, he guessed. And, the beer stash was a convincing sign of a pro drinker. Landon had his suspicions of who had tucked these things away. But, regardless, all three items, beer, blanket, and porn, raised his spirits. He switched his smartphone to camera mode, touched the red video record button, and panned over his collected treasures, narrating in an exaggerated Texas twang.

"Five circa 1970 O-ranj personal life preservers; one length white nie-lon rope; one gray coast guard-ishoo stitched blanket; two extra-large cans of malt likker; one well-thumbed porn-O-graffick magazine. Hell, a fella could have a pretty good time in Vegas with all this." He sniggered at his *Dr. Strangelove* riff, wondering who it had been for. Never mind, it felt good to break the stress, even fleetingly. And now, thank you, Victor Frankl, he had a purpose. Laughing, feeling human again, was a big part of the work of surviving. Means and end. Just like the sign over the gates of Auschwitz that had falsely entreated ARBEIT MACHT

FREI, "Work sets you free." Landon had visited there, impressed to learn that the Auschwitz prisoners forced to make the sign had turned the "B" upside down. A tiny but enduring act of defiance. There was purpose in that too, Landon imagined. It was time to get out of the water.

The stink of fuel, stomach acid, urine, and feces that had flowed back down the anemic marine toilet's pipes after the capsize made Landon want to retch again. His senses were becoming more acute as his fight-or-flight response began to wind down. He felt the pain of the violence his body had absorbed in the sinking, but even worse, he felt the cold. Because water was so much denser than air, it displaced body heat twenty times faster. He had to get above the waterline, or he'd lose his ability to regulate his own temperature. He looked around. There was no ledge or indentation he could use to push himself higher. He could use the life preservers to insulate his legs, but half his body would still be underwater. He looked between the bins and then got an idea.

He reached into the right bin and found the gray wool blanket. He unrolled it and pulled one corner diagonally across to the opposite corner, creating an isosceles triangle. He knotted the triangle's three corners. Next he took the coil of nylon rope and pulled apart the braids, making three even lengths of about five feet each. Landon tied slip-knots at one end of the lengths and looped them around the base of the knots he'd made in the blanket, using them as stoppers for the rope. On the other ends he tied bowlines, which created loops about the diameter of a paper cup. Landon threaded a bight of each rope strand through the bowline, turning them into lassos. He placed the lassos at the wide ends of the blanket's triangle over each of the oval door bins at their hinges, and then closed and latched them with the knot pinched inside. The final lasso, from the tip of the triangle, he looped around the base of the upside-down marine toilet, cinching it tight and pulling out the slack in the blanket, which was now suspended between three points. Resting his elbows in the base, he pushed down, slowly lifting his body out of the water. He grinned at his own ingenuity.

But then the edge of the oval door on the right began to pull away from the bin opening. The knot slipped under Landon's weight, dropping him into the water. The fall jarred his broken rib, setting off an intense torment. He stayed motionless until it finally subsided, then tried again, pushing the knots back toward the hinge points of the door frames and latching them shut. This time they held. He had choked up on the blanket knots enough to keep the base taut even when he was in it, elevating him above the water by eight inches. It wasn't much, but it got his body out of the wet and cold.

"I made a hammock," he said quietly, in disbelief. Then, defiantly, he said, "I'm Bear fucking Grylls!" He used his bare feet to push out the point attached to the toilet, creating a larger surface area for him to recline. Vanessa might even be impressed. He smiled at the thought. He hadn't been very handy around the house when they were together. In fact she'd laughed at him once after studying his Home Depot receipt and discovering that he'd spent nearly $100 on a shiny leather tool belt, then filled it with twenty dollars' worth of crap tools. Yet he'd made the hammock without using any tools at all aside from his own ingenuity.

Landon got back into the water, opened up one bin at a time, and piled up all the treasures from inside onto the blanket. First, he loaded up the five life vests, then the magazine, the beers, and finally his smartphone, sealed in its plastic baggies. Then he slid the knots back toward the hinges, shut the oval doors, and pushed their metal latches closed again. With all his worldly possessions now within arm's reach, he wouldn't need to open the bins again and keep readjusting the ropes of his platform. Carefully he climbed back into his hammock, holding for a moment to let the water drain from the legs of his jeans. Once slung inside, he stretched out, positioning the life vests around him, making a nest of sorts to both cushion and warm himself. He placed each of the beer cans inside one of the vest neck holes—their own insulated koozies, though not really necessary this far from the warmth of the sun. The beer continued to tempt him. He was already parched, but thought it better to wait, ration it carefully. As it was his only source of potable water.

Landon imagined dying of thirst would be even more agonizing than drowning. He'd read from accounts of shipwreck survivors that extreme thirst could become so excruciating some experienced psychotic breaks—a terrible torture as kidneys and other vital organs began shutting down, signaling the slow march to death. But Landon had other reasons to be cautious about rationing his beer. He'd read once in a *Men's Health* article that the lower atmospheric pressure at altitude or flying on a plane could speed up and amplify alcohol's intoxicating effects, because oxygen levels at higher altitudes are already lower, meaning less O_2 in the brain. Maybe that explained all the bad behavior by so many air passengers, he mused. But what about the higher atmospheric pressure at depth—and breathing a dense concentration of oxygen as he had been? He puzzled over this problem. Would it offer protection, slowing the circulation of alcohol in his bloodstream, or would it compound it? He simply couldn't risk it—until thirst forced him to drink. He needed full command of his wits, something he wasn't certain he had even now. The final argument for not drinking yet was both physiological and psychological. It would speed his dehydration further by making him urinate. He wasn't eager to add to the stink of the growing cesspool swirling about him. He'd also been dry for the month prior to coming aboard *Philomena*. He had gotten past the cravings, felt better in the mornings, and enjoyed increased clarity in his thinking. It was nice not to fight through the nausea and muddled mind of his typical waking hours. So the thought of drinking alcohol again nagged at him, despite the extremity of his circumstances. He sat back and propped the magazine on his chest. He held it up for a moment, thinking that Junior had probably been in a similar position on *Philomena*: beers on either side—this just the last of a six-pack stash—spank rag in his hands, but on top of the toilet instead of underneath it. He silently thanked Junior for his preparation and foresight. The beer cans were intact and the magazine dry. Landon looked at his phone in the plastic bag. He needed to preserve the battery, and this meant not only limiting his use but keeping it from the cold. He tore away the magazine's cover. Same with the next page and two more after that. He wrapped the magazine pages around his phone, as if he were wrapping a birthday present, then placed the smartphone back in its bags and sealed them shut. He looked at the remaining pages of the magazine and then began tearing them off one by one, balling each up, stuffing them inside his sweater sleeves.

"Thank you for your service, ladies," he said out loud, cracking himself up for what he'd been reduced to doing.

He tucked the sweater's hem into the waistband of his jeans, pulled open the neck, and filled it in with more balled-up magazine pages. The paper was scratchy against his skin, but then the warming insulation outweighed the discomfort. By the time he was done, Landon felt like a Halloween scarecrow stuffed with leaves and grass clippings and propped up on the front lawn. He was sure he looked like one, especially with his missing teeth. He nestled back in his makeshift hammock. Now that he was out of the water and warming up, his focus shifted away from the cold and back to the pain. His rib stabbed and ached, and his facial contusions were swelling fast. Weirdly, the sockets where his incisors had been throbbed in time with his heartbeat. Mother of madness! He was a garbage piñata stuffed with porn and appropriately suspended beneath a toilet. If he didn't make it out alive, would those who found him think him resourceful or batshit bananas? Like it mattered.

CHAPTER 6

WHITE GOLD

Second in a Globe-Democrat series on South Carolina's beleaguered commercial shrimping industry.

Our features editor Lukas Landon is filing dispatches all this week while aboard the trawler Philomena as her captain and crew make one last run in an attempt to stay solvent at the end of a brutal season. (Globe-Democrat print and digital editions, published 12-17-18.)

BITTER SEAS
Working Together?

In war, Clarita Esteban's orders were law. But at sea, nature and shrimping crews don't always comply with the chain of command.
—*Lukas Landon*

Captain Clarita Esteban called it quits at half past noon as the hauls got lighter with every sweep. Floyd "Junior" Swain and Jesus "Chuy" Ortiz winched up the twin outrigger arms and popped the nets one last time on the morning run, sorting through the teeming sea life that turned the deck into a writhing mass of translucent gray.

They tossed the unwanted bycatch overboard and shoveled what was left, about two hundred pounds of white shrimp, into the center chute. Below deck, Olveda Esteban, the captain's daughter, fed the shrimp into narrow aluminum trays for flash freezing then transferred them into crates to store in the "cold" hold, a space big enough for six hundred boxes. Factory ships have long used freezer-plate technology, but it's less common on medium-sized trawlers like Philomena, an expensive part of Captain Esteban's retrofit after purchasing the vessel. It allows multiday fishing while keeping fresh what's already been caught, a wise investment that may already be paying for itself on this trip.

Only after the outriggers were secured and the nets folded and stowed, necessary preparations for moving on to a new location, did the deckhands peel off their gloves and boots and descend to the galley for lunch. In the galley, cook Emmanuel Etienne stirred a hot, milky, peppery broth of fish stew crowded with potatoes, carrots, and chunks of fresh snapper over blue-gas burners while Junior and Chuy waited for him to fill their bowls. They eat first and they eat fast, because they only have twenty to thirty minutes before they need to be topside again to work the trawler's nets in a new spot. The engineer and first mate, Lorenzo Ortiz, sat quietly at the end of the table, sipping his "morning" coffee, having just awakened at half-past noon. Ortiz is Philomena's steward of the night. Meanwhile Captain Esteban was at the wheel, guiding her ship to a new fishing hole hopefully as rich in shrimp as their morning's first two strikes.

Just a day and a half into their last late run of the season, Captain Esteban and the crew of Philomena are settling into a comfortable yet cautious rhythm. So far the catch has been steady, and the sizable hold of the 110-ton ship is beginning to fill. It seems that the captain's late-season gamble has paid off, and the early tension onboard, once as taut as the nets pulled in from the seas behind them, is starting to slacken. This is apparent throughout the ship, the burgeoning haul of "white gold" feeding the crew's optimism that they'll have a shorter trip and a bigger payday back at Port Royal. Shrimping work is usually done just a few miles out, often within view of the shoreline. This typically allows boats to set out early in the morning and return to port the same day. But sometimes circumstances require another approach, especially late in the season, like now, when boat captains look at the numbers for the year and see a tide of red ink that might sink their operation for good. This is exactly the situation Captain Esteban and her crew are facing in their freshman year together, but something she says her military training helped her anticipate. In these situations ships might stock up on fuel and provisions, maybe even take on extra hands, and not plan on coming back until their holds are filled, sometimes for days or even a week at a time. While this reduces expenses, like the costly diesel fuel spent shuttling back and forth to their home port each day, it creates other pressures on the captain and crew, and even on the ship itself, especially with older trawlers like Philomena, already prone to mechanical failures.

Shrimping crews can expect long hours of setting, hauling, emptying the nets, sorting, shoveling, and packing in two-hour intervals from dawn to dusk. Mealtimes refortify the crew and provide a welcome respite from their taxing labor, so much so that Captain Esteban, anticipating the food-productivity connection, has hired an extra crew member to work not the nets but the galley. She discovered cook Etienne while eating at the King Creole Restaurant in Beaufort, where he typically works the breakfast and lunch shifts. The rail-thin Haitian migrant is preternaturally quiet, preferring to let his food do the talking; it's only noon, and he's already dishing out a Michelin star–worthy meal. Quite the feat, considering he must cook this crew of six three meals a day in a tiny galley with just a two-burner propane stove and an oven no bigger than a breadbox.

Even with these culinary delights at every meal, some in the crew have not warmed to Etienne. "In the army, we called it herding cats," Esteban confides wearily, "trying to get skeptical, independent-minded individuals to work as a team. Here I gotta create some sorta small unit cohesion in just one season, not over year-long combat deployments. Danger can help bind you together. We got that here too." She nods. "But once deployed, you faced that danger with people that you trained over and over with, possessing all the mighty resources of Uncle Sam. Here, even though some of us are family, it doesn't mean we've all done this work together—and we're also doing it on the tightest of margins. I'm telling you, give a cross look to that old Cat D343 below, and she'll fold on you faster than a trailer park in a tornado. And this late in the season, the only thing it's really about is the money. You're just protecting your investment." She pauses, looks off into the distance. "Trying to make sure you end up whole, so you can do it again next year. Money is everything right now. As long as you're making it you have their loyalty. Once you stop . . ." She glances back, shrugs.

IMAGES: 1. Deckhands unloading nets on deck.

CUTLINE: Philomena deckhands Floyd Swain Jr. and Jesus Ortiz sort through the first haul of the day. Shrimpers say bycatch— anything netted other than shrimp—used to be an issue, but new devices allow turtles and other larger sea life to escape unharmed. Environmentalists disagree.

IMAGE 2. Cook stirring in the galley.

CUTLINE: Meals onboard can be one of the few respites for shrimping crews working long hours, sometimes for weeks at a time. Cook Emmanuel Etienne, a Haitian immigrant, says his grandmother taught him to cook back in Haiti, combining the best of Creole, French, and Caribbean flavors.

IMAGE 3. Captain's daughter alone on top deck at night.

CUTLINE: While her mother was deployed overseas, Olveda Esteban was living with her grandmother in Savannah, a high school basketball star point guard with a scholarship offer to play at UNC. A knee injury upturned those dreams, forcing her to trade hoop nets for shrimp nets.

CHAPTER 7

JUNIOR

Monday, December 17, 2018
Three days before the storm

After transmitting his second story and photos, Landon closed his laptop and pulled the cables that connected it to his BGAN modem, which was perched near the bow of the main deck and pointed at some unseen satellite in the eastern sky. He sat there unmoving, thinking about what he hadn't included in his reporting. Something that likely would've brought a swift end to his little expedition before it had really begun. On the mechanical side, the uncertainty of a sputtering engine. On the human side, a dispute between deckhand Chuy and Emmanuel the cook.

Even in his short time on board, Landon had heard Chuy refer to the cook as the Floater, a specifically cruel reference to Haitian asylum seekers who drowned trying to reach the beaches of Miami on homemade watercraft made of inner tubes and other unstable detritus. And in one incident he made the unfortunate choice to tease the cook by pilfering his prized possession, a hand-size black leather-bound book that he pored over at the galley table whenever he was on a break, absently unwinding and rewinding the leather thong that bound it shut. Landon observed that, when finished, the cook always put the book back into the fanny pocket of his sun-bleached multipocket fishing vest. The vest was also jammed with bottles of spices and seasonings, which Landon thought a clever solution to the galley's cooking challenges.

On the first night out Landon watched as Chuy lifted the book from Emmanuel's pocket, unwrapped the leather thong, and flipped through pages. He scowled, eyebrows arched. "It's just a recipe book or something," he said, squinting at the scribble. "But in French." Immediately losing interest, he handed it back to Emmanuel, no apology for the invasion of his privacy. "Le this and le that," Chuy teased. "Le boring shit, dude."

Emmanuel was impassive about the violation and continued cooking. But within five minutes after finishing his meal, Chuy raced topside from the galley and could be heard vomiting violently over *Philomena*'s port side.

"Something did not agree with him," Emmanuel said to no one in particular, scrubbing bowls in the sink.

"That something better be the last something," Captain Esteban said.

Emmanuel shrugged. "Too much cumin maybe."

The captain addressed this incident later with Landon in the privacy of the wheelhouse after supper. It was an early sign of the challenges she faced in unifying the crew and ending the season in the black, she said. "But writing about it won't help anybody," she added.

Landon said nothing, but he got the point. Back on the bow, he sighed and gathered up his gear, stuffing it in the waterproof black polypropylene bag he carried when using the expensive and fragile devices topside. As he walked toward the middeck, he saw Junior sitting cross-legged, whittling, and asked if he could join him. The deckhand looked up from his work and gestured with a hand for Landon to sit.

Landon watched him for a while, saying nothing. Junior put the piece he'd been working on back into the dusty velvet Crown Royal bag tied to one of his belt loops. He dug around in it, found a fresh plug of wood, and started carving it up.

VIDEO TEXT TRANSCRIPT AND DESCRIPTION: Floyd Swain Jr. is dressed in a blue denim work shirt, gray jeans and black rubber boots. On his head a camouflage ball cap, with the bill turned backward. A sprout of reddish-blond hair pokes through the inverted U made by the adjustable band, "Bear Archery" embroidered around it. He whittles at a little plug of basswood burl with a folding pocketknife, leaning against the portside gunwale at middeck. He has the face of a young laborer, colored by constant exposure to the sun but not yet turned by it.

[Globe-Democrat digital edition, published 12-17-18.]

BITTER SEAS
In Their Words: Floyd Swain Jr., Philomena deckhand, 30
—*Lukas Landon*

Lukas Landon, *voice off camera*: I'm talking with deckhand Floyd Swain Jr....

Floyd Swain Jr.: Just call me Junior. That's what everyone know me by.

Landon: ... thirty years old, originally from Florence, South Carolina. How long have you worked shrimping boats now, Junior?

Swain, *looking up from his whittling*: ... Hmmm, prolly ten seasons or more. Ever since I got done with high school.

Landon: So it's been your work for most of your adult life?

Swain: Yeah, you could say that. I do other stuff. You know, between seasons. Some paintin' and dry-dock work. Little maintenance stuff, outboards mostly. Two-stroke, some four. Nothing real big, no diesel work, like we got on the Phil. Take the captain or Lorenzo for that. Outa my league.

Landon: How'd you first get into shrimping, being from Florence, inland?

Swain: Yeah, well, my daddy's friend Roy had a small boat, docked outa James Island. Fished pretty much everything. We'd go out as day hands peak season, sometimes. Daddy didn't take to it all that well. Hard to get some sea legs on you when you stumblin' drunk most of the time. [*Laughs, but also can't contain an involuntary shudder. Turns shyly back to his knife work.*] Roy saw I took to it, though. Had me back over the summers. Taught me what I needed, and I went from there. After I graduated got me a full-time spot on a trawler outa Hilton Head.

Did that for about six seasons. Then a buddy a mine knew somebody on the Phil. Older boat, but bigger. Bigger hauls, more money, at the start, anyway. Stayed with her ever since.

Landon: That's one of the reasons I wanted to talk with you. You're the only deckhand from *Philomena* that stayed on after it was sold to Captain Esteban last spring.

Swain, *concentrating on his whittling now, rocking back and forth in time to a song only he can hear. Takes so long to respond, Landon prompts him:* Some of that crew, they were just old-fashioned. Used to the way things were.

Landon: That's not you?

Swain: Look, those boys get all hot 'n' bothered about removing the battle flag and all. You know what they always saying, "It ain't hatred, it's heritage." They think they all Stonewall Jacksons or something. Not me. Plus, I got what y'all call some sentimental attachment to the Phil. Been onboard a long time. Know all the nooks and crannies, you know what I mean. [*Stops, gives Landon a wink, before resuming his carving.*] Feel like she's part mine.

Landon: What about Esteban?

Swain, *shrugging again:* What about her? . . . You mean her being Black?

Landon: . . . and a woman.

Swain: Now, that's the way God made her, right? I ain't got no problem with that. Why would I? Besides, she's done served her country in Iraq, shed blood for it as I hear. And I've put in my time with some dumb-as-sheetrock male captains. Ain't no one saying a woman can't do it same or better. She done all right so far.

Landon: This season? Seems like you got off to a rough start.

Swain: None of that on Captain Esteban. Just some bad luck. Finding enough folks to run the ship right, engine problems. All good now. We'll do all right.

Landon: What about the rest of the crew? You've never worked with any of them.

Swain: Yeah [*smoker's laugh*], ain't that what makes life excitin'? The mystery of it all? Chuy's a piece of work . . . always doing some chuckleheaded nonsense. [*Laughs again.*] Don't use that. Yeah, they's all okay. Lorenzo Ortiz got plenty boat time, a good mate for a newer captain. Plus, he keeps Chuy's dumb ass in line. Them being related and all.

Landon: What about the captain's daughter, Olveda? She's got barely any time shrimping.

Swain, *becoming serious*: You want me to say something that could get me fired? We done here, if you is. [*There's a thin layer of sweat on Junior's forehead and upper lip, and he swivels his head from bow to stern, like a dog trying to avoid its master's reproach.*]

Landon: No, just, you know . . . she's a greenhorn.

Swain: We was all greenhorns once. And besides, if you can't take care of your family, why buy the boat? Olveda, she young. That's for sure. Got stuff to learn. But she strong. Was a ballplayer, so I hear. Besides, she got the shit job. In the hold most of the time and don't complain nothing about it. Messin' up down there ain't gonna kill nobody. It's just shrimping. Not like we're operating, you know, a supercollider or sumpin'. [*Grins.*]

Landon, *laughing, off camera*: Okay, just one or two more. Is it unusual for a shrimp boat to stay out for a week this late in the season? Isn't it usually day runs and back in to offload?

Swain, *keeps whittling for a time without looking up*: These days you do what you gotta do. When I first started, you could fill a hold in a day, then it started to take two, then three. Now we lucky if we get a big enough haul in a week. Cap'n doin' what everyone doing now, staying out longer, anchoring offshore, saving fuel not running to port every day to offload.

Landon: But then the catch isn't as fresh, right?

Swain: Naw, Cap'n was thinking ahead, put one of them freezer plate things in the hold. Cold stores it so good, it still taste like it just jumped on your plate. Wild catch always better'n what those fish farms do, anyway. [*Pauses.*] Only downside, makes us a little heavy in the water. Phil was never fast, but now we chug along like we got emphysema. [*Chuckles.*]

Landon: Got it. That's good for now. Thanks, Junior. [*Junior nods, smiles.*]

Landon touched his phone screen, stopped the recording, and pocketed it. He was getting up to walk away when Junior stopped him.

"You ask me a bunch questions. How 'bout I ask you one?"

Landon sat back down. "Shoot."

"Why you out here with us? Weren't you some big war reporter, got awards and all that? That's what Cap'n says."

"Any monkey can cover a war," Landon sniped. "Buy me a beer when we're back at Port Royal, I'll tell you all about it." He'd not intended for his reply to come out so curt, especially after the deckhand generously agreed to be videotaped for their interview.

Junior caught the brush-off. He said nothing for a while, just kept at his carving, working faster, scraping, prying, shaping, finally blowing on it to clear the shavings.

"Well, I don't know nothin' about monkeys, but this here seems right for you." He handed Landon the finished work. Landon brought it closer to his face. A tiny ocher-colored octopus, rough-hewn but impressive, with all eight arms and elongated head.

"This is for me?" Landon asked.

"Always try to make the sea critter I see in someone."

"I'm an octopus?"

"Yeah, on account you gotta juggle all that stuff you do." Junior pointed with his pocketknife. "You be better off with more hands like that lil' guy."

"Probably right. Thanks very much," Landon said, putting the gift inside his gear bag. "But seems like you're more octopus than me, always busy whittling when you're not setting nets or winching them in."

Junior closed his knife, an immaculate four-inch stainless-steel drop point with an oiled rosewood handle burned in with the letters FS.

He was about to slip it into the velvet Crown Royal bag when he saw that Landon had taken note. Tumbled the closed blade through his fingers like a magician doing a coin trick.

"Was my daddy's. Only thing he really gave me, besides a good beating now and then," Junior said, chuckling. "I like to keep busy. Idle hands and all that."

Landon looked into Junior's eyes. His pupils were the diameter of bottle caps and black as obsidian. When he saw Landon shift his gaze to the tremor in his hands, Junior thrust them into his pockets, chin-dipped a quick goodbye, and walked away.

CHAPTER 8

OPTIONS

Under the Sea: Day 1

Landon's improvised hammock had raised him out of the water before hypothermia could set in. But the process had taxed him. Following the mental concentration and physical labor of setting up the contraption, he found it increasingly hard to catch his breath. His lungs felt cheated, unable to get all the oxygen they needed from the space. He wondered if he had already sucked it all up, converted it to carbon dioxide waste. His head was pounding, a combination of his toilet-slam trauma and dehydration, he figured, and—oh yeah—that gnawing fear that he would die in this place. Then he considered the tiny triangle of the head's sink wedged into the wall space near the door. He'd wished he could simply open the tap and suck out all the pure, fresh water from the ship's holding tank. He sat up. Why not at least try? The sink was overhead, like the toilet, not submerged in salt water. He leapt from his perch into the pool of water and excitedly reached up, ignoring the ongoing affliction of his rib, desperate for his prize. He opened the single tap. A loud squeak, but then . . . nothing. Swiftly he ascertained that even if it had released water, the tap spout was pointed up and would probably trap it with no real flow pressure. Follow the source! He stretched higher, feeling for the flexible hose that connected the tap to the holding tank somewhere outside the walls. He found the base where the hose connected and, after a few cautious tugs, hung from it like an orangutan, his body weight breaking the connection. A small gush of water came out, splashing the top of his head. He squared himself under it, opened his mouth wide, and pulled the hose down. The tip brushed the flap of his empty gum socket. He nearly flinched away but held fast and worked the hose past his lips, as rewarded with several mouthfuls of sweet, potable water, the desert sands of his tongue awash in this heavenly flash flood. He closed his eyes and swallowed, grateful, careful not to let any precious liquid seep away. There was more in the pipeline, and he held it back with compensating pressure until he could open his esophagus and swallow again. He did this twice more before the hose ran dry. Enough, but never enough. He climbed back into his hammock, wondered if these small sustaining moments would simply prolong his misery before killing him.

Wondered if he did die down here, who would mourn him? His father, Tobias, was long dead from pancreatic cancer, his mother, Annabel, packed away in a home for Alzheimer's patients. Landon hadn't been in contact with his older sister, Michaela, for years. A high-end dermatologist, she had followed the money to Los Angeles in 2009 and established a lucrative practice in Manhattan Beach, shooting up wealthy soccer moms and desperate housewives with Botox and wrinkle fillers. That was just a year after his own divorce. He'd gone off everyone's radars then, not just family but colleagues and friends too. Stopped checking in, not knowing what to say or simply not wanting to say anything. He and Vanessa had been amicable when they split, but she'd been eager to move on after her mercy-kill of their six-year marriage, unfriending him on Facebook, Instagram, and other social media before the papers were notarized. But he'd heard from a few mutual acquaintances that she'd finally succumbed to her father's pressure to quit teaching, return to Jacksonville, and join the family business. Three years later she'd married one of his protégés at the firm. She was now living in a big house in the exclusive San Marco neighborhood, and pregnant.

Despite his relative anonymity, Landon speculated, the drama of his death by drowning in a capsized shrimping trawler would undoubtedly draw some news coverage. Keen-eyed media vultures like himself would seek out someone to dish on or decode whatever his Rosebud had been in life. Who better for that than an ex-wife? Landon imagined the cameras, microphones descending from all sides to the front door of Vanessa's impressive Spanish Revival house. She wouldn't like the media invasion of the family residence, but she would default to her impeccable manners, knowing from her time as an assistant television news producer that the reporters would not be deterred without something of substance. Yes, it was in Miami where she first met her ex-husband Lukas Landon, then a crime reporter for the *Herald* and later a war correspondent. No, she had not been in regular contact with him for years. The cameras would love her. Landon imagined her in a simple but elegant white linen wraparound dress that revealed the glorious three-quarter-moon outline of her near-term pregnancy and the firm bosom of motherhood that would sustain it after.

And then—cue the villain's theme—some impossibly sweaty, impatient print journo, jealous that a wall-eyed hack like Landon had once lived within arm's reach of this spectacular beauty, would ask her an impertinent question, both coarse and unkind.

Landon knew Vanessa would chide the reporter for his remark, giving him one of the looks of disappointment she'd so perfected in her years in primary school classrooms. Afterward, he assumed, she would continue patiently, poised and thoughtful, maybe proffering a final small gift of insight into the inevitable void of a man who asked much of others but gave little of himself.

"Some people believe that only soldiers are changed by war. I know this for a fact not to be true," she might say with an authentic, soft-voiced respect. "Those who bear witness are also haunted by its ghosts. Immersed in violence for so long and asked to make meaning of it, they rarely find themselves whole once that time has ended." Well, that was depressing, thought Landon.

Maybe his *Globe-Democrat* colleague and sometimes lover, Rhona, would shed a tear or two, though Landon was convinced the sadness would be fleeting. She was a strategic thinker, relentlessly practical.

She'd be initially impressed at the butch way he went out, but then the micro-nostalgia for a few booze-filled nights at bars followed by some rapacious time in the sack would be packed away. The next stage would be relief. The perfect permanent end to the temporary affair; an ex-lover exits the world, taking your bad behavior with him. Dead guys are the bomb. Dead guys never spill the beans. Dead guys never come to your house in the middle of the night, drunk, loud, and coke-buzzed, waking up your husband and kids in a pathetic attempt at explanation, resolution, or confrontation. All things that Landon knew he was more than capable of and had even considered. He was such a fuckwit when the booze and coke hijacked him. He remembered scratching out a stupid little poem for her after the first time she stayed over at his place. He'd torn open an empty pack of Camel Menthol Lights, wrote on the inside panel, left it on the pillow while she was sleeping, and showered. Clever title, he thought, and could still recite the last rhyming stanza.

Smokescreen
while this can't last more than a pack
lit by 20 matches
I still can't help but pity those who feel
fire never catches

When Rhona woke and saw it, she'd rolled her eyes in exasperation, told him to "stop going all John Cusack on me," crumpled it up, and tossed it at him before pulling him back into bed for one more before going home.

None of these projections and memories were helpful. Landon looked around his bubble. Homemade hammock and beers aside, it was still a literal shithole. And to make things worse, the shithole had a countdown clock that was still ticking away. He looked at his phone: 18 hours, 44 minutes. Trapped underwater for almost an entire day already. How could he stay alive in these impossible circumstances? What were his options? He considered the following:

OPTION 1: Supersaturate himself with breaths, open the door, and swim out of the head and down the short hallway to the hatch opening and the galley below. The galley also had a single portside door leading out to *Philomena*'s main deck. That would be starboard now, with the ship inverted. Details he had to be certain of, especially on a single breath of air. If he got confused while swimming around in the dark waters of the overturned trawler, that would be the end of him. Navigating the swim would be even further complicated by needing to maneuver through an underwater minefield of debris: pots, pans, bench cushions, possibly even bodies. And what would he do if he ran into one of those? The sight of the corpses of Captain Esteban, Olveda, or any of them, for that matter, would probably scare the air right out of his lungs. If he did keep it together, would he try to retrieve their bodies on the way out or leave them there? He felt his chest tighten as if he were already in the middle of the swim. If the galley door wasn't obstructed, he'd open it, then blow out a few bubbles and follow their direction to the surface.

Another idea would be to tie the life vests together, hold them like a bunch of helium balloons and ride them up and out of his nightmare. But that might cause him to ascend too rapidly, which could also get him bent. Then he'd have to let them go, hoping to find them at the water's surface, where he could lash them to his body like a visible makeshift raft. A lot could go wrong with this option. It was dark on the ocean floor. Even with his eyes open, the opacity of the salt water would make it difficult to find the galley door. Also, he had no idea how deep he was. Would he be able to make it out of *Philomena* and all the way to the surface with just the air in his lungs? Free divers could ascend from hundreds of feet, but they were trained athletes. Even so, some experienced shallow-water blackouts, drowning before they reached the surface. He'd been undersea for more than eighteen hours. He'd probably accumulated so much nitrogen in his tissues that it would come boiling out once the lid was taken off. Might even suffer an arterial gas embolism. That would hurt. But say he did make it to the surface and, through some miracle, escaped decompression illness altogether. He'd still be floating on the open seas, nearly impossible to locate—even if the captain or Lorenzo had been able to get out a distress call with coordinates. How long could he last up there, tossed around in open water, before becoming hypothermic—or shark bait? He was still spitting blood from where he'd knocked out his two front teeth. Shark Week had told him the apex predators could sense a few drops from miles away. Maybe the sharks were already waiting for him just on the other side of the thin metal hatch. No, this plan didn't sound promising. So there was always . . .

OPTION 2: Stay put and wait for rescue. The obvious arguments were convincing. In the marine toilet he had a small, but so far reliable bubble of air to breathe. With his improvised hammock and porn-insulated sweater he was above the waterline and, for now, free of the immediate threat of hypothermia. He also had two light sources: the red emergency LED—underwater but still aglow—and his smartphone, while the battery held. And finally, after sucking out the water in the sink hose line, he still had Junior's tallboy malt liquors for hydration. But option 2's downsides were equally daunting. Most worrisome was how long his air would hold out before he either used it up or poisoned it with his own CO_2. And if the Coast Guard was even aware *Philomena* had sunk, where would they establish a search grid? This was a big body of water. It could take weeks to locate the ship. Too late for him.

Unable to make a clear valuation on either option's probability of success, Landon instead reexamined each on the degree of suffering entailed with each option's failure.

OPTION 1: Get lost, panic, and drown swimming inside the ship. Get stuck, panic, and drown swimming inside the ship. Make it out of the ship and drown during a long ascent. Make it out of the ship, make it to the surface, get bent, drown. Make it out of the ship, make it to the surface, drown in stormy seas. Make it out of the ship, make it to the surface, drift in open seas, become a takeaway meal for sharks and other hungry ocean creatures.

OPTION 2: Use up O_2, suffocate. Poison air bubble with CO_2, pass out, suffocate. Water level rises, air bubble leaches out, drown.

The suffering ratio of both options sent his heart racing again. But option 1 seemed to have the edge in greatest misery before death. He pushed back in his hammock, silent except for the soft, shrill whistle of air working its way through his crooked nasal passages. He used Vanessa's breathing technique to calm himself yet again. His chest rose and fell with his gradually slowing heartbeat. The sound from below broke his concentration. His heart accelerated again. Landon sat up as the noise became more insistent. *Chk, chk, chk, chk, chk, chk, chk.* Clicking, skittling? Something inside the ship! Below him in the galley or the hold. Landon closed his eyes against it. *Chk, chk, chk, chk, chk, chk, chk.* He placed a hand on the wall. Vibrations. Something there separated only by the thickness of the metal walls surrounding him. He put his ear against it. *Chk, chk, chk, chk, chk, chk, chk.* Pulled back. So close! Sea life? He knew the creatures of the deep sought out and found dead things very quickly. Had they gotten inside the ship? Crabs, sea lice, urchins, jostling with tarpons, sharks, and barracuda for the endless buffet of white shrimp in the hold? Or had they found a larger meal with the bodies of the crew?

Landon was seized by two opposing instincts. He wanted to retreat far back into his bubble, away from all the potential horror. Yet he also fought the strange urge to push open the door and shoo the predators away from his crewmates. Morbidly, he imagined each of them in circumstances sorrier than his own. Emmanuel the cook, ironically, now food for the fish while suspended in the galley. Captain Esteban's body surviving enemy explosives only to be shredded by sharks. Olveda's limbs being pulled apart like wishbones in a tarpon tug-o-war. Chuy and Junior suspended in the blue-green water of the hold, nosed by a cautious bull shark, sifting for lines or hooks before chowing down on the deckhands. Finally he considered Lorenzo inside the wheelhouse, an army of white-bellied crabs picking at the soft parts of his exposed flesh: his eyelids, the hollows of his nose, his lips, the skin over his jaw and cheekbones, the folds of neck, all being nibbled away, peeled back, finally revealing the dull block of his skull and the gray matter within, once the seat of his knowledge, experience, animation, now exposed and decomposed in the time it might take to watch a television sitcom. The horror of those images displaced everything else. Out of options, out of breath, out of his mind, paralyzed in place. Septimus impaled on his metal fence.

CHAPTER 9

CAPTAIN

Third in a Globe-Democrat series on South Carolina's beleaguered
commercial shrimping industry.

Our features editor Lukas Landon is filing dispatches all this week
while aboard the trawler Philomena as her captain and crew make one
last run in an attempt to stay solvent at the end of a brutal season.
(Globe-Democrat print and digital editions, published 12-18-18.)

BITTER SEAS
The Fighting Season

She left the army as a sergeant to go to sea as a captain. But for
Clarita Esteban the turmoil of the shrimping business, complicated
by a bad first season and lingering racial and gender discrimina-
tion, make the waters off South Carolina feel like just another war
zone.
—*Lukas Landon*

As an army staff sergeant in Iraq, Clarita Esteban drove a ten-ton
wrecker known as an M984 into combat, hauling away Humvees dis-
abled by roadside bombs, many still smoking, stinking of sulfur and
stained in blood when she hooked them up. She remembers her first
recovery operation. It was April 2006, springtime in Anbar Province,
and a little over three years since the invasion. But the "victory" was
not going well. Insurgents had launched a series of coordinated at-

tacks against the local government center, two U.S. combat outposts and even heavily fortified Camp Ramadi.

"My team got the call for a recovery of a QRF (quick reaction force) convoy just outside the gates of our own location at FOB (forward operating base) Blue Diamond," she said, disappearing into the memory instantly. "Insurgents daisy-chained three 155-millimeter shells together and concealed them in the rusted-out hull of an old Fiat. The blast was so big it turned one of the Humvee wheels up. The turret gunner had been tethered in. When it came down, that plate armor that was supposed to protect him, well . . ." She sighed. "It cut him in two. That was how my first tour started. Only got worse after that."

Esteban did another tour of Iraq and one to Afghanistan, earning a Purple Heart and Combat Action Badges for each theater before leaving the military in 2010 after a decade of service. She had an 11-year-old daughter by then, mostly raised by her mother while she was deployed. She was through with the explosions, twisted metal and mangled bodies. She wanted to trade the desert for the sea, trade the present for a slice of her past. Now she's at the wheel again, trying to do a job some would consider only a little less dangerous and possibly even more unpredictable—that of shrimp boat captain. Esteban has Latin American ancestry; her great-grandfather emigrated from Panama not long after the building of the canal, and put down roots in the Carolina Lowcountry. That's where she grew up and had been raising her daughter until her overseas deployments. But both the military and shrimping run in the family. Her father served in the infantry during the war in Vietnam, and was in civilian life a longtime shrimping hand.

"My daddy did all but die hauling in nets for other folk," she said, hand on the wheel as the seventy-foot Philomena departed from her base in Port Royal for the Atlantic. "He didn't have any sons. So I was it. When I was in my teens, sometimes the boats Daddy worked for let me come out for day runs in May, June. Early season. Haul salt for the holds and pick out the bycatch that got their gills net-stuck. Had me some guns after those summers." Esteban laughed and flexed her left bicep, exposing the white slash on its underside where she caught a dime-size piece of shrapnel from an improvised explosive device while on a recovery mission during her second Iraq tour.

After she left the army she used her GI Bill benefits to study for her master operator's license. She apprenticed as a mate on trawlers up and down the Carolinas and the Florida coast, "working for pennies," to get all the hours and experience she needed to helm her own vessel. Now she exudes the confidence of someone who has more than earned their place at the wheel; a life spent on the cusp of danger and unwilling, or perhaps unable, to turn back.

Last May, using much of her life savings along with two small business loans, Esteban cobbled together enough cash to buy the converted trawler Philomena for $90,000. She dropped another $25,000 to update the electronics, change out some engine parts, put in a plate freezer and paint and reseal the hull. But even the improvements can't hide the fact that Philomena was built four decades ago, in 1976, when disco was ascendant and Jimmy Carter would be elected president of the United States. And while the ship may be familiar to these mid- and south Atlantic waters, a Black female captain is a rarity of the first order—particularly in a state that was first to secede in the Civil War and which, up until the Charleston church shootings in 2015, still flew the Confederate battle flag over the state capitol. That mindset may have been one of the reasons Esteban had problems putting together a crew.

"The ways some of 'em looked at me on Philomena, you'd think I was Robert Smalls steaming away with their rebel paddle wheeler again," she said, referring to the 23-year-old slave boat pilot who made an audacious nighttime escape, navigating the Confederate supply ship Planter through Charleston Harbor and delivering it right into the hands of the Union Navy.

"There's a lot a good ol' boys still around." She clicks her tongue at the thought. "None of 'em want to say so, but most have trouble with cap'n being a woman"—she paused, lets out a short, full laugh—"and Black. Not sure which one unsettles 'em most. Served my country for 10 years, half that in war zones. Not one male soldier ever had a problem doing what I told them. And it wasn't just the stripes. I earned it."

It took her time to round up a full crew, causing Philomena to miss the month-long June roe shrimp season altogether. To finally get out to sea she had to enlist her own 19-year-old daughter, Olveda, a onetime high school basketball star. Having been deployed to war for so many critical years during Olveda's childhood, the captain hopes it's a chance for them to reconnect. But she concedes her daughter may see it otherwise, perhaps just one more in a long list of compromises she's had to make with a mostly absentee mother.

Philomena finally put out in July and had a solid six weeks, before its big Cat diesel cut out and needed even more expensive repair work. That took the ship out of commission during the last couple weeks of August, peak fishing for brown shrimp. And with all that, Esteban's entry into the field couldn't come at a less propitious time for the industry as a whole, beset by the double blows of declining hauls, some say due to global warming, and fierce new competition from cheaper farm-raised shrimp in Asia, specifically Thailand and Vietnam.

IMAGE: Clarita Esteban behind the wheel of Philomena, face bathed in early-morning sunlight.

CUTLINE: Former army veteran Clarita Esteban cleaned up the wreckage of American wars in Iraq and Afghanistan, but now she's traded the desert for the sea as a shrimp boat captain. Being one of only a few Black women doing the job on the Atlantic seaboard has had its challenges—like finding a crew willing to serve under her.

But Esteban seems to know how to drive in only one direction—forward. While it's December, late in the last month of this year's season, she's taken Philomena and her crew back out and plans to stay out for as long as a week, provisioned for this one final run. She's worried she could finish the year deep in the red, possibly making her delinquent on her boat loans or even default, unless they can fill the hold.

"Got people depending on me and this ol' ship." Esteban shrugs. "Ain't no Plan B."

There is a lot working against her. Esteban knows this late in the season, shrimp are much scarcer, mostly fished out. And while it's possible to find coveted large white shrimp this late, they're not always easy to capture in the surly waters of winter. Which means she and her crew will have to run their nets day and night, hoping her gamble pays off.

"MOWING THE LAWN" was the way Captain Esteban described it to Landon. It was their third day at sea, and the ship was dropping nets five miles offshore, working a straight compass heading on a north-south line between Beaufort and Charleston. Late in the morning, the captain was still at the wheel and buoyed by their good fortune. The hold was filling fast. Maybe things had finally turned for *Philomena*, even if their namesake was one of the pitiful patron saints of lost causes.

Enzo had shared the legend with her early on, during their meticulous preseason inspection of the ship. He'd sheepishly asked her permission to tape up in the wheelhouse the holy card that the ship's original owner had given him after he and his family disembarked at the Port of Miami on their trip to America. Though Adventists didn't put much stock in Catholic saints, he'd kept it all these years, a lucky charm with a horrific backstory. Philomena, he told Captain Esteban, had been just a young girl, thirteen or fourteen, when she caught the eye of a Roman emperor. But as a Christian she had made a vow to remain chaste. The emperor, not one to take no for an answer, sent his minions to change her mind, "wooing" her by torture. It didn't work.

"That's when they decided to just kill her," Enzo had explained. "They whipped her, shot her with arrows, and tossed her into a river with an anchor around her neck. But even after all that, she still lived. Finally they just chopped off her head. But she never gave in."

"Tough little chica," the captain said at the time, impressed. "No better name for a ship than a girl who won't go down or stay down." Enzo agreed, despite knowing that there was scant evidence Philomena had ever existed. Better to believe in something than nothing.

Where Enzo had disagreed was with the captain's decision to let a journalist come onboard. Things were tough enough without putting their whole operation under a media microscope, he'd argued. Captain Esteban countered with a different perspective. The attention from Landon's stories might help them get a better deal for next year—if they could make it to next year. Maybe offloading at Hilton Head, where they fronted you fuel, salt, and ice, instead of second-tier Port Royal. They might even get higher prices per pound, wholesalers and restaurants wanting some of that goodwill PR that comes from supporting a veteran/minority owned business. In the end Enzo deferred to her judgment without bitterness or acrimony, simply respect. She savored that in the man—a fine and rare trait.

But if fate forced her to have a reporter onboard, there were worse picks than Landon. He seemed curious, polite, and willing to share parts of his own history in her early telephone and email encounters with him. He'd reported for years on the wars in Iraq and Afghanistan. She was surprised to learn they'd even both spent time at FOB Blue Diamond in Ramadi, although two years apart. Landon had been there briefly in 2004, early in the war, while Esteban had done her first Iraq tour there in 2006, during the period of near constant unrest sometimes referred to as the Second Battle of Ramadi.

Still in the getting-to-know-you phase by email, she had asked Landon, Why *Philomena*? He wrote back that he'd almost given up after months of searching. Then a standing Google keyword search captured an article for him in the *Port Royal Reader*, a small blurb actually, noting that she'd bought *Philomena*. He sent her the link even though she had seen it already. The only real press she'd gotten. Carried a photo of her, which answered the question.

Esteban decided to try the same technique with Landon, scouring the internet for nearly everything he'd written reporting overseas.

She discovered Landon didn't just write about soldiers and guns, but also spent time living and reporting among civilians. From his more personal, behind-the-scenes dispatches, titled "Reporter's Notebook," she learned he sometimes took off his body armor and dressed in a dishdasha (what the soldiers derided as man-dresses) and head scarves, eating the locals' food, sleeping in their homes. The arc of many of his stories seemed to show a broader dimension to the conflict—not just the "bang-bang" but the full picture, especially when it came to Iraq. He was making an effort to understand and explain why some, who had initially welcomed the American toppling of Saddam Hussein, now took up arms against them as unwanted occupiers. But his dispatches from 2004, the time of some of the war's greatest violence, were understandably disturbing. Esteban noted that Landon appeared nearly obsessed with "collateral damage," a noxious euphemism she'd heard often in her military career used by both military officers and politicians to minimize civilian deaths, displaced families, and other civil destruction caused by war.

Landon's later writings were staked to the topic, reporting on civilians caught in the crossfire, while acknowledging the spiritual damage that did to the soldiers responsible. That was admirable, she believed.

But something troubled her about Landon too—the way he tried to sell her when she deliberated too long about bringing him onboard. Her story, he had said, was not just that of the shrimping industry's struggles but of a woman still fighting to make it in a white man's world.

"You are the rarest of the rare in South Carolina," he'd said to her one night over the phone. "A Black female shrimp boat captain and an Iraq/ Afghan War veteran with Combat Action Badges and a Purple Heart. Who isn't rooting for you?"

He'd said the last part with the peculiar familiarity that sometimes comes with drink. But more than the *way* he said it, it was *what* he said that bothered her most. It felt manipulative, like naked flattery. He characterized her struggle in a way that made her accomplishments seem too unique, reinforcing the notion she was the exception that proved the rule. Every Black woman she'd ever known had been strong and resourceful: she'd been raised by a strong Black woman and given birth to one. All her aunties and cousins, all the Black female soldiers working above or below her—every single one of them was solid. Being a Black woman meant the world gave you no other choice. It was either push back or knuckle under, fight or submit. And she knew that if she didn't fight, didn't do something to promote her boat and business, she was likely to lose everything. She didn't have the capital or the energy to start over again. She had to make this work, especially since Olveda's future was now back in her hands. Enzo was right; Landon was a risk. But most men were. That was a lesson made terrifyingly clear when her boot camp drill instructor pinned her to the back wall of his office and began fishing for his cock through the zipper of his fatigues. She didn't wait for him to find it. She stepped outside his stance and with mantis-like speed backhanded his nuts so square and so hard she swore they traveled his height and rang a bell in his head, like a carnival striker game. She walked out of his office mostly intact, while he ended up in sick bay with an exploded testicle. He blamed it on an off-duty biking accident, but was reassigned; higher-ups figured this had not been his first try. But while Esteban had learned to recognize threats, she also knew a gift when it was offered. Landon, she hoped, was a gift.

But who was to know if that gift was also a Trojan horse? She needed some insurance. After Landon told her he'd been at Blue Diamond in 2004, she reached out to folks in her noncom network and asked if anybody had rubbed elbows with an embedded journalist named Lukas Landon at that time. A handful of former colleagues responded. Landon was all right, they mostly concurred, but he had some unreported history of his own. They told Esteban he'd likely be fair with her, but if he wasn't, here was the leash that would make him heel.

CHAPTER 10

LORENZO

Tuesday, December 18, 2018
Two days before the storm

Late in the afternoon, near the end of their productive third day out, Landon noticed Captain Esteban's momentary look of surprise as she throttled up. Outwardly, she dismissed it. No big deal. Just a brief loss of engine compression, she explained. Similar to what she'd felt heading out from Port Royal, but this was the first time it had happened since, and Landon sensed there might be more to it. Confirmed when she told Lorenzo to check it out. Landon asked to tag along. The first mate gave an ambivalent shrug. Landon accepted that as progress, since the number two had mostly ignored him since he came aboard. They climbed down into *Philomena*'s engine room through a pull-away hatch in the galley floor.

The ship's Cat D343 diesel engine reminded Landon of the Beatles' infamous yellow submarine, a match for shape and color. He kept this observation to himself, fearing that Lorenzo would send him right back up the ladder. Earlier, he'd overheard the captain mention to the first mate that *Philomena* was underpowered. Landon found that hard to believe. At 5,500 pounds, the engine weighed nearly twice as much as a Mini Cooper. Also, the engine room was directly underneath and just aft of the staterooms, separated from them by only a quarter-inch steel plate, and while it was running, the combined heat, noise, and vibration made it nearly impossible to sleep even in calm seas.

"Okay, shut her down," Lorenzo spoke into his brick-size handheld two-way radio before clipping it back on the waistband of his work pants. Without forward momentum, *Philomena* began to pitch and roll in the windswept seas. Landon steadied himself with difficulty. Even with its 365-horsepower centerpiece, the engine room itself was a medieval dungeon on water; a dank, wet pit stuffed with metal housings, fuel pipes, thermostats, water pumps, compressors, base plating, and hundreds of other parts clamped to its walls or bolted onto the ship's steel subflooring. The acrid stench of fuel and fetid water brought a rise from his stomach, but Landon swallowed it back. Looking to the right of the ladder, he was surprised to see a full-face gas mask, its straps looped on the overhang of a pipe. He made a note to ask Lorenzo about that later. Lorenzo meanwhile heightened the whole creep factor by choosing to use the most primitive of shop lights, a single bulb in a wire cage shaped like a lacrosse stick, to illuminate his work. It bathed the engine room in a rude glare, casting deep shadows from the obstructions all around. Lorenzo was about five-foot-nine, Landon guessed, stocky, with Popeye-wide forearms and short, thick legs. Still, he moved with a fluid grace within the confined space, weaving through the maze without ever brushing a shoulder or even a pant leg. Landon observed as Lorenzo pulled the rubber tubing from the underside of the piston's engine casing and threaded a compression meter to its tip. He tested its hold, then keyed the two-way.

"Bring her up slowly, please." On the bridge, Captain Esteban twisted the ignition key clockwise, brought the engine back online. Landon flinched at the roar when it ignited. Lorenzo held the gauge in his large, leathery right hand and the radio in the left. He eyeballed the meter as it rose steadily in an arc.

"Throttle up. Slow." Lorenzo watched the black needle ride out to 100 psi, then to 300. "Little more, little more." The meter bounced at 350. "Now slowly, all the way up." Landon watched the mate's deep-set eyes follow the needle into the red at 500 psi, let it hold there for a second before going back to the radio. "Okay, ease it back, slowly, slowly, all the way." Lorenzo watched the needle tremble, then settle back into the black of zero. "Okay, shut it down."

Landon observed silently for a full hour as Lorenzo and Captain Esteban worked through every cylinder.

"Rings are good all the way around," Lorenzo spoke into the radio when they were finished. "Probably just some wear in the seals." He used the back of his right hand to wipe the sheen of sweat from his cheeks and forehead. "Should hold until we put back in at Port Royal. I'll replace them all then. Let's keep fishing while we can."

"Copy," the captain's voice came over Lorenzo's radio.

"But, Clarita," he said into his radio again, "don't drive her like she's one of your wreckers back in the sandbox. She cleans up good, but she's still an old girl, all right?"

"I hear you, baby," the captain said. "You old girls need to stick together." Landon stifled a laugh at the deft sting. "Don't worry, Enzo," she continued, "I'm not gonna break your childhood sweetheart, as long as she does what I tell her." A suppressed giggle on the click off. Lorenzo smiled to himself, pulled the radio to his mouth, then changed his mind. Let the captain have the last word.

"Is that true?" Landon asked softly, as Lorenzo reached for the light hanging from a steel bracket above them and hung it waist-level, leaving their faces in shadow.

"Is what true?" Lorenzo responded, winding up the orange extension cord.

"What the captain said. That *Philomena* was your childhood sweetheart, brought you from Cuba to Miami when you were a kid? During the boatlift. Mariel?"

"I know what it was called," Lorenzo said. He seemed reluctant to engage in questioning, maybe afraid of saying something wrong to the reporter that might damage what Clarita was trying to build. But Landon waited him out. Standing there in the dark, patient as a wildlife photographer. He wasn't some sloppy hack looking for a quick soundbite or a headline; he genuinely wanted to know what they were up against.

Finally, Lorenzo surrendered to the inevitable questions that would follow.

Landon looked in the corner. "What's with the mask? Huns about to send a volley of mustard gas into the trenches?"

"Right," Lorenzo said, wondering just how recently the reporter had arrived from Planet Wackadoodle. "Left over from the last owner. Things get smoky down here sometimes. Not exactly well ventilated, as you can tell. Might be handy in a fire too."

"You expecting one?" Landon asked, concerned.

"Hope not, but better to have and not need, I expect."

"Agreed," Landon said. "But it might be better suited in the wheel-house with the first aid supplies. I mean, how are you going to find it down here if the place is already filled with smoke and flames?"

"Knock yourself out."

"Okay, but I was hoping we could talk a little first."

Lorenzo shrugged, as if to say, Might as well get it over with now. Landon pulled out his phone and began to record their thirty-minute exchange on video.

VIDEO TEXT TRANSCRIPT AND DESCRIPTION: Interview recorded in the dimly lit engine room of the shrimp trawler Philomena following repairs. [Globe-Democrat digital edition, published 12-18-18.]

BITTER SEAS
In Their Words: Lorenzo Ortiz, Philomena first mate/engineer, 46
—Lukas Landon

Lukas Landon: You've got a connection to Philomena that's deeper than any other member of the crew. Maybe deeper than the captain's— even though she owns it.

Lorenzo Ortiz: Yes.

Landon: That connection goes back almost four decades, to 1980, when Philomena was almost new, just a handful of years after she'd been christened. Tell me about that journey from Mariel Harbor to your new life in America.

Ortiz, *considering the question*: My parents were Seventh-Day Adventists, had raised me the same in a barrio on the outskirts of Havana. I was their only child.

Landon: Was that a little unusual? Cuba, like most of Central and South America, was and is predominantly Catholic, even after the revolution in 1959.

Ortiz: Yes, Fidel [*Castro*] was baptized Catholic and studied under the Jesuits. But when the church spoke out against communism, it became an enemy of the revolution. He expelled the priests and then took over all the Catholic schools, turned them into Cuban public schools. I wore a red handkerchief tied around my neck for all of first and second grades.

Landon: So why did you leave? Were your parents opposed to the revolution?

Ortiz, *shrugging*: Not necessarily. My father worked as a mechanic at a local garage in our barrio. It was work, but he never got paid much. Mi madre . . . my mom was a housewife. We were the kind of poor people Batista's goons preyed on, the kind the revolution was supposed to help. But there was a problem.

Landon: Your religion?

Ortiz, *nodding*: Fidel had a hard-on for the Catholics, but it was even worse for Protestant convert groups like us. We weren't a threat to anyone, but some thought we were, I don't know, weird.

Landon: Vegetarians, pacifists, celebrating the holy day on Saturday rather than Sunday . . .

Ortiz: Some eat meat and fish, but not my parents, not us. Mostly you're supposed to keep it moderate and no pork or shellfish. [*Landon raises his eyebrows.*]

   I know. [*Nods, a tiny smile indicating the irony isn't lost on him.*] I'll get to that in a bit. But the point is . . . our barrio's CDR . . .

Landon: CDR?

Ortiz: Committee for the Defense of the Revolution, kind of like neighborhood watch, but for the purpose of outing supposed traitors and counterrevolutionaries. To us, they were just rats, snitching on their neighbors to get a few more ounces of rice or chicken bones for soup.

Landon: So they outed you?

Ortiz: No, it's not like we were practicing in secret or anything. There were ten thousand of us around the country. They just started calling us antisocialists. That was enough. Once it started, Fidel wanted us gone. We were among the first to have our papers processed, and when Carter said he'd take us in—

Landon: U.S. president Jimmy Carter, at that time.

Ortiz: Yes. All the Cuban exiles who'd left for Miami right after the revolution began chartering boats and sailing down to get us in Mariel Harbor and bring us to Miami and Key West. It was like a revolving door. My parents weren't sad at all; my grandparents on both sides were already dead, and we had some family in Miami. There was nothing really to stay for. We waited in the harbor for three days before the first boats arrived. I remember seeing Philomena almost immediately. It stood out because of the brightly painted red hull. It looked almost brand-new, with no rust or wear at all. I'd never seen a ship like that in Havana.

I remember pulling at my father's sleeve, telling him that was the ship I wanted to be on, the one I wanted to take us to America. He was a kind man, not pushy or aggressive, but he seemed to understand how important it was to me. He asked others to let us move to the front of the line as the Phil docked. Many seemed annoyed, but I remember them looking down at my face and then giving their assent, to go ahead. [*Pauses, recalling.*] Once we were onboard, he moved my mother and me to the very front of the bow, where we'd have the first and best view of the Miami skyline.

As we got adjusted, wedging our few bags into the V space made by the metal railing, I remember a very tall, bald man coming up to us. Well, tall to me. He was wearing a spotless guayabera and slacks with a crease so sharp you could cut a rope with them. But despite his nice clothes—rich-guy clothes, compared to my father's—he had this deeply tanned face; not the tan of a man of leisure but of a guy who obviously worked in the sun. You could see it by his hands too, all rough and calloused. I could see them closely when he shook my father's hand and then tousled my hair. He squatted down to my eye level, pulled his fat Cohiba from his mouth, and said to me, "Hola, hombrecito. Come se llama?" I told him my name and then he said, "Me llamo Capitan Bustamante." His voice was deep, his surname coming out like cannon being fired, Booooo-sta-mante. To me it was like the voice of God himself. "Este tu barco?" I asked him, is this your boat? "No. No!" He laughed. "Este es tu botero a Miami." This is your taxi to Miami. [*Landon laughs off camera, while Ortiz breaks out in a wide grin.*] Then I remember him putting his cigar back into his mouth and standing up. "If you stay here for the trip, you may end up getting wet," he said to my father, who immediately looked down to me and my pleading face. "Estamos muy contento aqui," my father said to him and smiled at me. "This way we'll be clean before we arrive." I was so happy I grabbed my father's hand and jumped up and down. Mr. Bustamante smiled, gave my mother and father a polite nod, and saluted me.

"Buena suerte, mi valiente amigo," he said, glancing down at me, and then walked back to the bridge.

Landon: That's remarkable. Riding the bow of Philomena to your new life in America, and now, so many years later, behind the wheel as her first mate and keeping her running as engineer. What does it mean to you to be back on board? A completion of life's cycle, nostalgia, something else?

Ortiz, *staring at Landon, silent for a moment, then looking down*: All of that. But there's more to it. There are also ghosts here. The ship needs to be cleansed so it's the same for Captain Esteban as it once was for Captain Bustamante. A vessel that carries good people to better places.

Landon, *silent for a beat, then*: What kind of ghosts?

Ortiz: It's hard to explain. This ship brought many like me and my family to a new life here. But after a few months, toward the end of the boatlift, that changed. Fidel saw a chance to poke America in the eye. Can't really blame him, they'd tried to kill him for years. He opened up—

Landon: The jails and mental institutions.

Ortiz, *nodding*: Pushed the undesirables out. It wasn't just ordinary Cubans anymore, those with "questionable" loyalties. It was criminals, troublemakers, the feebleminded. Bustamante and some of the others who had embraced the exodus early on began to see what was happening. After a few months and a couple of bad trips—boatloads filled with predators and prey, reports of rapes and murders taking place on the ships and other boats capsizing because of overcrowding—he pulled Philomena out of the people-ferrying business and went back to work fishing. But it was rumored never to be as profitable as it once had been, before Mariel. Bustamante sold the ship in '85. Some claimed Miami was never the same after the boatlift either. Crime and chaos unleashed.

Landon: The damage was already done.

Ortiz: Worse—it was just beginning. But it wasn't just the exodus causing all the problems, it was the influx of drugs too. Coke. But many of the new refugee families were victims as well. We'd simply traded one set of oppressors for another. Snitches for psychopaths.

Landon: Okay, but I don't understand. You got through those tough times, made a life and career for yourself there. Why move to Port Royal from Miami at this stage? Captain Esteban said with your chops on diesel engines and all the thousands of mate hours you've logged, you had your pick of boats down there. Could've captained one of your own if you'd wanted.

Ortiz nods.

Landon: So why give all that up to come here? Oh, and why a Seventh-Day Adventist making a career on shrimping boats? Can we get back to that?

Lorenzo didn't answer. Landon hit pause on the video recording, put the phone in the pouch pocket of his gray hoodie.

"Why do you want to know all this? I thought you were here to do stories about shrimping?" Lorenzo asked, more curious than irritated.

"I am," Landon said earnestly. "But every story has a human face. You, Captain Esteban, Junior, Emmanuel, Olveda . . . even Chuy."

Lorenzo laughed.

"You're all the real story," Landon said. "It's like a book. The characters are everything."

Lorenzo nodded, but turned his gaze back to Landon. "So what about you?"

"What about me?" Landon asked, confused.

"You spend your whole life watching other people, telling other people's stories. Who tells yours?"

Landon blinked, then shifted from one foot to the other. Lorenzo continued to look at him, saying nothing more.

"This is my life," Landon finally answered. "I report and write about people who don't get a lot of attention from the world. Like you guys."

"Okay." Lorenzo crossed his arms.

"What?" Landon said, irritation showing.

Lorenzo remained silent.

"This isn't about me," Landon said, defensive. "It's not my story. It's yours."

"Yeah, that's what you said. Time for us little guys to have the spotlight." Lorenzo paused, realized he might be doing exactly what he feared. Messing things up for Clarita. "All I'm saying"—his voice softer—"is that you're here with us now, living on this ship, sharing our food, sharing our danger. Can't you find a way to tell our story without disappearing? Still be a part of it?"

"That's not how we work," Landon responded, impatient to continue the interview. "People don't tell us the important things easily. We do have to disappear, almost, lose ourselves in the story so we can ask you the right questions." He hesitated, redirected. "Like, why are you *really* here, Lorenzo? Back aboard *Philomena* after all these years?"

Lorenzo nodded ever so slightly, then pointed to Landon's hoodie pouch. Landon took out his phone and started recording again.

Ortiz: After I came to Miami with my parents, they both found jobs. My dad in a garage, my mom cleaning houses. They worked hard, saved enough to get us out of a crappy apartment in Opa-Locka to a decent place in Hialeah. It was almost all Cubans there at the time, and there was an Adventist congregation in our neighborhood. It's really why they moved there. We all watched out for each other, and since all the early exiles thought we were anti-Castro, we were welcome there. It was pretty normal for me after a while; grade school, then high school. After years of working, my dad got his own garage with a loan from the church. I apprenticed with him there after I graduated, became a grease monkey. I didn't love it, but it came natural. Time went on. But, I don't know, I was twenty-two, still living at home. Then one Saturday in church something changed for me. I saw this girl, Lena, I'd known practically my whole life. Her family—Adventists too—came to Miami a short while after us. We went to school together, but you know, we were just kids. I mean one day she's all knobby knees and elbows, frizzy hair and thick glasses. And then, on that day, she transformed in front of my eyes. I looked at her sitting in the pew with her family. She was this striking beauty. [*Looks up, remembering.*] She was tall, taller than me. [*Laughs.*] Long, shiny black hair. When she walked, she now had this grace, but she still had that bashful smile that I first knew her by. I was a year older and hadn't seen her for a while. After she graduated from high school she'd gone away to Orlando to the church's health sciences school there. Got a nursing degree, but came back to work at Palmetto

General. I went up to her after the service and talked to her, but there was real attraction now. She could smell it on me. Not like before, just goofing on each other as kids. After the service, we began spending all our time together. I would clean up after a long day at the garage and pick her up after her shift at the hospital. We'd have picnics at dusk on the beach, eating arroz con frijoles out of plastic bowls and pouring cortadito from my work thermos into small paper cups.

Landon: Cuban coffee.

Ortiz: Yes. We got married a year later. My parents were so happy. Our wedding was probably the best day of their lives. Even better than their own wedding. They loved her. She was smart, kind, beautiful. And she was in the church. But most of all she was willing to settle for someone like me, their mechanic son. [*He laughs.*]

Landon: Your parents have passed?

Ortiz, *frowning:* Why do you ask that?

Landon: You said "loved." Past tense. I just thought maybe they weren't around anymore.

Ortiz: You're right, they're not, but I didn't mean them. I meant her.

Landon: I'm sorry.

Ortiz, *nodding, gazing into the light below:* Ovarian cancer. We'd been trying to have a baby, but weren't having any luck. Had some tests done, discovered why. She had some pain there, but no other real symptom. By the time we knew, it was already too late. She needed a full hysterectomy. I didn't care. Kids didn't matter anymore. I just wanted her to live. It was tough after the operation. She was depressed for a while, but at least she was okay. It helped when she was able to go back to work. But then, two years later, during a checkup, it was back. We had one more year together. Seven total. Everyone said we were lucky to get that. Like cancer is a fucking winning lottery ticket or something if it doesn't kill you immediately. With all the pain and suffering she went through, I wish it would've been quicker, if that meant my Lena had to suffer less.

Landon: I'm sorry.

Ortiz, *shaking it off, now matter-of-fact*: You asked me why I'm here. Well, that was sixteen years ago. I've never remarried, never forgotten her, never wanted anything else. After I buried her, I felt like my life had ended too. Nothing could be the same. I quit the garage, then quit the church. I blamed God for letting my only love die. I defied him, defied the church, started doing coke, hanging out in dive bars around the port area, where I could stagger out after I was done and scream obscenities at him into the streets while no one gave a damn. This went on for a while.

But then on a typical night pounding rum, getting drunk out of my mind, I ran into an old guy, Martin, that used to come into our garage. He was coming into the bar as I was headed out. He turned me around. Made me come back in and sit down. Forced me to sit with him drinking cup after cup of cortadito, until I sobered up enough to have a conversation. He wasn't in the church, but he lived in the neighborhood. He had a fleet of three small and very old shrimping boats, all with engines so bad that one or two were always in port getting repaired while the other was out fishing. He knew I was good with car engines and figured I could quickly learn what I needed to about marine engines to help keep him in business. He set me up with a bunk on one of his boats in repair, let me sleep for a week, weaned me off the coke and booze, fed me, helped me regain some strength, and then put me to work.

He became my tio. I wanted to repay him. I read all the manuals on the old marine diesels and found they weren't that different from what I'd been working on at the garage. After three or four months I had all his boats in good enough shape to fish every day. Tio Martin started making more money, and as a reward he gave me more responsibilities. First I worked the nets as a deckhand, and then I started driving the boats. When I was on the water or working, I could forget losing Lena for part of the time. After three years my tio told me it was time for me to move on—sign on with bigger boats, make real money, and find another woman to share my life with.

I knew no one would ever replace Lena, but it was time for bigger challenges. The work had become too easy, too routine. I felt my mind drifting back to the past. It was easy for me to get work because I could handle both the bridge and the engine room. My skills grew as I worked bigger and bigger boats—sixty, a hundred tons, even two-hundred-ton trawlers. I was making more money than I ever had. I got a new apartment, but this time in Miami. I began going out, started drinking again, little coke now and then, not really dating, but you know.

And then, five years after I lost Lena, both my parents died in the same year. First my dad from a heart attack, and then my mom from an embolism, a deep-vein thrombosis that moved up her leg to her lungs and suffocated her in her sleep. After that I could've died myself and wouldn't have cared. They were really the last people that meant anything to me. I found myself at that same threshold I'd been at after Lena. Ready to dive into the abyss again. But at my mom's funeral, I saw her youngest sister.

She'd come to America like us, but they hadn't talked much over the years. This auntie was fifteen years younger than my mom and had been wild. And then she just disappeared. Rumor was she got pregnant. Found out later it was true, and she wasn't even sure who the father was. She did her best to raise her young son right, but as he got older, like his mom, like me, he fell into a bad crowd. At the funeral she approached me. She'd heard about my meltdown after Lena died, but also that I got back on my feet and was doing well. She asked me to help her out with her son, Jesus.

Landon: Chuy!

Ortiz, *chuckling*: The one and only. The timing was good. It gave me a reason not to jump off the cliff again. I had a project now. He was eighteen then, and I took him out of there and had him live with me in my apartment. It wasn't easy. He never had a real father, just the parade of losers my tia had been with. He was lazy at first, entitled, and didn't want to do anything but party with his friends. I took him out shrimping a couple times on day runs, and they were disasters. He was hungover, puking off the back of the boat.

But then one night after he did too much coke, I found him at home in his bed, sweating and scared. He was coming down, didn't really have anything to soften the drop. No downers and no booze, too fucked up to go out and get some. So I went to my local mercado, bought a cheap bottle of rum, and made him drink a third of it. I eventually got him to fall asleep. The next day he asked me to take him out again on another day trip, promised me he'd clean up his act. For the most part he did. After a few more outings he showed me he could do the job, found some peace for himself on the water, just the way I had. I made him part of my package as a deckhand on every boat I worked after.

He's still a broody little pendejo, but he knows the business now and knows I'll crack his head if he doesn't work hard every single day. He supports his mom, sends her money. He turned out okay. I was glad I could help a little, felt like I owed that to Tio Martin. He believed I deserved a second chance, and he gave it to me. It would be insulting to his memory not to do the same for Chuy.

Landon: So things were going well in Miami. Why change the routine?

Ortiz, *nodding*: The last couple years, I could see Chuy was starting to get bored like I had. Getting into trouble in his downtime when we weren't out fishing. I started looking for options to get him away from Miami and his friends, the bad influences.

I saw Clarita's ad in the *Maritime News*. Couldn't believe it was the same Philomena until I checked the registration number, tracked down its provenance. After all my screaming at God, I thought maybe now he was finally answering back. The ship that first brought me to my new life here was calling out to me again. We had at least one more journey we needed to take together.

Landon: Where will this one lead?

Ortiz, *gazing off to the right*: I don't know . . . I don't think it really matters. I just know when it finally comes in view, I'll still be in the best spot to see it. Until then I'm going to keep her running good, exorcise some of those bad ghosts from her past. Some of mine and Chuy's both.

Landon stopped recording. His phone was warm from the lengthy session and needed a charge. He slipped it back into his sweatshirt pocket.

"Thanks," he said to Lorenzo. "That was powerful. I can edit some of the more personal stuff if you want."

"Aren't you the one who just said people don't share the important things? And when you finally get it, you want to cut it out? Do what you want," Lorenzo said. "Not like Chuy and I are gonna get fired after you reveal our sordid past."

CHAPTER 11

DEAD IN
THE WATER

Thursday, December 20, 2018
Into the storm

Captain Esteban gripped the wheel tight, guiding *Philomena* up the steep face of another oncoming wave, small relief that at least everyone was accounted for. Or were they? She allowed herself another glance back. They were just six.

"And where the hell's the reporter?" she demanded.

"Still racked out," answered Chuy.

"In this weather?" asked Lorenzo, incredulous. Then shot a look at the cook, leaning into the back frame of the pilothouse. Emmanuel caught the stare, gave it back without reacting.

Lorenzo turned to his cousin. "Go get him. Bring him up."

Chuy nodded, uncertain at first, but steadied himself, then, favoring his right ankle, limped past the others to the back and opened the door. A cold spray of seawater filled the wheelhouse, soaking everyone, until he pulled it shut behind him.

Chuy had just cleared the wheelhouse door when *Philomena*'s engine fell silent.

He stopped in his tracks, and turned to look back inside. The captain was still at the helm. Lorenzo darted to the rear and lifted the hinged lid from the bench where the personal flotation devices were stored. Within seconds he'd handed them out to Olveda, Junior, and Emmanuel and slipped his arms through a vest of his own before rushing over to the captain and cinching her into another.

"Looks like those gaskets couldn't wait," she said to Lorenzo, trying to force calm into her voice. "My fault though, shouldn't of pushed it. Now we're dead in the—" Before she could complete the sentence, *Philomena* rose up on the swell of a towering black wave. "Everybody grab something!" she yelled, looking back at her crew, horrified to realize Chuy was still standing outside on the wheelhouse platform. She watched him raise a hand as if to say he was okay.

"Enzo!" she shouted, directing his attention to Chuy just as the ship came slamming back down. In one step Lorenzo was out the door, but the platform was empty.

"Man overboard! Man overboard!" he shouted, pointing in the direction where Chuy had been just moments before, the way all sailors are trained.

"Enzo!" the captain called again, this time pointing to the starboard view port. With no propulsion, *Philomena* had slipped into a deep trough, exposing the right side of the ship to a monstrous wall of water, a predator wave that the captain knew, with no power to escape, would crush them. Lorenzo snatched the two portable emergency-position-indicating radio beacons clipped to the right of the console. He attached one of them to Olveda's life vest while she tugged nervously at a chain around her neck, pulling it so tight it finally snapped and fell to the floor. He squeezed both her shoulders, reassuring her silently, before flipping the switch on the EPIRB to activate it. A small red light inside a transparent, acrylic cone began flashing. Lorenzo did the same with the other, attaching it to the captain's vest while she was focused on the radio handset, punching the distress button to automatically raise Channel 16, the emergency frequency.

"Mayday! Mayday! Mayday! This is Captain Clarita Esteban of the ocean trawler *Philomena*. I repeat, this is Captain Clarita Esteban of the ocean trawler *Philomena*. We have lost power and are adrift in heavy seas approximately twenty-five miles due east of Tybee Island. Our current position is north three-one degrees, five-seven-point-five-six-three, west eight-zero degrees, one-eight-point-one-four-two." She repeated the coordinates twice more, slowly and clearly. For the crew, the sound of each number dialed up their fear, crowding out any disbelief that this was actually happening. Junior picked up on Lorenzo's cue, placed an arm around Olveda, but his comforting gesture was canceled out by the captain's final radio transmission.

"Request any assistance, immediately. We have a man overboard."

PART TWO

FIGHT

The desolation of that place was a thing exquisite.

—Cormac McCarthy, *Blood Meridian*

CHAPTER 12

ESCAPE

Friday, December 21, 2018
Under the Sea: Day 2

Landon shivered. Even out of the water, his body temperature was dropping again. His headache was getting worse, and he felt desiccated as sun-cracked shoe leather. Severe dehydration could send him into shock, and maybe he was already on that threshold, his small drink from the sink now a distant memory. He looked at the beers in their life-jacket koozies. He imagined the crack of the key tab, the first pour coating his tongue and the back of his throat in a wash of malt and bitters. But the consequences of giving in to his thirst too early could also be fatal. Malt liquor was almost twice the alcohol content of regular beer, as much as 9 percent, and that, amplified by the effects of his current depth, could incapacitate him, maybe even render him unconscious. It was too much of a wild card. It was more important to stay sharp, keep his wits about him, even if that meant holding off a little longer—at least until he decided on a survival plan.

Normally before any reporting trip, he would research and create a logistical operations scheme. Determine the regional language and dialects, currency, cuisine, cultural considerations, medical facilities, embassy locations, emergency contacts, as well as the average high and low temperatures at that time of year, rainfall, power, and digital access. But often it was his own experience, or talking to colleagues, that provided the best intelligence. Obviously, he'd never been in this situation, but he'd read about other underwater escapes that could be helpful in surviving his own predicament. He mentally reviewed them.

Just that summer there was the inspiring case of the Thai boys' soccer team known as the Wild Boars. In late June twelve members of the team, along with their twenty-five-year-old assistant coach, Ekkapol Chantawong, went exploring the Tham Luang cave network near Chiang Rai. But within just a few hours the passageways they'd just trekked were flooded by monsoon rains, and they were trapped inside a small cavern. Landon had followed the story closely, as had much of the world. He was rooting for the boys, who even before their fateful hike had been the most heartbreaking of underdogs—just twelve to sixteen years old, some orphans and stateless refugees living on the precipice of the messy, fluid, and often lawless Thai-Myanmar border. The boys had survived an astonishing nine days in the cavern before being discovered by rescue divers. For all that time they'd perched on jagged outcroppings, sharp rock slicing their bare feet. To sustain themselves they ate the meager snacks they'd brought with them and tried to slake their thirst by licking fresh water condensation off the cave walls, a trick taught to them by Chantawong.

Chantawong himself was an orphan and had been raised in a local Buddhist monastery. During the ordeal he proved himself an able and selfless leader, refusing most of his share of the food to help feed his younger charges while teaching them to curb both their hunger and their fear through meditation. A team of international divers from six different nations eventually got all the boys and their coach safely out of the cave network in a painstakingly, intricate rescue operation, moving them through two and a half miles of pitch-black passageways, some as narrow as fifteen inches, against a strong current of frigid water. Most of them didn't know how to swim, let alone use scuba gear. The news stories highlighted the remarkable patience and teamwork of the rescuers; how the divers fitted each boy, one at a time, with a wetsuit and full-face scuba mask, sedated him with ketamine, Xanax, and saliva-suppressant atropine so that he didn't choke, and placed him in a wraparound stretcher that they threaded through winding passageways, with one rescue diver in front, working in relays over the course of a five-hour journey, readministering sedatives and switching from depleted to fresh air tanks along the way.

Landon remembered being surprised that there had been only one fatality in the whole rescue: a Thai Navy SEAL rescue diver who ran out of air as he pre-positioned scuba tanks along the escape route. While the man's family was undoubtedly sad to lose him, Landon envied him. He'd achieved in death what so many longed for but never got—an enduring nobility. No matter how he'd lived before, his final act was one of ultimate sacrifice, wiping all other sins clean. Landon had hoped to find that kind of death in war, but found instead his own betrayal and shame. Drowning at the bottom of the sea in a shitter was either karmic retribution or, in a phrase Rhona liked to use, the hand of the divine. The only way to avoid it? Stay alive.

Landon wondered what the Wild Boars' rescue could teach him. As he lay on his hammock, he looked at the wall directly behind him, slid his fingers across its moist surface, and placed them in his mouth. Condensation. Fresh water. Propping himself up on his knees, he drew his tongue across the walls in broad swaths, lapping up the moisture, young Coach Ekkapol Chantawong's guiding hand stretching past the months and miles to reach him here at the bottom of the sea.

His jaw ached and the gap were his incisors had been was throbbing again when he stopped twenty minutes later. While he felt a little less parched, the effort had sapped his energy. Still, he probed his mind, hoping to recall other stories of undersea survival. Eventually he remembered a twenty-nine-year-old Nigerian cook whose predicament seemed close to his own.

In late May 2013, Harrison Okene had been crewing on an oil service tugboat in the Atlantic, just off the Nigerian coast. Landon remembered reading that like himself, Okene got up very early one morning, before dawn, to use the restroom. The sea had been choppy, but not unusually so. And then suddenly a large ocean swell struck, flipping the tug upside down and sending it to the ocean floor.

Okene later told reporters he'd been knocked violently from side to side, but managed to scramble to the engineer's office, where there was still a small pocket of air, as the tugboat settled nearly thirty meters beneath the surface. All eleven other crew members died, having been locked in their cabins as a precaution against pirates who regularly raided vessels working in that area.

In interviews Okene said he could hear them shouting, "God help me, God help me, God help me," as the boat went down. He said his own faith had been shaken in the weeks after, as he wondered why he was the only one to survive.

Favorable circumstances had increased Okene's odds of survival. He was able to locate a mattress in the engineer's quarters that, like Landon's makeshift hammock, got him out of the water and helped him stave off hypothermia, even though he had been wearing only boxer shorts when the tugboat sank. Okene survived nearly three days in an air bubble that was reportedly only four square feet in size, comparable to Landon's own. And scientists studying the case in the aftermath later determined that, true to Boyle's law, the bubble had to be oxygen-dense to sustain him as long as it did. Another threat to his survival was the buildup of carbon dioxide waste from his exhalations. Once the CO_2 level reaches 5 percent in a confined space, a person can't take in enough oxygen and will start to hyperventilate, and eventually pass out. Scientists were at first puzzled why that didn't happen to Okene. He later revealed to reporters that he'd splashed around in the water sometimes as he moved about. This, scientists figured, helped increase the surface area of the water and dispelled some of the CO_2 waste into the liquid. His own movements had helped extend the half-life of the breathable air in his bubble.

But Harrison Okene's biggest break came on his third day underwater, when salvage divers were dispatched to recover bodies from the sunken tugboat. Okene reportedly saw the glow of their dive lights and left his bubble briefly to swim toward them. He said he tapped a diver on the back of the neck and sent him reeling in fear. "Corpse!" the diver called into his face mask microphone, according to the reports. But when the cook pulled on the diver's hand, the refrain changed to "He's alive, he's alive!" As a diver, Landon had been fascinated by the story, even watching an online video made by the divers of their first contact with the cook.

The video had a claustrophobic quality: the slightly chubby, round-shouldered Okene inside his bubble, harshly illuminated by the diver's canister light, his shirtless figure surrounded by floating debris. The curve of the ship's hull was visible to his right, while the left disappeared into blackness; the same blackness that Okene had endured for days after the batteries in a flashlight he'd found had burned out. The water was opaque and had risen to a frightening level, past the nipples on his chest. The expression on Okene's face was hard for Landon to read. Was it shock? Fear? Relief? He felt he could now interpret it as that of a man on the threshold between hope and despair; a man who even in his new circumstances hadn't quite determined which to feel.

Because of the intense pressure he'd endured, a hundred feet beneath the surface, Okene's tissues were saturated with nitrogen gas. It had to be released slowly, or a sudden decrease could release the gas into his bloodstream all at once. Moving into Okene's joints, lungs, and heart and in a unique case, these bubbles would almost certainly be fatal. He was first evacuated from the sunken tugboat into a diving bell lowered from the salvage boat. After off gassing there for several hours, he was finally brought up from the deep and spent the next two days in a decompression chamber until all the nitrogen was cleared from his system. When it was finally over, the young cook returned to his home and wife in Nigeria, telling reporters he would never again go back to the sea. Impossible to blame him, Landon thought.

But Okene's survival tale didn't have a storybook ending. Though he was alive and reunited with his family, later reports told how the cook suffered both physically and mentally. Layers of his skin had peeled off from his long submersion. His nights were plagued by nightmares, his days by the paralyzing effects of post-traumatic stress. But perhaps most upsetting was that some in his own community, including a local pastor, had accused him of summoning black magic to survive while his shipmates died. Brain-dead idiots! Landon remembered thinking at the time. A man's will to survive dismissed as conjuring and spells by the superstitious. He promised himself, if he ever got to Nigeria, he'd look up Okene, shake his hand, maybe do a follow-up story on him.

Landon didn't relish getting back into the water now, but he felt he didn't have a choice. He splashed, kicked, and slapped at the water, a giant carp in a tiny pond, trying to do as Okene had done inadvertently, increasing the surface area of his bubble to soak up the toxic gas he'd been breathing out. It was bracing, the cold water lifting some of the fatigue of being sedentary and giving him another bump of temporary purpose. His mind raced along with his movements. He was a human blender now, unable to contain his panic or euphoria or whatever was coursing through him, spinning and slashing at the water, thinking of the sounds he'd heard earlier outside the door of the head, the chilling *chk, chk, chk, chk, chk, chk, chk* skittling that made his skin crawl.

He imagined his hands and arms as chain flails, striking at the crustacean swarm that worked through the flesh of the captain and crew with their clicking pincers and chitin mandibles, exposing their organs for the sharks and barracuda to finish off. But it was impossible to fight them. There were too many, and every time he pushed them back, more would appear from the dark edges to feast. He thought he might collapse from a stroke. Finally he surrendered, sinking to his knees in the water, panting, drawing in deep breaths, exhaling in long gasps, sabotaging the very CO_2 experiment he'd hoped would prolong his time and lengthen the window of opportunity for his rescue.

He felt lightheaded. Was he already low on air? He was an idiot and a fool to believe he could save himself. To believe he was worth saving. Defeated, he crawled back into his now-wet hammock, reached for a can of Cobra, and guzzled down half.

"Thank you, Junior," he said, making an air toast. He could've finished it in one gulp, but he held back, a single thread of pride forcing him to halt, a tiny victory for self-control. At depth, the beer barely fizzed when cracked open and tasted flat, yet it was a sip of heaven for his dehydrated body and spirit. The alcohol almost instantly calmed him. He felt like a lazy cat on a sunny window ledge, wanting to do nothing else but curl up and sleep. That lapse, he knew, could be a death sentence. So what?

He lay back in his hammock, closed his eyes, sipped his beer, and imagined he was kicking back at Virginia Key Beach Park, a gorgeous and uncrowded spit of sand just off the Rickenbacker Causeway south of Miami and just north of Key Biscayne. The place had an easy tempo and an antique carousel that he'd almost had to bribe Vanessa to ride with him. She said it was loud and all that spinning around made her dizzy, but Landon loved the thing. It reminded him of the Old Man, his paternal grandfather, and his tales of traveling carnivals and their infamous midways. Among the Old Man's many other jobs, including jazz trumpeter and used car salesman, he'd once been a carnival barker, luring "suckers to see sideshow freaks" like the Wild Man of Borneo and Dippy the Pinhead. But what the Old Man lacked in morality he made up with cunning and charisma, every decision connected to a caper or machination to get more of something—money, booze, pussy. The world was a competition, and he came ready to win. He always seemed impatient and hungry, cracking the bones and chewing the marrow out of life like a ravenous tiger. Maybe that's why Landon's own father, Tobias, was intent on being the Old Man's opposite. Tobias was a study in temperance, fidelity, control. It made for a less colorful but more consistent character. Likely that was what Tobias had been aiming for, never trying to compete with the Old Man's antics when he was alive or with his reputation after his death. Tobias focused his full energy and enthusiasm on only one person in his life: his wife and confidante, Landon's mother, Annabel.

The alcohol made Landon wistful. He had wanted with Vanessa

what his father had with his mother. But that took full devotion, something he'd never given his ex-wife, an insistent and permanent regret. He took another sip of beer, pretty sure he was fully inebriated on just three-quarters of a can of malt liquor, savoring it and the bittersweet memories it unearthed.

CHAPTER 13

TICKLERS
AND TEDS

Fourth in a Globe-Democrat series on South Carolina's beleaguered commercial shrimping industry.

Our features editor Lukas Landon is filing dispatches all this week while aboard the trawler Philomena as her captain and crew make one last run in an attempt to stay solvent at the end of a brutal season. (Globe-Democrat print and digital editions, published 12-18-18.)

BITTER SEAS
Reporter's Notebook:
Question: How Does a Shrimp Boat Work? Answer: Only with a Lot of Effort.
—*Lukas Landon*

Most of us have only a vague idea of how a shrimp boat works. It leaves port empty and comes back, captain and crew hope, full of shrimp. It's that time in between that you don't see where the magic—or, as deckhands say, the donkey work—happens. Truth is, while there have been some advances in fishing technology—marine radar, more stable boats, more sophisticated netting—shrimping remains backbreaking work requiring days or weeks at sea, setting and hauling nets from sunup to sundown. The crew are usually paid out of the ship's gross profits, meaning the captain covers the cost of food, fuel, salt, and other expenses. If the picks are good, a deckhand can make a couple of thousand per week. If the picks are bad, they can walk away with just a few hundred, or even go away empty-handed.

Many shrimping crews are like well-oiled machines, having put in so many seasons together year in and year out that they know each other like family, able to anticipate each other's actions, sometimes wordlessly. And sometimes, just like family, they fight over things petty and large after spending too much time together. Philomena has a unique crew, in the sense that some members literally are family. Captain Esteban's daughter, Olveda, is a greenhorn getting broken in this year, and the ship's engineer, Lorenzo Ortiz, had been working with his younger cousin, Jesus Ortiz, for years in Miami prior to their both joining Philomena together this season. Floyd Swain Jr. is the only old hand on Philomena, a holdover from the crew of the boat's previous owner, Low Country Holdings LLC. So while all have some familiarity either with each other or the ship itself, working well together as a crew takes time, and sometimes the connections can make things more difficult. Shrimping requires a complex choreography of people and equipment. Doing the wrong thing at the wrong time on the razor-thin margin of safety on the high seas can cause injury or death faster than you can say "slippery deck" or "loose outrigger."

So exactly how does a shrimping boat work, at least on the mechanical side? It starts with the iconic objects that make shrimp trawlers so distinctive-looking: the large steel poles called outriggers, mounted both port and starboard behind the wheelhouse (see the infographic below, "How a Shrimp Boat Works," and a video of Philomena in action at the Globe Democrat website, www.globe-democrat .com/bitterseas), which reach high into the sky while the ship is heading out from or back into port, but stretch out over the water once it's at sea. These devices both stabilize the ship and act like giant knitting needles, allowing the nets to be stretched across a wide surface area while also keeping them from getting tangled up.

Once the outriggers are deployed, big wooden planks called doors—because that's what they look like—are hoisted out to the outrigger ends on both sides. The doors help keep the nets open while the ship is dragging them behind. Then the nets, threaded with float buoys and weights, are unfolded and connected to the outrigger by leg lines. The nets are conical in shape, often two per outrigger pole. The boat drags these nets along the seabed, their weighted bottom lines skimming the seafloor while float buoys lift their top edges. A chain called a tickler drags ahead of the net opening, forcing the shrimp to jump into the nets from the sea bottom where they feed.

But that's not all the nets catch. Deckhands say their picks can be sometimes as much as 40 percent other fish, including kingfish, croakers, menhaden, blue crab, starfish, and jellyfish. But one of the most controversial catches that ends up in shrimping nets is the loggerhead turtle, the largest and most common turtle found off the U.S. Atlantic coast.

It's estimated that more than 4,500 loggerheads are killed in the region by fishing operations every year. But shrimpers like Captain Esteban see that number as a point of professional pride, citing the fact that it represents a whopping 90 percent reduction in turtle deaths compared to the previous decade.

"Don't do us any good to haul up anything aside from shrimp," says Captain Clarita Esteban, poking through the bycatch of a recent Philomena haul. "See all the jellies? Just dead weight in our nets. Croaker and other stuff, we push it right back over, hopefully swims away. All my guys know we need to clear the deck fast. Now gotta say, not everybody does it like us. But we're all required to have the BRD [bycatch reduction devices] now. It's not perfect, but it's a lot bettr'n it was."

Outcry from advocates of more sustainable fishing has led to greater awareness of bycatch's cost to the marine environment, resulting in some encouraging solutions. These include the development of special devices that help prevent the netting of unwanted species like BRDs and TEDs (turtle exclusion devices), funnels that allow bigger creatures to pass through the otherwise fine mesh of the shrimping nets. Failure to use these devices, or to use them properly, can lead to hefty fines or even, for repeat offenders, pulling a boat's fishing license—if those responsible can be caught.

"It's a desperate situation right now, and the laws and new technologies only help so much," says Shay Sobel-Masters, executive director of the Charleston-based environmental group Blue Oceans Outreach. "Especially if we're not supplying resources to enforce them. We're not even adequately policing local fishing operations, so what happens with the factory ships operating twelve miles out, beyond U.S. territorial jurisdiction? This is going to end in our worst nightmare—a planet of empty oceans."

The captain and crew of Philomena believe they're at least doing their part. "This is our livelihood. We feed ourselves by puttin' food on your table," Captain Esteban says, watching as the outriggers are raised with mechanical winches and swung back over the top deck, in an operation that's probably been done already a dozen times this day. Once in place, the baglines, a clever double half-hitch of knots at the bottom of the nets, can be undone with a single pull. In unison, Chuy and Junior "pop" them, spilling hundreds of pounds of teeming sea life over the deck. Flashes of silver signal significant amounts of fish, jellyfish, and other bycatch, which is funneled away from the hold by a wooden divider and pushed overboard. The remaining shrimp are swept through the hatch belowdecks and into cold storage. Repeat this six to eight more times in a day, and that's how a shrimp boat works. "Done right"—Captain Esteban makes a nod to her crew—"it's a beautiful thing."

CHAPTER 14

VANESSA

Under the Sea: Day 2

In his short and murky sleep, Landon had momentarily, mercifully, forgotten where he was. Then he awoke, needing badly to piss. He felt like his bladder was going to burst, and as much as he hated the idea of further contaminating the cesspool that surrounded him, he inched to the edge of his hammock, unzipped his fly, and got ready to relieve himself. When the first dark stream hit the water below, though, he clamped down. Remembering the empty beer, he swallowed the last few drops, then placed the can between his dangling legs and resumed. It was difficult to keep his urine stream in the can's keyhole opening, but his aim was mostly accurate. The red emergency light didn't allow a fully accurate reading, but his urine was dark, indicative of dehydration. The beer can grew heavier, and before his bladder emptied it began to overflow. He tilted the can, draining some into the water below. But as he was rezipping his jeans, he knocked over the can, dumping half the contents onto the suspended blanket.

"Christ on crutches," Landon shouted, frustrated to the point of tears again, his earlier calm giving way to a creeping hopelessness. He touched the urine on the blanket, noted its sour, ammonia smell. Gripping the can firmly, he felt the contents of his body's internal warmth within. He considered trickling it over his bare body, but realized how quickly the heat would evaporate, leaving him both colder and stinking of piss. Instead he lifted his sweater and placed the can under his right armpit, then his left, then to each side of his neck. These, he knew, were major arterial circulation points. The can of his own warm piss was like an old-fashioned hot water bottle, heating the blood as it flowed through his body and helping to keep him from slipping into hypothermia.

Once the heat of the can dissipated, Landon placed it on one of the shelves in the cupboard, hoping he wouldn't be forced to drink it as a last resort. He pulled at the collar of his sweater, felt the coarse wet wool around his neck. It resurrected the memory of that Christmas more than eleven years earlier, shortly before the divorce, when he and Vanessa had nothing left to give each other but a few sad gifts, one of which he was wearing now. It had been wrapped loose—no box, no bow, no note, just holly-green paper decorated with red-and-white-striped candy canes. He recalled her handoff, his peck-on-the-cheek thank-you, pulling it over his head to model the fit. Snug, especially around the waist, but that didn't matter. He never saw himself wearing it. Ever. He'd gotten her a yoga mat made from bamboo fibers and a ridiculously expensive yoga hoodie, the kind with thumbholes in the sleeves and formulated from some magic material that promised fast-track enlightenment, but only if paired with perfect karma and the destruction of all desire. The memory pressed down on him, squeezed against his chest. Wanted more. The masochistic pleasures of resurrecting his long-dead marriage. He felt for his smartphone, pressed the home button, relieved to see he still had a healthy charge. He checked the stopwatch: thirty-seven hours, seven seconds. He swiped it away for the photos app.

He'd been through countless devices since his divorce, but with every new phone he migrated a few dozen photos and a handful of videos from the cloud onto its internal storage drive. Though they ate up the phone's true memory, he wanted them there, decade-old muses that he could summon regardless of phone service or Wi-Fi in conditions like his current one. He pulled up the index of thumbnails and began opening them one by one. There was an image of him and Vanessa smoking shisha at an outdoor café on the Istiklal Caddesi in Istanbul. Kissing in front of the Castillo de la Real Fuerza on their honeymoon, about to take a giant stride off a dive boat's swim deck into Belize's Blue Hole. And the more ordinary stuff, the stuff he loved, silly shit like holding kitchen strainers over their faces and fencing with whisks in a French cooking class, pretending to hang off the edge of a cliff while hiking a section of the Appalachian Trail, Vanessa feigning shock when she realizes she's snagged her husband by the shorts with her fishing line, her hair blowing seductively across her face while riding shotgun in his Jeep on a drive to Virginia Key Beach. There were more photos, but only one video of her. It wasn't even sentimental, but it had proved prophetic. In 2006 she had entered a half marathon. She'd been doing a lot of running that year, and this one landed on a weekend when Landon wasn't working. He positioned himself at the end so he could capture her final sprint across the finish line. She seemed to explode over the last quarter mile, her long, lean legs pumping, ponytail threaded through the back of her visor like a Roman Praetorian's plume. But it was the determination on her face as she passed through the finish arch that made him keep the recording. It was a look that said to him that there were things she wanted for herself too, and that he would either have to run with her or be left behind. She'd finished third in her age category that day. It was the last time he would ever see her run. He played it once again, wondering why he had not run after her. Or even walked alongside when she hadn't been running at all.

She had been the true love of his life and the only person, besides his mother, able to see past what he felt was the striking imperfection of his surface. Lifelong strabismus hypertropia meant the iris of his right eye was asymmetrical in position to his left. Flaring slightly up, not cartoonishly so, but enough to be noticed and acknowledged, silently or otherwise. Landon felt it sent a subconscious signal to others that he was not fully present during their conversations, that his right eye was exploring the realm of his own thoughts while the other stayed locked on target. He compensated with positioning. When seated across from someone during an interview, he would turn his head to one side like a bird, cheating the angle for a better view—in his case that of a man gazing calmly, purposefully, with an eye that didn't wander.

Most did not notice what he was doing, but Vanessa did, immediately. For a short time in the late 1990s she had been a field producer for one of the local television affiliates in Miami. She'd been sent with a crew to the *Miami Herald* newsroom to produce a remote live interview with Landon. It concerned an investigative series he'd done on a chain of pet stores being used to launder drug money for a West Palm Beach businessman. Landon had been with the *Herald* just two years after being hired away from the *Plain Dealer* in Cleveland, but he was already making a name for himself as an up-and-coming crime reporter. He'd done radio interviews about his stories, but this was the first time a TV station had taken interest. As the crew planted tripods and light stands around his cubicle, he began to cheat to the left, as he did during in-person interviews.

"What are you, a Hollywood gossip columnist or a crime reporter?" Vanessa teasingly admonished him. She took his shoulders and squared him up to the camera. When he watched a recording of the interview later, he saw that she was right. He was not an aberration, just another asymmetrical face among billions. What did stand out was his confident recap of the story and the short question-and-answer with the Ricardo Montalbán lookalike anchor that followed.

He was even more polished when the station brought him back for additional live shots on other stories. After one of their segments together, he felt bold enough to invite Vanessa for a drink. She accepted without hesitation. A dinner followed, and soon enough they were dating. Ever skeptical, Landon considered he might simply be her ladder up, a newspaper reporter connection boosting the street cred of a future star in the oft-maligned and shallow TV news industry.

That was not Vanessa's intention. In fact, she didn't want a journalism career at all. Within a year after meeting Landon, she submitted her resignation to the TV station and went back to school full-time for a master's degree in primary education. Within fourteen months she was teaching fourth grade at Paul Lawrence Dunbar in Overtown, one of the lowest-rated public elementary schools in Miami–Dade County. The school was an overcrowded nightmare, populated with children from impoverished new immigrant families as well as poor locals. It was such a basket case that the teacher and administration turnover was one of the highest in the nation, and the students routinely tested at the bottom of all of the standardized testing regimens. Even in grade school, gang affiliations were crystallizing, and the school district had both armed school police and metal detectors to greet students each morning.

Landon supported Vanessa's desire to give back, but this was a position that should've come with combat pay. She was lucky if she could teach for twenty minutes each hour, between the fights and the emotional breakdowns that went with empty stomachs, broken families, and the hopelessness of knowing you've been abandoned by the system before you even made it to your twelfth birthday. But Vanessa loved it, especially after the vapid, self-serving wasteland of local TV news. She'd recharge with long runs after school, but got right back to work, preparing and grading assignments late into the night. She possessed the zeal of a CrossFit convert and would not fail her kids, even if everyone else had.

He'd seen the same dedication with his mother, Annabel, a high school physics teacher, but she had worked in the infinitely more forgiving environment of a fully staffed, well-resourced, mostly white suburban Ohio school district, the kind where no one went to school without a warm, hearty breakfast in their belly. Landon admired Vanessa's drive and hoped that flame would never burn out, though he knew it would someday. No one could keep up that pace, hold up a social contract that lopsided. But she was determined to try, so he supported her the best he could with soft encouragement and hard insider information. He'd glean school district politics and policies from a colleague on the *Herald*'s education desk and pass that information on to Vanessa so she wouldn't be ambushed by the news of a new round of budget cuts or some other injustice passed on by Florida's governor and state house to its struggling schools. Landon had even shown up for a special schoolwide career day seminar. He presented a jazzy PowerPoint that highlighted some of his more sensational stories, stuff he knew the kids couldn't resist: big drug busts, the octopus escape from the Miami Aquarium, the local homeless boy who defied the odds to get accepted to all the Ivy League schools. He was proud to be able to keep the students engaged, to do that for Vanessa.

Landon shifted in his hammock and felt the stab of a chef's knife buried in his back. A pain of the mind swallowed by the pain of the body. Then, as if on a timer, his gums began to throb again. He was wet, cold, insufficient, feeble, paralyzed by his suffering. He thought of *Philomena*'s crew, how each and every one of them would've endured this better than him. Fearless Captain Esteban, chaining up Humvees still smoking and hot to the touch in the middle of a combat hellscape while absorbing shards of exploding metal. Lorenzo, losing the person he loved most in life but withstanding his grief to pull himself together, and Chuy too. Landon couldn't even get over his decade-old divorce.

He released a long, pitiful sob. Why had he thought he belonged on-board among these magnificent individuals? He was nothing next to them. He didn't deserve to live. What value did he provide to the world? Lorenzo had been right to question his purpose. He'd lost that trail so completely, it would never be found. He thought about Viktor Frankl again, another passage from his book that he'd highlighted: "When a person can't find a deep sense of meaning, they distract themselves with pleasure." Scratch out *person*, insert *Lukas Landon*. He took another sip of the malt liquor, laughing at the irony that for years he'd been slowly poisoning himself with alcohol, and now the shit was keeping him alive. He wanted to travel further back, to lose himself in the misery of the past rather than live in the misery of the present. He closed his eyes. Thought again of his life with Vanessa.

Within a year after she began teaching at Dunbar, Landon and Vanessa got engaged. It was something his own family quickly embraced, along with his beautiful, intelligent, compassionate fiancée. Her family, however, had trouble hiding their concern. His soon-to-be father-in-law, Nate Taylor, was founder and president of Taylor Materials, a company that supplied concrete to commercial construction firms. His was one of the most successful minority-owned businesses in Florida. And because of this, Landon figured, Nate had higher hopes for Vanessa than marrying a weird-looking white newspaper guy who would probably never make more than $70,000 a year. Just one more in a series of poor choices she'd made, the first, giving up her career in broadcasting to teach.

Nate had adjusted his view of his future son-in-law slightly upward after 9/11—or perhaps he was just relieved to see the wedding postponed while Landon went off to war. After the initial shock of the terror attacks played out in the media across the country, Landon began investigating follow-up stories about the hijacker pilots who'd flown the planes that crashed into the Twin Towers, the Pentagon, and a field in Pennsylvania. He contributed to reporting that revealed that two of the four hijackers, Mohamed Atta and Marwan al-Shehhi, had received training from a South Florida flight school. Landon knew this ongoing story would likely be the biggest of his lifetime. He badgered his bosses to send him to Afghanistan for America's impending retaliation against the 9/11 mastermind Osama bin Laden and al-Qaeda and the Taliban-controlled Afghan government that had given them safe haven. Eventually they relented—as did Vanessa. She was disappointed at their postponed wedding, but more concerned he might not come back at all. She sent him off to war with a photograph of herself and a love letter slipped inside the fabric lining of his body armor, never mentioning its presence—and was saddened to realize he'd never discovered it there.

Landon had gone in just weeks after 9/11, joining a few dozen men and a handful of women, independent journalists like himself who weren't going to lose this moment in history on a phone behind a desk. On a cold October night, by the light of the harvest moon, they crossed the Amu Darya River into northern Afghanistan on a pontoon raft operated by Tajikistan border guards, once soldiers of the former Soviet Union. Landon buzzed with anticipation and fear. It was a moment of inflection for him. The threshold he'd sought his entire life. Once across, they'd linked up with fighters from the opposition Northern Alliance and followed them into the trenches of Kalakata. Watched as the Taliban line disintegrated and fell back, pounded by US air strikes. In November he followed the fighters farther south, over the Hindu Kush and into the Afghan capital of Kabul to witness the collapse of the Taliban government, its quick dissolution surprising everyone. Finally, he traveled with them as they chased their enemy to the border. There, along with scores of other journalists, he watched as American B-52 and B-1 bombers dropped hundreds of thousands of pounds of explosives on the mountains of Tora Bora. He was the first to report the use of the most powerful bomb in America's nonnuclear arsenal, the Blu-82, a monstrous fifteen-thousand-pound explosive nicknamed the Daisy Cutter for the distinctive pattern of "petals" it cut, hundreds of yards long, into the rice paddies and jungles of Vietnam when deployed there. But even with that kind of firepower raining down, most of the Taliban's high-level leaders, their wealthy Saudi patron and onetime tenant Osama bin Laden, and the remnants of his al-Qaeda network managed to sneak through the porous passes across the border into the safety of Pakistan.

After five long months covering that conflict, Landon finally returned home, war-proven and bristling with the confidence of a man who'd found himself a worthy companion to the world's violence. He and Vanessa wed that summer.

Vanessa quickly learned that her husband's change was a beast that needed to be fed. Following the afterglow of the wedding and a short unconventional honeymoon in Cuba, she found Landon was restless, impatient, maybe even bored with their brand-new life. He seemed charged by risk-taking, driving too fast, drinking more heavily, and becoming argumentative during social gatherings. It was as if he'd started taking steroids and was growing outsized, and easily triggered. This plateaued only when the *Herald* tapped him for a new overseas assignment: the imminent US invasion of Iraq. This time Vanessa had pleaded with him not to go, screaming at him when her sound arguments didn't take.

The malt liquor curtain was descending on Landon, but not quick enough to mask those awful moments. "Easy now, V," Landon had said, his face flush with his second double Maker's and a smile so infuriatingly patronizing that Vanessa nearly squared up on him. "I've learned a few things from Afghanistan. I won't be taking any stupid chances."

She sucked her hands into her face, squeezed them against her cheeks. This was like explaining existentialism to a child.

"It's the unprovoked invasion of another country!" she shouted at him. "It's nothing but stupid chances."

Sitting in his hammock in the dark, Landon now knew he should've listened to his wife. America's hubris, as well as his own, would cost everyone it touched more than they could imagine.

The person he was then had needed another ride down the rabbit hole as badly as he needed another drink. He'd needed to go back to where he believed the best version of himself had lived. Luckily for him, neither of his wars would end quickly. And with each subsequent trip, usually three months at a time, Vanessa heard from him less and less. Sometimes he wouldn't come home to Miami at all, leaving her hurt and frustrated when he'd skip Christmas to fuck off by himself in Israel or spend spring in the wet gloom of Germany and Poland. One summer he even abandoned her to get certified as a scuba dive master in Sharm El-Sheik between his war zone deployment cycles, telling her that being underwater soothed his frazzled nerves. Excuses, Vanessa knew, from a man who simply didn't want to talk and, despite the violent drama surrounding him, felt like he had nothing to say.

In Afghanistan he'd seen the typical talismans of war—brutal killings, sadistic violence, sexual predation against children. But he seemed capable of defusing those mental time bombs with his stories and photographs. The work was cathartic, but Iraq demanded some unpayable debt to his soul, the inexplicable carnage growing more absurd every day, every week, every month, every year. His work couldn't explain it anymore—not to his readers, not to his editors, not to himself. It failed the all-important "why." Why had they gone into this place, and why wouldn't the Iraqis gratefully accept this new government the US and its unwitting allies had so graciously bestowed on them? The understanding didn't come with the violent deaths of Saddam's sons Uday and Qusay. It didn't come with finding Saddam himself, bearded and unkempt, hiding in a spider hole near his hometown of Tikrit. It didn't come after Saddam was executed. It didn't come with the twin uprisings of both Sunnis and Shias, or with the ascendance of Abu Musab al-Zarqawi, the Jordanian petty criminal who pledged fealty to Osama bin Laden and became leader of al-Qaeda in Iraq. In fact, that was when the real chaos started, when the evil on both sides just multiplied: rapes, extrajudicial killings, the revelations of what had been going on at the American prisoner-of-war camp at Abu Ghraib. Perhaps that was the most puzzling betrayal of all. Why had supposedly democratic American soldiers and civilian intelligence agents become sadistic monsters whose brutal deprivations had become iconoclastic images of what it means to lose touch with one's own humanity? Why had they created a living chamber of horrors, preposterously, absurdly, and unimaginably in the name of spreading American values within a military designation so ironic as to end all ironies? Operation Iraqi Freedom. No one would be free. If the conflict ever ended, it would still follow all of them for the rest of their natural lives. What they saw, what they did.

Same, Landon lamented, for himself.

There were no weapons of mass destruction, no single moments or identifiable turning points that changed everything. Not even Ramadi. Like everyone else who participated in the Iraq War, Landon hadn't lost his humanity in one great climax. He'd lost it in a thousand small decisions. He'd lost it in the miasma of bad choices, huffing from one to the next without pausing for the lessons they should've taught him. His downfall was the same as his country's, that arrogance of hope that he was one of the good guys. That he'd done nothing wrong. Or at least that the wrong he *had* done was accidental. And the accident was in the service of something good, or at least not making something worse. War was not the only place that challenged the perceptions of your own goodness, but it did it, Landon realized, the hardest and the fastest and the most unalterably.

Violent conflict had become this self-perpetuating thing that he'd seem to be covering forever and always would. But by 2006, while both wars were still going strong, the public spectators were feeling war fatigue. America was losing interest. Getting bored. And so the *Herald*, hemorrhaging money like every other news organization in the country, pulled the plug on Landon's regular reporting trips to both Iraq and Afghanistan. But by then, nearly six years of continuous war had left him incapable of being stimulated by anything else. Landon pleaded, threatened, cajoled; the withdrawal was brutal. And, knowing their contribution in getting him addicted to war, his editors had given him a new one—or rather an old one with some new kicks. Nixon's 1973 war on drugs had been upgraded with police deputized as soldiers in surplus military gear from Afghanistan and Iraq. It was perfect, poetic injustice. American cops from Miami to Mills Creek now rolled in armored Humvees, carried M4s underslung with M40 grenade launchers. Fuck serve and protect—it was time to dominate the battlespace. This was something Landon knew, something he could work with as a reporter. Time to gear up. The difference now was that his war zone was also his home.

Landon had contacts all over Miami on both sides of the law. He'd report on the war on drugs during the day and participate in it, wildly, at night. He was living the hack life now, with a ready-to-roll playlist of war stories that kept coked-up friends and colleagues in wide-eyed awe, but not necessarily his bosses, who instead keyed in to the missed deadlines and reporting that was incomplete or, worse, inaccurate. Vanessa had seen a counterclockwise click in his devolution after nearly every reporting trip overseas, aside from his very first. Most troublesome, though, was a homecoming after his 2004 trip, the one where he spent time in both Ramadi and Fallujah. Some of her teacher friends were married to servicemen or reservists who had been deployed to both wars too.

He was in Fallujah? Okay, that was it, they told her. Bloodiest battle of the whole war. No wonder your man is messed up, they said, thinking this explanation was somehow comforting. He just needs some time away, talk with somebody maybe. But you know men. Rather drink the problems away. That'll slow down after a while. Nightmares will taper off too. It's all part of it, girlfriend, even worse for my man, since he had to pull the trigger. Yours was just watching.

But it didn't. Any of it. When he did come home right after work, it was worse than when he went out with his colleagues. A slow, quiet solo desperation, rather than a frantic social one. He'd walk in the door and, his messenger bag still over his shoulder, go to the fridge in the kitchen, fill up a water glass with ice, vodka, and a small splash of lime and soda, and head to his office upstairs, where he said he was going to work on some book ideas or follow-ups to current stories. Vodka was his weekday drink, bourbon only for the weekends. Like it mattered. She'd find him at nearly 11:00 p.m. dozing on the old overstuffed couch he'd brought from his former life as a bachelor, but which she'd made presentable with a dark-gray cover from Crate & Barrel. There would be a dusting of white powder from a spent line or two next to the workstation keyboard on his desk. Not enough to keep him at it. She'd urge him to come to bed, and he'd promise, "Soon, soon." But instead he would refill his glass, get back on his couch, and eyeball the laptop on his chest until he drained the fresh drink and passed out again. Eventually, he'd wake up around 3:00 or 4:00 a.m., pee, and come to bed. There was no affection, certainly no sex, not even any conversation.

He was physically transforming too. His face was bloated, his dress shirts were stretched tight at the waist, and he was developing fine, spidery red lines on his cheeks. It was unsustainable, yes, but honestly, he couldn't get worked up enough to give a fuck. While he wasn't a soldier, he'd spent more time in war zones, seen more killing, than most of those who were paid to do it. This was the cost of that knowledge. If you didn't die there, then it seemed only right to kill yourself once you got home. Some did it fast, jumping from the workbench in their garage, noose wrapped around the rafters—or if you were really inconsiderate, sucking off your Glock in the den before your wife got home. Landon thought that was selfish. Best to pace yourself, do it slow, make them hate you enough to leave on their own. Make them so miserable that they don't really think about you at all while they're backing out in the family minivan. Just the overwhelming desire to escape before the walls cave in on everyone. Then, after that, you could do what you wanted, fast or slow; the last dance was yours alone.

Landon didn't believe he'd deserved Vanessa anyway. It was a fluke. She'd fallen for some idea of him, a crusading reporter who cared about ordinary people the same way she cared about her students. So he stopped caring—had to—because he knew she would leave him eventually. He wouldn't arrest his own decline. Initially he'd been a sought-after speaker and dinner guest because of his colorful war experiences, but now his stories took on an increasingly cynical and maudlin tone. He became argumentative, sloppy, a bore. His editors at the *Herald* accepted it for a while, were willing to pay for him to talk with someone, but he refused. Eventually they refused, too, and gave him an ultimatum. He took it and tendered his resignation, ending a decade at the paper, but not before winning one final Headliner Award for his series on the skyrocketing suicide rate of returning war veterans.

In the aftermath, she watched him do little for several months but sit on the couch in his study, drink, and rewatch the director's-cut DVD of *Blade Runner* on his laptop. Didn't even read books anymore, his original passion. Then one day after school, when she poked her head in to check in on him as usual, he pressed the pause button on the remote and casually told her he'd gotten an offer from the *Charleston Globe-Democrat*. Some colleague, Rhona or something, he knew from last year's online journalism conference in DC had told him about an opening there. Why hadn't he ever mentioned it to her before, or said anything about looking for work outside of Miami? He shrugged. He'd already sent his clips and had an offer. They'd need to move to Charleston.

Vanessa was too shocked to be angry. They'd agreed early on that they would both pursue their professional passions, even though journalism and teaching meant humble incomes. But they needed consistency to sustain them. Lateral job changes were okay; downshifting was not. And this, without question, was a lurch downward. Once in the grips of that gravity, it was nearly impossible to escape. She breathed, calmed herself, as she did during yoga. Then slowly, deliberately, as if she were speaking to one of her fourth-graders, she explained that this was not a good career move, that he shouldn't take the job in Charleston, especially for that shit money. Where would it lead next, the *Hilton Head Advertiser*? The *Charlottesville Courier*?

He looked at her, sighed, told her he'd already taken the job. She could either come or stay in Miami. No discussion, no compromise, no resolution. Though it seemed impossible, he hated himself even more for giving her no choice. He knew she would come, at least try. Vanessa was no quitter. She'd taken vows; she considered them inviolable, for now at least. Too much riding on this life choice she'd made. Instead she'd have to betray her students, though they probably needed her more than he did. She was only in her fifth year of marriage to Landon, though it seemed both less and more—less because of his time overseas, more because of his inertia and seeming lack of enthusiasm for anything but vodka, bourbon, and coke, and sometimes a story. Still, she wasn't ready to give up on him yet.

But one year in Charleston convinced her she was wasting her time. She had done everything right; she'd established herself in another underserved school district, made a new circle of friends, and attempted to support Landon through his rough transition. His work was erratic, mostly pedestrian and serviceable. But every so often, if he was interested enough, his stories would read like the ruminations of an off-kilter genius, unimpeded by creative boundaries or sober thinking.

It was nothing that made his new editors or his wife comfortable.

His editors, knowing his professional pedigree and promise, held fast. Vanessa did not—could not, anymore. Betraying yet another group of students, she finally ceded to her father's persistence and returned to her childhood home in Jacksonville. She and Landon owned so little that the breakup was simple: no property, a couple of used cars. Each would keep one, and everything they'd individually brought into the marriage.

The parting wasn't so much amicable as just numb to the point of indifference. They didn't even hire attorneys, just a mediator. Vanessa's father was relieved that Landon hadn't asked for some kind of consolation prize, since Vanessa filed first, on the grounds of irreconcilable differences.

Landon was once again left to his own devices, as he knew he would be, deserved to be, as he had always been. And after Vanessa left, his work got better, more consistent. He still partied, but he paced himself. Applied minor discipline to his routine to keep afloat amid the chaos. A slow dance.

And from where he lay now, in a ratty old blanket strung under a toilet at the bottom of the sea, remembering, it seemed very little had changed at all. The way he'd lived his life over the past decade had insulted everyone who ever cared about or loved him, but most of all himself. And that would simply not do. He had to find his purpose again, or die honorably in the attempt.

His stopwatch app read thirty-nine hours, eleven minutes.

CHAPTER 15

MOVABLE
FEAST

Tuesday, December 18, 2018
Two days before the storm

Landon studied his notes on his laptop while lying on the top bunk in
the stateroom. His head barely cleared the ceiling. He knew he'd never
make it in the navy. He'd been at sea with the crew of *Philomena* for two
and a half days now, working ceaselessly. He took notes on his observations and talked with the crew through the day, wrote his stories in
the afternoon, edited video in early evening, and finally transmitted everything late into the night using his laptop and satellite modem while
trying to keep a steady signal in rolling seas. This left just a few hours
of fitful sleep in the cramped, stacked triple bunks of one of the two
so-called staterooms. A first-class seat on an airplane had more room.
Space was so tight on *Philomena* that both staterooms were also used
for storage. In addition to their crew occupants, they were stuffed with
tools, spare parts, lubricants, patching kits for the nets, and extra food.
Bags of onions and oranges, tins of milk, and cartons of eggs were all
lashed against the walls with bungee cord netting, creating just enough
room to walk inside.

But the discomfort was part of the adventure, and Landon was feeling good about the larger story coming together from the accumulation

of smaller ones he'd done so far. He liked the crew too, an intriguing mix of characters. They'd been refreshingly open with him so far, but Landon knew that was partly due to his incongruous secret superpower: being an introvert reporter. Most people didn't trust loud, gladhanding extroverts with their secrets and stories, but they'd readily talk the ears off the weird, quiet ones. Impossible to believe that those would betray your confidence, even if they were paid to do otherwise.

As a teenager, Landon had filled the void of friends with the introvert's security blanket of choice, books. He did not discriminate, devouring *Mrs. Dalloway* and *The Bell Jar* as readily as the testosterone-filled tomes of Conrad and McCarthy. He had read Homer's *Iliad* and *Odyssey* and Virgil's *Aeneid* before the start of his junior year in high school. In his early teens, reading lessened the sting of not being invited to sleepovers or birthday parties. In his later teens, it salved the isolation of being alone in his room on dateless weekends. The upside was that he'd crushed most of what would be on his college reading lists before he ever got there. The downside of all this knowledge was the absence of people to share it with—one of the reasons he'd been drawn to war. He discovered that his loneliness was an unsustainable luxury in that environment of institutionalized violence.

Landon closed his eyes. Exhausted, he slept deeply at first. Then the dream: a sandbagged rut in the desert at the edge of the base. Landon's hands in a choke grip around a projectile, raising it shakily above the rim, threading the hole, then releasing it to slide down the hollow of the mortar tube. He lunges left, fast and low. A deep thump and a smoke puff belch from the tube. Over his shoulder a more confident soldier repeats the routine, followed by another thump. A radio crackles to life. And it is this that rouses him from his dream, willing himself awake before he can hear the message.

Landon extended outward in a violent, waking spasm that connected the crown of his skull with the bunk's metal frame. The structure shook, but made no noise. He looked down to see Chuy still curled up, undisturbed. Heard Junior's snoring even before he saw him. He reached into his sleeping bag, found his smartphone, and clicked the home button: 2:20 a.m. His mouth was dry and his water bottle empty. He decided to go to the galley and refill it from the five-gallon jug lashed to Emmanuel's food prep counter. Believing no one to be awake at that hour, he skipped putting on his pants and went out in his boxers, but when he climbed the ladder that led from the staterooms into the galley, he saw that Emmanuel was still awake. The cook was seated on the built-in bench around the dining table, reading his leather-bound book. He looked up at Landon, but showed neither surprise nor interest and returned to his reading.

"Sorry to bother you," said Landon, embarrassed. "I just wanted to get some water." He held up his empty bottle to prove he wasn't spying on the cook. Emmanuel lifted his eyes again momentarily, throwing a nod to the right to indicate the placement of the water container. Landon walked over, unscrewed the cap of his own bottle, and placed it under the plastic spigot, turned its little rudder valve to release the water. When he looked back at Emmanuel, the bottle overfilled, spilling onto the floor before Landon could shut the valve.

"Shit," said Landon, prompting Emmanuel to look up. "Spilled some." He screwed the top back on and placed the bottle on the counter.

"Behind the refrigerator," Emmanuel said with his Haitian accent, still reading.

"What?"

"Behind the refrigerator. A mop."

Landon found the mop along with a broom and other cleaning implements, all secured by a bungee cord. He freed it, then dragged its filthy, stringy head back and forth across the floor where he'd made his mess. When he'd finished, he grabbed his water bottle and made his way back toward the ladder, but then stopped.

"Hey, I can't really sleep right now, and I don't want to invade your privacy, but would you mind if I just sat out here a minute with you?" Still reading, Emmanuel gestured with his left hand to the open cushion on the bench beside him. They sat in silence. Ten minutes went by, then twenty. Emmanuel continued to read; Landon, eyes closed as if meditating, sipped his water.

Suddenly Emmanuel snapped his book shut, wrapped the leather cord around it, and set it on the table. "Why can you not sleep?"

Landon opened his eyes. He saw that for the first time the cook was actually looking at him. Since boarding *Philomena*, Landon had never had a close look at Emmanuel's face. He'd been aloof, unwilling to engage with others with the exception of serving them food and picking up after them. Even when Landon complimented him on a delicious meal, the most he'd ever gotten was a brief nod. But now the cook was laser-locked on him. Landon returned his gaze, noting the man's broad forehead, cliff-high cheekbones, and eyes so deep-set they seemed to be peering from a cave.

"You cannot sleep. Why?" Emmanuel asked again, now drawing Landon's eyes to his prominent Adam's apple, which moved like a mouse in the belly of a snake.

Landon was so surprised by the question, by any words coming from Emmanuel's mouth, that when he finally did answer, he simply blurted the truth. "I have dreams sometimes."

He was mortified by his own unguardedness. As part of his journalistic tradecraft, he had at times shared secrets with strangers, the give and take, making them feel better, ungrifted in an exchange of information. But what he proffered was usually premeditated and of little real value. This was a tangible piece in the jigsaw puzzle of his psyche. He wondered why he'd offered it up so readily to Emmanuel, but strangely, he didn't regret it. Vanessa and Rhona both knew of his night terrors. He'd woken them too many times with his shouting, sobbing, cursing. He wondered why they ever spent time in the same bed with him again.

Emmanuel stared at Landon for a beat, as if he were diagnosing him. He nodded, got up, and stepped to the cupboard beneath the stove. He reached under, twisted the valve on the large propane bottle, then clicked the button adjacent to one of the two stove burners, igniting a blue flame under the metal fins.

"I will make something, and it will help you to sleep," he said, filling a kettle from the water jug. Landon glanced at the leather-bound book left on the table in front of where the cook had been sitting.

Emmanuel unlatched a bungee cord across the cabinets that held the plates, cups, and flatware, and took down a tin mug. From another he found a pint-size container that, when opened, filled the room with the smell of lavender.

"Tea?" Landon asked.

"Yes, tea. But also more than tea." Emmanuel turned to face Landon so he could see him pull a small vial from one of the many pockets of the khaki fishing vest he always wore. He held out the vial for Landon to inspect, pinched between his index finger and thumb.

Landon took it from him, rolled it in his hands. Its contents were granular and, in the hue of the galley light, seemed an off-white color.

Landon laughed, handing it back to him. "I usually use this stuff to stay up, not sleep."

The cook smiled, the first time Landon had ever seen him do it. It was a night of firsts. Perhaps he was more comfortable in the nocturnal hours. "With this you will sleep. I am certain." He unscrewed the top of the vial and tapped the bottom twice into his open palm, then dumped the powder into the mug with the raw tea just as the kettle began a deep, low whistle. He poured the steaming water into the mug, stirred it with a teaspoon, and placed it in front of Landon.

"Take in the smell." Emmanuel mimed, wafting his hands in front of his nose. "Before you drink," he told Landon, "it is as much for that as to be consumed. The smell." Emmanuel could see Landon's wariness as he looked into the steaming mug. "Do not worry," he said, his white teeth nearly glowing in the low light of the room. "If I thought to poison you, I would have done so earlier. That way I cook only for six, not seven."

A rare joke from the cook? Landon hoped so. He smiled nonetheless, closed his eyes, and waved his hand over the mug, wafting the heat and steam into his face as he inhaled deeply. Maybe it was just a placebo effect, but the remaining tension of the dream stored in his body seemed to dissipate, the knots in his shoulders slowly unwinding, the tightness at the back of his neck loosening. Encouraged, he took a sip. At first the flowery lavender was all he could taste, but as he swallowed, there was a tiny bitterness to the tea. Anise? Valerian root?

"What is it?" Landon asked, touching his tongue to his lips.

Emmanuel resumed his place on the bench next to Landon. He picked up the book, unwound the cord, and opened the book again. "A family recipe," he said, then began reading again, as if the entire encounter had not happened. Landon feared that the small window for a conversation with Emmanuel was about to slam shut. The tea was already making him drowsy, but he reached for the place where he thought they might best find dialogue.

"You know where I had the best goat I've ever eaten?"

Emmanuel shut his eyes, lowered his book.

"Tanzania," Landon said, not waiting for an answer. "I went on a safari. Tried to forget about the wars for a while. My guide had taken me to meet with a group of Masai. They killed the goat right in front of me, and I helped skin it. They started a fire hours earlier to burn the wood into coals. Then we took green sticks, spitted the chunks, and roasted it slowly over red-hot embers. The fat dripped onto the coals, hissed, and popped. When I finally bit into it, it had a crispy outer texture. I plucked it away with my teeth and the juice dribbled on my chin. There was nothing on it. No seasoning, just goat meat slow roasted. That was thirteen years ago, but I can still taste it when I think about it."

"No, no, no," Emmanuel protested, closing the book and putting it down on the table. "The best goat you will ever taste is *cabrit en sauce,*" he said with passionate insistence. "If I had a goat here, I would prove to you."

"How is it made?" Landon asked, smiling inside, knowing that it was through food he'd found his breakthrough with Emmanuel. He thought of Anthony Bourdain, who had said that food was the key to unlocking people's stories.

For the next hour he and Emmanuel spoke of nothing but food.

The key ingredient to *cabrit en sauce*? Sour orange juice. Best bread? Landon: Afghanistan; Emmanuel: Cuba. Best falafel? Landon: Syria; Emmanuel: Detroit. Weirdest food, and where eaten? Emmanuel: tarantula on a banana boat; Landon: Mom's tuna-helper casserole after his pop's funeral. He explained that his sister had secretly laced the dish with weed. Admittedly one of their best moments together, despite the circumstances.

Finally, the tea and whatever Emmanuel had put in it began to overtake Landon. He could no longer keep his head off the table. He was tired to the point of feeling intoxicated. He said good night and headed back to his bunk. Once in his sleeping bag, he pulled his smartphone out from under his pillow again: 3:40 a.m. He'd feel like shit tomorrow. Scratch that, it was already tomorrow. He'd feel like shit today.

When Landon did wake up, he was surprised that only a few hours of sleep had refreshed him. The quality had made a difference: deep REM, no dreams, no anxiety, no dread slamming into his brain like a torpedo, destroying his peace. He wondered what was in the powder. Whatever it was, he wanted more—he hadn't slept that well in years. When he came into the galley, Junior and Chuy were already at the table, gobbling down platters of Spam and bowls of scrambled eggs and grits.

"Hey look, it's Peter Parker," Chuy said while chewing, releasing tiny flyers of yellow and white onto the table. "Ready to blow the lid off the shrimping business, dude?"

"Gaddamn, Chuy," Junior said, covering his plate from the other deckhand's mouth eruptions. "If you really do need to speak, can't ya least try *not* to do it while your yap's full of food?" He nodded to Landon. "Sit down, have some breakfast. Emmanuel outdone hisself as usual." Landon slipped into the bench beside Junior.

"It's just fucking grits and eggs, man. Redneck food," Chuy said, after taking one more bite and dropping his spoon on his plate. He took one long, last gulp of coffee and turned toward Emmanuel. "Hey, floater, when you gonna make some real food again? Frijoles negros, tostados, and some café con leche, instead of this instant shit?"

Emmanuel kept working the propane burners, not bothering to turn around. Landon looked at Chuy, surprised the little chucklehead, as Junior had aptly referred to him, hadn't learned his lesson about screwing with the cook.

"All right now," Junior said, a weariness in his voice, "you've made enough friends this morning, Chuy. Let's get topside, may be the only time you work something besides your mouth." He stood up and put his plate with other dirties in a bussing tub on the counter.

When both of the deckhands were gone, Emmanuel set a plate and fork in front of Landon.

"Thanks," Landon said, and began scooping some eggs from the serving bowl on the table. "And thanks for the sleep aid last night. That stuff really worked." Emmanuel nodded, said nothing. Night and day, Landon thought.

Then the main deck door to the galley opened and Olveda stepped in, followed by the captain. Landon stood up to greet them, but bumped his knees against the table, spilling the eggs off his plate and knocking the fork to the floor. Olveda brought her hand to her face, stifled a laugh.

"Sit down, Landon," Captain Esteban said, sliding into the booth next to Olveda. "This ain't the royal navy." Landon reached for his fork on the floor, but Emmanuel picked it up first and gave him a clean one.

"Sleep all right?" Landon asked, looking first to Olveda, then Captain Esteban. Olveda nodded politely, reaching for the open jar of Nescafé Red and spooning out two scoops into the empty mug in front of her before filling it with hot water from the thermos on the table. Emmanuel put plates and forks in front of them both, as he had done for Landon. The captain ladled out some grits, topped them with scrambled eggs, and took a couple quick bites before making herself some coffee.

"Sleep better once the hold is filled," she finally said, grabbing some buttered toast from a small wicker basket on the table.

"So what's the plan?" Landon asked.

She shook her head, annoyed. "You gonna start interrogating me before I take my first sip of coffee? Keep that up, and I'll have Junior and Chuy chum the waters for your morning swim."

Olveda and Landon both laughed.

"Sorry," Landon said. "Occupational hazard. Forgot how to have a normal conversation. Everything's a question."

Captain Esteban shook her head again. "And here I thought your momma must've dropped you on your baby head." Half smiling, she put three tablespoons of sugar into her black coffee and took a big gulp, let out an audible sigh of satisfaction. "Now, that's better. Okay, so Landon wants to know what the plan is."

THE CAPTAIN EXPLAINED that Lorenzo had been driving *Philomena* southeast during the night, and from here they'd drop the outriggers, set the nets, and start dragging from this point south toward Georgia, but outside the state's boundary waters, see if the change in location might yield some larger shrimp. These shrimp had eluded capture so far and lived longer into the season, the captain explained. They might be bigger than what they had netted on earlier runs. If they had a good haul today and one more tomorrow, the six-hundred-box cold hold would be close enough to full to head back to Port Royal. Besides, they were getting low on fuel, food, and patience. She also confided to the reporter that Lorenzo took in a National Weather Service flash overnight, warning of a possible winter storm in two days. All that to say, she figured she'd pushed it as far as she could this season. After breakfast, the captain swapped out with Lorenzo in the pilothouse while Olveda climbed belowdecks to await the white-gold avalanche everyone hoped would soon be filling *Philomena*'s hold.

Landon went out on the top deck to watch Junior and Chuy at work. The wind had picked up considerably. The ship dipped from side to side as it pulled the huge nets behind it, the wooden "doors" that kept the nets open skating across the surface. Landon had earlier asked the Captain how they knew when they had enough shrimp in the nets to haul them in.

"You feel the drag," she told him. "Those nets fill up, and as big and heavy as the Phil is, that drag can still pull you down a couple of knots. When that happens, you throttle back and haul 'em in."

"What happens if you don't?" Landon asked. Captain Esteban shook her head as she steadied the wheel, still scanning ahead.

"You're in for a world of trouble. You can snap the outriggers, tear a net if you haven't been maintaining them proper. And if you're the one driving the boat when it happens, well . . . you best be looking for a new career. Preferably something on land."

"Ever happened to you?" Landon asked.

Captain Esteban turned toward him and raised an eyebrow.

"Not even early on?" he persisted.

"After hauling blown-up Humvees, Brads, and tanks out of the sandbox for so many years, I kinda got a good sense of the drag."

The captain's sense of the drag was indeed on as the crew put in a marathon day, starting at half past six in the morning and finishing a few minutes before 6:00 p.m. The only downtime was when their line sweeps played out and the captain moved to new spots, each one seemingly better than the last. Landon pulled out his phone and documented the maritime ballet of each new haul: setting the nets, dropping the outriggers, pulling them in again, popping the nets, picking out the bycatch, and squeegeeing the twitching pink masses into the hold for Olveda to scoop, flash-freeze, and store. The short tempers and moodiness that characterized the crew at the beginning of the day had disappeared with the prospect of returning home after just one more day of fishing and with enough money for a good split that would hopefully tide them over for winter.

What the crew hadn't anticipated was the special meal Captain Esteban had asked Emmanuel to prepare that evening to reward their hard work. While no one was popping champagne corks yet, the meal, she knew, would help maintain the crew's momentum and carry them through the final stretch. It was the very reason she had hired Emmanuel in the first place, even though Lorenzo had argued against the additional cost. But no one was complaining after seeing the four-course movable feast of classic Haitian dishes he created in his tiny galley.

He started by placing on the communal table a generous tray full of kibbe appetizers made by frying a mixture of minced lamb and bulgur wheat. This was followed by a dish that Emmanuel called *mayi moulin*, a Haitian staple of cornmeal grits cooked in butter, shallots, and garlic and served with smoked herring. While Chuy rudely questioned Emmanuel about the "look" of it, after a taste, he readily gobbled it up just as enthusiastically as everyone else at the table. The third course—and the crew's favorite—was a spicy stew called *lambi guisado*. This was another Haitian classic, the shy cook reluctantly explained, consisting of conch cooked in tangy spices and served with rice. For his finale, Emmanuel served a platter of marinated fried pork called *griot* with a side of sautéed jute leaves mixed with rice and beans, known in Haiti as *lalo legume*. For the next hour and a half everyone ate with gusto, laughed, and chatted excitedly about what they were going to do with their share of *Philomena*'s shrimping profits. While Emmanuel was proud of the extraordinary meal he'd put together, it seemed to Landon the cook hated the limelight so much, he might crawl away into the engine room when the crew gave him a round of applause. Even Chuy gave the cook his well-deserved acknowledgment.

Later that evening Landon stood alone on the deck rubbing his belly, smoking a Kool he'd borrowed from Junior, and looking up at the dull and distant December moon. When he finished, he turned to go belowdecks and caught a glimpse of Captain Esteban and Lorenzo in the wheelhouse, embracing and sharing a brief but passionate kiss. He smiled. Well-earned happiness, he thought, but the stingy universe parceled it out way too slowly and in too small portions. Unlike the Haitian feast he'd just eaten.

While everyone else was preparing for bed, Landon sat down next to Emmanuel at the galley table and typed out his latest dispatch. The main story was titled "Pink Christmas?" Subhead: "Despite the trials and tribulations of their maiden voyage, the crew of *Philomena* just may end the season in the pink with a hold full of shrimp and the knowledge that together they can take whatever the sea dishes out." He figured both the print and online editions would carry a half dozen of the candid photos of the crew he'd taken during the voyage so far. The website would post those as well as embedded videos of the interviews he'd done and action clips of the thick hauls of shrimp scattering across the deck as the nets were popped during the day's fishing. It was a rare story for him, not of soul-destroying misery and carnage but of small triumphs within the grasp of the underdogs. He read over his lead.

This old ship with its checkered past, refit and given new license, motored back into the sea determined to still find profit in an industry beset by uncertainty as both climate and competition abroad seek to transform it. But Philomena's battle-scarred captain and her atypical crew have parried, pushed back, mostly defeated these challenges . . . for now, at least. With one more day of fair seas, good luck and a hold of the tenuous bonds Captain Esteban has knitted between them, they will return to Port Royal to end the season, loaded with shrimp, debts paid, defiant, humble, whole. As much as each of them can be.

He proofed the work while Emmanuel remained absorbed in his black book, as usual. Landon was fine with that, especially since the notoriously shy cook had done an interview with him earlier that day. There were conditions, of course. Emmanuel said it had to be audio only, since he was busy preparing for that night's feast. He also made the reporter promise to tell him a story of "equal value" about himself later. "It will be not official. How do you say it?"

"Off the record," Landon said.

"Yes, off the record, so as not to embarrass yourself," the cook teased.

About 2:15 a.m., when he'd finished writing and editing and Emmanuel was already asleep, curled up in a spot on the padded bench around the galley table, Landon climbed above deck once again, struggling to keep his balance in a building swell. He took out his phone and opened the compass app to locate southeast, the approximate direction of the satellite he needed to hit with his BGAN. He set up the satellite modem and then sat down, bracing himself against the starboard gunwale, and opened his laptop using an adaptor plugged in through an HDMI cable, the other end already attached to the modem. He opened the modem's interface on his laptop. It began chirping loud and fast, a mechanical indication that the signal was strong. According to the interface, it was in the high nineties. Perfect to transmit. Hopefully he could send all the compressed files in twenty or thirty minutes. He felt full, fat, and exhausted. Content for the first time. Maybe this might signal the break in a seemingly endless bleak streak of personal destruction.

CHAPTER 16

EMMANUEL

AUDIO TEXT TRANSCRIPT AND DESCRIPTION: This audio interview took place in Philomena's galley while the ship's cook Emmanuel Etienne was preparing an elaborate four-course Haitian meal at the request of Captain Esteban. The ambient noise is that of a chef, busy in his kitchen. We've provided text descriptions of his specific prep work for audio context.

[Globe-Democrat digital edition, published 12-19-18.]

BITTER SEAS
In Their Words: Emmanuel Etienne, cook, 37
—Lukas Landon

Lukas Landon: Emmanuel Etienne, thirty-seven, originally from Haiti, but raised in Miami and now a short-term contract cook aboard Philomena. First, what brought you from Haiti to Miami and now the Charleston area, and how did you end up becoming a cook?

Emmanuel Etienne, *chopping garlic on a cutting board*: You are a journalist. So you know of the Duvaliers?

Landon: The Haitian dictators, Francois "Papa Doc" and Jean-Claude "Baby Doc" Duvalier.

Etienne: You may also know, then, how Papa Doc used his secret police, Tonton Macoutes, to murder tens of thousands of Haitians.

Landon, *nodding*: When I reported on the earthquake there in 2011, I learned from locals that the name Tonton Macoute derived from Haitian folklore, a monster that ate children?

Etienne, *putting garlic in a pan with shallots*: My parents, when they were children, they were told bad uncle Tonton Macoute would come and take them away in a gunnysack. That is, if they did not behave. As they became older, what they learned [*pauses*] . . . Tonton Macoute was not only about children. The monster came for adults as well. Many, many people disappeared or were taken to the lair of the monster, the prison Dimanche. [*Shakes his head.*]

For those that lived by Dimanche, the screams never stopped, night or day. When Papa Doc died, Baby Doc was just a teenager. He became the ruler. A ruler who behaved like a spoiled boy. He liked all fancy things—houses, cars, boats, clothes. His wife was the same, buy, buy, buy everything! This while people were starving in the streets. But Baby Doc learned from Papa Doc that the US would give them money, weapons . . . almost anything they wanted, and not care anything about what they did. If they do one thing more. Be against Castro. Be against the Communists. So Baby Doc did just that. He and his family played in their mansions, only a little way from Cité Soleil, a slum so large and so filthy you get bumps [*touches his forearm*] on your flesh just if you walk by it. America gave him all he wanted, not once worrying how he used it. But then the problems of Haiti begin to wash up on beaches in Florida.

Landon: The Haitian diaspora. And you and your family were a part of that?

Etienne, *nodding as he hand-squeezes overripe oranges into a plastic container and adds spices from his vest*: People were angry. The people began to rise up against Baby Doc. He fled Haiti, but the military took over and did the same things.

My parents, they had a small food stall in Port-au-Prince, but they never made enough money. Every day Tonton Macoute threatened them. Took what they earned, and when they earned nothing, took the food they tried to sell. Sometimes . . . [*He pauses, collects himself.*] Sometimes threatened my mother with rape. My father said, Enough! He bought six old tire tubes, lashed them together. He covered the holes with sheets of plastic and made a sail out of broom handles and a bedsheet. [*Stops his prep and stands still, recollecting.*]

It was 1990, November. I was nine years old. I remember my father, who was not very good with such things, trying to make this boat in the dark. That morning when the sun came up, my parents put me and my sister on the raft. She was my elder by two years. They put us in the middle tubes, one of us on each side. Inside the others they put jugs of water and plastic bags filled with bread, bananas, dried fish.

Our belongings—extra clothes, a little money—my father stuffed into thick garbage bags. He tied them to the raft with twine or wire. Whatever he could scavenge. When we pushed off from the beach, others were also leaving. Nearly all had better boats. Rowboats, fishing boats with motors. So many people trying to leave, and no one to stop us. My mother in front, my father in back, they paddled with two planks of wood so dried out they looked as if they would snap with every stroke.

Landon: That must've been terrifying as young children.

Etienne, *laughing*: Not for me. I was too young and stupid to know what it really was. For me, it was an adventure! But my sister, she knew better. She was quiet, did not say anything to frighten me or to dispirit my parents. Still, she saw their faces. Full of fear. She knew there was something to cause worry.

Landon: What happened?

Etienne, *removing eight conch steaks from the small galley fridge and placing them in the plastic juice container to marinate*: This will make them soft, give them spice. [*Turns back to the camera.*] On the first days, it was [*hunches his shoulders*] . . . okay. Once away from shore, my father, he put up the sail and there was some wind. He followed the coastline of Cuba. He hoped to get us to Santa Cruz del Norte. This was a fishing village. He heard we can fill air in the tubes. They were always leaking. Also, we could get water and more food before the big crossing.

My parents also heard that if we said we were Cuban, the Americans would let us in, no question. All because they hated Castro. But if they believed we were Haitian, they would send us back. It was not a good plan. My parents only spoke a little Spanish. They knew almost nothing of Cuba.

Landon: Tell me about the crossing.

Etienne, *stirring a pot of rice absently while recalling the journey*: In that little raft, my father did reach Santa Cruz del Norte. [*A tiny smile.*] I think he was proud he had done something good for us. I learned later the town was in between Matanzas and Havana. Me and my sister, we wanted to stay there. My mother also. Mostly because she feared for us. But my father had another fear. It was a fear greater than the sea. He had been poor too long. I think he felt if we stayed, it would be the same forever.

He had heard from so many about the American dream. He became, what you say, brainwashed. He heard Haitians have their own neighborhoods where French is spoken on every corner. A man could give his family all the things he could not in Haiti. I remember drinking guayaba juice and eating fried bananas with my sister in the shade of a palm tree. But I could still hear. My mother whispered to my father. She told him Santa Cruz del Norte was a good place, a place we could all be safe. She begged him—she told him that the ninety miles of the crossing would feel like nine hundred miles or even nine thousand miles. There was no coastline to follow. Only open ocean. At one point, she saw that we could hear. She lowered her voice. But she pointed at the raft on the sand. It looked like a pile of melted tar.

My father, he would not agree. We stayed for three days and three nights, eating and drinking as much as we could afford. My father patched the leaky tubes, tightened the wires and twine, refilled the water jugs. He filled plastic bags with mangoes, grilled corn, tortillas, and cans of black beans. I think he felt for the first time he had control over something. He felt strong. He knew I could see that also. [*Shrugs.*] Maybe that is the best a boy can give his father.

But others knew better. Some local fishermen looked at the condition of our raft. Also at how young were me and my sister. They tried to convince my father not to go, to stay for winter in Santa Cruz del Norte. He was too stubborn. But they took rowboat oars and sawed them in half, made paddles to replace the old wooden planks. They also gave him a cane fishing pole wrapped with heavy line, also a handful of rusty hooks. My mother thanked them but tried not to look at their faces. She knew their doubt.

Landon: You were only nine at the time? How do you remember this in such perfect detail?

Etienne: All people have gifts. [*Pulls a tray of pork cutlets from the fridge, covers them with salt, pepper, cayenne, and other spices, pats them down, and puts them back.*] Mine is memory. I do not forget. Also, it is the last memory I have of my family. [*A long silence.*]

When we woke the next day, the ocean was calm. My father decided that this was the day we would go. After breakfast, he loaded the raft with all our supplies. Me and my sister got into our places, and my parents paddled out to sea. I looked out and thought there could be nothing beyond this sea. To me it was endless. It was also too calm. My father put up the sail, but no wind to catch. So they paddled. My mother tucked her knees under her. My father straddled the middle of two tubes in the back. They paddled until we could no longer see the shores of Santa Cruz del Norte, until their hands blistered and bled, their skin so raw they could barely hold the water jugs we passed them to drink.

That first night, when the sun finally went down, it felt like a gift. The sky was clear and the moon bright. [*He stops his work, seeming to ponder the image.*] It was quiet, beautiful, calm. We all might have felt very good if there was something more between us and the bottomless ocean. Only six black tubes. We were exhausted, but even on the tranquil sea we could not find sleep. Then we saw dark shadows beneath us, and fins broke the water around our raft. Sometimes they came close. My father would raise his oar and swat them while our mother held us tight in the center of the raft.

On the next day, the sharks went away. We ate breakfast of mangoes and shared two of the grilled corn. Each of us bit from them until nothing was left but stalks. [*Takes a long pause.*] That was to be our last breakfast together. Then we wrapped my parents' blistered hands with rags and they paddled again. They paddled for hours and hours, but on that day the sun was shielded by dark clouds. The sea was so big, we wondered how my parents knew which way to go. We had no compass. We had no land to show us the direction. We had nothing.

But I heard my father say to my mother, there is a special current. One that will take us right to the Keys of Florida. "The Gulf Stream," he said, "just like a taptap, it will take you to town." This was to keep her spirits up. She put on a strong face, but I saw she was tired and worried. [*Emmanuel works faster, seemingly keeping pace with the building climax of his story. Note: a taptap is a type of Haitian bus.*]

But then there was a change in the sea. It was no longer flat but [*searching for the word*] . . . choppy. There was something else too. Wind. My parents tied the paddles to the raft, and my father raised the sail. As the wind filled the old stained bedsheet, his face filled with a smile. We began to cut through the water. But I looked back and saw his dark fists clench at the knots he made at the end of his sail. He used all his own strength to hold against the wind.

At that moment, I thought, this stubborn man who knew nothing about the sea, who never sailed before, he might do it by force of his own will. I was proud. But then the wind grew stronger, the waves larger, and the sky opened up with a rain that stung and blinded us. My father, his smile disappeared. He told my mother to tie us against the tubes so we won't be swept away. She got to the center of the raft, she looped one end around my waist and the other through the opening of the tubes. Before she could do the same with my sister, the raft rose up on a wave, the cotton sheet pulled between the broomstick mast and my father's grip. [*Emmanuel stops working, looks into the distance.*] At the peak the raft, the front it lifted from the water and turned on itself. We were all dumped into the sea. I was pushed down. Deep under the water. I felt the darkness, but I also felt calm. Maybe I was dead?

But then I feel something rub against me, burn my flesh [*points to his stomach*]. It is the rope my mother tied around my waist. To the tubes above me I am tethered like a goat. I wave my arms, I kick my feet. I try to reach the light I see above me. I pull at the rope so I can get above the water. When I do, I breathe like I will never breathe again. And the sea, it rages around me. The rain, it feels like it wants to push me back under. But the rope is not long, and when I come up, I am next to the raft. The sail is under the water, and I can see the raft is turned over [*cups his hand and rotates it downward*]. I pull myself on it. I shout for my mother, my father, and my sister. [*Pauses.*]

But . . . I knew I would not find them. None of us knew how to swim. That is not something a poor family has time to do [*laughing*]. Can you believe going into the depths of the sea without even knowing how to . . . how do you call it? The doggie stroke? [*Shakes head.*] That wave took all from me. My family, our belongings. It was only me the sea rejected. I hung on the tubes and cried. I waited for the next wave to bring my own death. That was the moment [*long pause*] . . . I was most afraid.

Landon: I'm so very sorry. [*Silence.*] What were their names? [*Silence.*] Your father, mother, and sister?

Etienne: My father was also Emmanuel, my mother, Henrietta [*pronounces it Ohn-ree-etta*], and my sister . . . Fabienne.

Landon: Fabienne. [*Pause.*] What happened after? How did you survive that?

Etienne: I did nothing. I was so afraid. I held to what was left of the raft. The storm, it finally passed. But I felt the tubes beneath me giving up their air. The wire my father scavenged to tie them together, it had cut them.

I held on to this black jellyfish and waited to die. Maybe it would be thirst, I thought, maybe it would be to sink below, maybe the shark would eat me. But after a day and night like this I felt a light around me. It protected me. At once, I knew. This was the presence of my father, mother, and Fabienne.

This was a sign for me. They died, but their spirits stayed with me to guide the raft. I could see that it was moving again. It was then I understood! They led the raft into the special current my father had whispered of to my mother. The Gulf Stream.

But another day passed. I grew weak without food or water. I lay on my stomach on the raft and drifted. Night came, and I hoped I would die because I was mad with thirst. Finally, I pressed my lips to the sea and drank. I drank even though my parents told me not to. The salt burned my mouth and my throat. I spat up and felt sick. I was so young, but still I knew death was nearby. I fell asleep, or unconscious.

Then, as if I was in a dream, I could feel myself lift into the air. Yes, I thought, I will join my family. I will be with them in heaven. But like the rope, something pulled me back. Something tilted my head and pushed a cup to my lips. Water, beautiful fresh saltless water. I drank without even opening my eyes. I heard voices speaking . . . they spoke in Spanish.

Landon: Cuban Coast Guard?

Etienne, *shaking his head*: When I opened my eyes, I was on a boat. It was a shrimp boat, but that is something I learned only later. The one who gave me water, I remember first his hands. They were thick, with hard skin. But they were gentle as they pushed my neck forward to drink. I remember second his face. It was deep with lines and dark. But not like mine. Also, he wore a baseball hat. I know this because it poked me in the face as he asked questions in Spanish. "Que lo que, muchacho? De donde?" I drank three cups of water before I could talk. My French and my skin told them everything they suspected.

They laid me on a bench in the pilothouse. Placed over me a blanket that smelled of fish. In that place I watched the man in the baseball hat drive the boat back to the port.

Landon: Cuba?

Etienne, *shaking his head*: Stock Island.

Landon: Florida?

Etienne: Yes. The captain, the man in the baseball hat, he was Dominican but immigrated to the US and married a woman half Dominican, half Haitian, who had come to the US many years before, as a girl.

Landon: So what happened then?

Etienne: The captain, his name was Jorge Ramos. [*Opens the door to a small oven, uses a dish towel to pull out a flat pan for closer inspection, returns it.*] He took me to his home. He knew that if he went to the police I would be sent to a detention camp or something worse. At that time the US government believed all Haitians were sick with the AIDS. They stopped boats and rafts and took the Haiti people to Guantanamo before they could ask for asylum. There was an HIV detention camp there, just for Haitian people. [*Shakes head with disgust.*]

Landon: Sounds similar to the policies we have now. Go on.

Etienne: So this man who plucked me from the black jellyfish, he took me to his home. And then I understood why. In his family was a matriarch, his wife's mother, Myou. This was his wife's Haitian side. Myou looked at me like I was a lost grandson. She told me later that three spirits came to her the night before. Told her I was coming.

Landon: Three spirits? Your parents and sister?

Etienne, *with a "maybe" shrug*: Jorge and his wife Keekah had no children. Could not have children. Myou believed I was their gift from the sea. She said she been praying for me to come. They took me to her room in their small house on Stock Island. There she fed me soup made with the broth of fish and chicken, she placed rags on my head that smelled of rosewood and cinnamon. She said it was to heal my mind, to make me forget what the sea had done to me. What it had taken. But I never forgot. She spoke to me in French. She sat with me for hours, she stroked my face, she soothed my spirit. She brought me back from the dead.

Landon: So this family just ended up taking you in. Raising you?

Etienne, *nodding, but continuing his food preparations*: Yes. Mostly because of Myou. Jorge and Keekah were kind to me, but they were also frightened of me. I survived when the rest of my family did not. They were unsure what force saved me.

Myou was not. She was certain the good spirits of my family had brought me to her. She knew also what could happen to me if I did not stay. I would be sent back to Haiti to live with my cousins or to an orphanage in Miami. She would have neither. Myou became a grandmother to me, but my teacher also.

Landon: Your teacher? In what way?

Etienne: In all ways. [*Pausing.*] It was she who taught me to cook. Recipes for the body. But also [*smiles*] remedies for the spirit. The ways of the invisibles, the loa.

Landon, *after thinking for a moment*: Ahhh, the black book! Is it voodoo?

Etienne, *smiling*: Do not be naive, Lukas Landon. It is not like what you see in movies, zombies and such. Loa is our healing legacy. It was brought here by my ancestors when they were stolen from their homes in West Africa. [*Takes out the pan from the oven again and cuts a square from the browning concoction.*] Taste this. [*Hands Landon a square resembling a slice of brown cornbread.*]

Landon, *taking the square, distracted*: So it's rooted in the legacy of slavery, right?

Etienne, *nodding*: Eat, it's only kibbe. [*He smiles.*]

Landon: What's written in it? The book.

Etienne: As I said, the things my grandmother taught me. Remedies for all. Things for a bad stomach, and even things for a bad heart. I have made them all at one time or another.

Landon, *taking a bite, chewing*: Good, like sticky rice, but with wheat?

Etienne: Bulgur, parsley, lemon.

Landon: So you are much more than a cook. But back to the remedies. If you've made them all, why are you always reading the book, studying it even?

Etienne, *shrugging*: Someday the book may be lost, or taken, like has happened once on board this ship.

Landon: I heard about that. [*Smirks.*] I doubt it will happen again.

Etienne: I doubt so, also.

Landon: So you're memorizing it.

Etienne: I have done so already. I test myself only. It also keeps me from tedious conversation.

Landon: Yes, that tiny book can create a big wall around you. [*He laughs.*] In fact, until the first night when I couldn't sleep and sat out here with you, I wasn't sure you would ever speak to me.

Etienne, *shrugging*: I speak when I choose to speak and to whom I choose to speak. When there is equal value to the conversation.

Landon: That's the reason you agreed to talk with me now? If I would tell you a story of equal value?

Etienne: Yes. Balance. Then you are not just taking from me my story, but also giving your own.

Landon: Balance is good.

Etienne: I have told you the moment I was most afraid. Now it is your turn to tell me yours.

L andon nodded. Tapped his smartphone to stop the recording. Turned to Emmanuel. "Do you mind if I ask you just one more question first, off the record now?"

Emmanuel held out his palm in a sign for Landon to continue.

"You're a very talented chef, not just a cook, and obviously you know many other things as well. So why work on a shrimping boat, endure the hardships of the sea, even if it's just for a week? And for that matter, the abuse . . . from Chuy."

Emmanuel paused. "It is quite simple. It was at sea I lost everything, and at sea I was reborn. Captain Esteban did not know this, but she gave me an opportunity to be close to the spirits of my family again."

"What about the teasing? The disrespect?"

Emmanuel closed his eyes for a moment, thinking. "We all suffer. That is what my grandmother taught me. Sometimes when we suffer too much, we do not share it as we should, but we inflict it on others. That is Chuy."

Landon looked at the cook, head cocked. "I don't understand."

"Chuy, he hates himself, and I make it worse for him."

"How?"

Emmanuel smiled as if it were obvious. "He is drawn to me. It is possible he believes he is in love with me."

It was an answer Landon hadn't been expecting, but it seemed to make sense. Chuy was obsessed with Emmanuel. And in his machismo heritage, that was unacceptable, unthinkable. Emmanuel was probably right; he acted out against the target of his affections because he was angry and confused.

"We have said much tonight. Your mind is no longer calm." Emmanuel pulled a small vial from one of the pockets of his vest and handed it to Landon.

"The sleeping powder?"

"Yes, keep it. Sprinkle only a little under your tongue, and it will work the same. But only a little. Too much and you will have trouble waking."

Landon stuck the vial in the small rivet pocket inside the front pocket of his jeans.

"Also, I cannot have you disturb my work in the day and my peace in the night with your talking and questions." Emmanuel smiled.

"But what about my most frightening moment?" Landon asked.

Emmanuel turned his back, continuing with his meal preparations. "I will ask you again," he said, "when I think you are ready to tell it. Truthfully. That is not tonight."

CHAPTER 17

TRUMPETS

Under the Sea: Day 2

Landon snapped awake, uncertain if he'd just microdozed or if he was already passing out from an oxygen deficit. He looked at his phone, watching as the numbers continued to rack up: forty-six hours, fifty-three minutes, and fuck all seconds. His earlier resolve to find purpose, to scrape and claw and fight to survive, was crumbling away on him. With every inch the water rose and with every molecule of air lost, his world was shrinking, one step closer to sealing him inside the bathroom walls forever. He was cold and racked with thirst. His broken rib ached, his gums still throbbed, and now the top of his jaw was beginning to swell. Swallowing the blood that dripped from his tooth sockets had made him nauseous.

He patted the tiny rivet pocket of his jeans, felt the two lumps again, the teeth still there. He didn't know why he kept them. They'd never be replanted. He wasn't going anywhere. This was his tomb. The crabs and sharks would be coming for him soon.

He didn't fear being dead, just the pain of dying. Would he suffocate or drown? Drowning scared him most, since it allowed for anticipation. Landon would see the water rise around him as his bubble shrank, forcing him to squeeze his face into a corner, desperately sucking at the last air pocket until there was nothing left. The sea was a creeping ghost crab, inching closer every time he closed his eyes. When it finally climbed over him, he would try to hold his breath. That's what the drowning studies reported. The science was terrifying. Once his face was submerged in the cold water his heart would speed up, but then his mammalian diving reflex would likely kick in. His blood vessels would constrict, his heart rate would decrease, and his nervous system's hard-wired attempt to stave off drowning by slowing down his overall metabolism to conserve precious oxygen as long as possible would kick in. A last desperate attempt to keep brain and body alive.

Next, the carbon dioxide would build up in his blood in a condition known as hypercampia. That would trigger an irresistible need to breathe, and he would gasp involuntarily, trying to suck up air while completely submerged. The water would enter his trachea, causing his vocal cords to seize up and his neck muscle to contract in laryngospasm in an effort to keep the water from entering his lungs. But it would be futile. They would fill with liquid rather than air, and the lack of oxygen to his brain would, mercifully, cause him to black out. Finally, all his muscles would go slack, including bladder and sphincter in the body's own excretory coup de grâce, leaving him suspended in the final rapture of the deep, a lifeless floating meat bag soiled by its own waste.

He imagined his body curled around itself, floating like a fetus in a specimen jar. Felt the self-pity well up inside him, let out a deep, prolonged wail, a surrender to his helplessness. A death sob.

Ah, yes! This was the Lukas Landon he recognized. The nihilist who would gladly exchange all the experiences of his life for that gorgeously empty box of nonexistence. Nothing and no one would miss him, anyway. He'd been a ghost when he was alive, so why did he fear becoming one in death? He leaned his battered head against the white porcelain bowl above him, his Liberace shit chandelier, and wept. It was poetic justice that he die here, in a cesspool at the bottom of the sea. He felt his heart sinking in his chest, gave in to it fully. This was the hole he would never climb out of. Fleetingly he wished he could construct a god, a demon, or an adorable sneezing puppy to console him.

Landon hadn't been raised with religion. His parents had been fervent nullifidians, and any vestigial, organic curiosity he might have had about deities and life after death had evaporated completely in him in adulthood. But the existential void he now found himself in forced some latent proofreading of his belief system. If he did die, and there actually was an afterlife, he figured that by default his father would be there to greet him. Yet what would they say to each other in the hereafter, considering the sparse and halting dialogues of their earthly lives?

For decades Landon had painstakingly attempted to deconstruct his father's stolid, measured façade, in a lifelong effort to crack the enigma code of his life. He eventually arrived at a maddeningly simple conclusion: Tobias had lived his life purposefully, antithetical to the Old Man, Lukas's grandfather. His father was determined to be a steady orbiting moon, rather than an exploding supernova like his grandfather.

The Old Man had believed himself to be a giant of the universe. He filled his lungs with the limelight and attention of lesser mortals, burning out their retinas and, over time, their patience with the atomic wattage of his self-regard. As a boy, Tobias had admired the Old Man's many real gifts: a jaw so square it led as his weapon of choice, hazel eyes that made you feel like a diamond in a pile of dog shit if they happened to alight on you. But beneath the superficiality of his rogue charm and outlaw handsomeness, the real magic of the Old Man lay in what he could produce from his lips: the ethereal, supernatural music he could make when they were pressed against the polished brass of his trumpet's mouthpiece. And because of that, it had been the only thing the Old Man had ever loved.

Landon had met his grandfather just a handful of times, and at an age when it was difficult to remember faces clearly. But he'd heard the stories of how the trumpet, not his family, was the Old Man's real passion. How he dented the rim on another man's head in a bar fight, how he'd played the instrument with an untaught virtuosity and hedonistic abandon, like a pied piper, a lothario enticing young women to follow him home from the broken-down jazz joints of Cleveland Heights to his apartment nearby. The Old Man's trumpet was something Tobias had always wanted, even though he freely admitted he was not half the musician the Old Man was. Landon figured Tobias simply wanted acknowledgment that the Old Man had loved him too, and would eventually prove it by surrendering the very totem of his immortality. And then, one day, he did. But only after the thing sat coated in dust, untouched, unplayed, for years, only after the Old Man had already lost his lips, did he part with it. Figured Tobias had finally suffered enough, earned the trophy the same way he had his purple heart from 'Nam. By surviving his wounds.

After the Old Man died, Tobias built a kind of living shrine for the horn in the basement of their Sandusky home. It wasn't much. Just a partially enclosed sound booth made from squares of plywood, tacked over with carpet samples that surrounded the three-legged stool in the center, trumpet case resting on top. And on snowed-in winter weekends Tobias would make his pilgrimages there.

The sound had lured Landon from his warm bed as a child. He'd creep down the basement stairs and, with his father's back to him, he'd conceal himself in a dark corner (the place he'd first learned to disappear). From there he'd watch his father's ritual, Tobias rubbing the mouthpiece up and down against his thigh to warm it, wetting his lips with a roll of his tongue, and puffing out the skin of his cheeks. Watched as his father tilted the warm metal to his mouth, wondering if Tobias ever saw the reflection of the Old Man in the dented bell. How could he not? He thought then that if the trumpet was ever passed down to him, he would learn to play it like his father and grandfather. Before blowing a single note, he'd look for both of them staring back at him from the brass.

Anticipating the moment Tobias would bring the brass to his lips, Landon could barely breathe. Then he'd hear the golden noise, the breath traveling through the reservoir of his father's lungs through the dark, hollow curves of the Old Man's trumpet, sliding into the dusty air of the basement, wafting through heating vents—one long D-flat, the most melancholy note in music. The Old Man never blew that kind of sad indulgence, but for his Tobias, it was the switch that turned the whole thing on; shook up the ghost that haunted the horn. He would play for as little as a few minutes or as long as an hour.

Not the legendary staccato acrobatics of the Old Man's playing, but the steady rise of a seabird, lifted into the clouds on a warm offshore breeze. Landon always wondered what it was his father was trying to say in his music, but he never found the courage to ask him. Maybe if they met again, after all that had happened, that would be his ice-breaker; the gift of being brave enough to ask difficult questions of each other.

It was something he'd given to countless strangers over the course of his professional life, but never to his father, mistaking Tobias's reserve for lack of interest. Landon had never asked him about Vietnam, even after his discovery in the attic. It was Annabel he later approached, and who had told him the story. That his father had been drafted into the war at eighteen and served with the Twenty-Fifth Infantry out of Cù Chi. But just five months into his deployment he'd been out on patrol in the infamous Iron Triangle when a soldier, brand-new to the unit, stepped on an antipersonnel mine. The young man was killed and To-bias wounded when he caught a twist of metal to the skull. He was flown to the US military hospital in Wiesbaden, Germany, where the square of crumpled skull fragments were removed in surgery and patched over with a permanent titanium strip. Metal in, metal out, Landon had thought, first hearing of it. The story filled in so many gaps: his father's mellow demeanor, the constant rubbing of his forehead, the desire to quietly indulge his passions without needing to be the center of atten-tion. All that the Old Man was not.

But Tobias, while steady and consistent, was hardly colorless. Landon recalled his fifteenth birthday, when his father had given him an expensive leather-bound copy of transcendentalist Henry David Tho-reau's meditation on isolation, *Walden; or, Life in the Woods*. Typically, Landon's first reaction to any gift was to decipher the intention behind it. But in cracking the spine and seeing what his father had written, all he could think was how he'd underestimated Tobias. It read:

Lukas, Happy Birthday. Between these covers, sage advice for your own life's journey. Love, Pop

It told him all that he needed to know—that his father was indeed much more than the sum of his ordinary and extraordinary (titanium) parts. Landon wished now that he had taken that revelation, used it to build a bridge to the man before he died. But he did not. The book did start a conversation in Landon's own head, though. He consumed it the way only a stay-at-home-every-Saturday-night, *Dead Poets Society*-obsessed high school bookworm could do. Felt compelled to take it with him the first time he went to war, and when he came home alive, figured it was charmed. Had taken it with him on every dangerous assignment since. Now it was sitting at the bottom of his duffel bag in the underwater stateroom.

He needed these memories—fuel that would prompt him not to give up. Resilience was a muscle that needed exercise to get stronger. On *Philomena* he'd been surrounded by stories of resilience: Captain Esteban reclaiming her life and family after her wars, Lorenzo fighting through a husband's greatest grief. Even the cook, Emmanuel, surviving the open sea at just nine years old after it had taken his parents and sister, leaving him alone and floating among the sharks. And resilience had been evident in his own family, if he'd just bothered to look. Tobias had adamantly refused to live without both love and music, in spite of the exploding insanity of a world that had tried to kill him and nearly succeeded.

Landon exhaled, feeling minor comfort from those memories. Was roused by a slow tympanic pulse emanating from the porcelain against his forehead. He pressed his hand against the bowl. It was still there, so soft, he followed it with his fingers to the bowl's flared edges. No, he'd been imagining it. The stress was finally eating away at his brain. But he stayed, tilting his head, hoping to hear it again. And there it was, wafting from the opening, faint but clear: the sound of the Old Man's trumpet, as if it were emanating from the basement of his childhood home. He couldn't be imagining this. It was too clear, too perfect, the dozen or so trumpet stings that followed the piano and bass intro to Miles Davis's "So What," his father's favorite composition. What he almost always played first during his basement sessions.

Landon grunted as if the sound pulled air from his own lungs. The hairs on the back of his neck rose. He pulled his knees under him, pushed up. His improvised hammock clenched, ropes straining against his weight as he steadied himself and then lifted his head higher, deep into the porcelain, until he could go no farther, until the top of his head touched the bottom of the bowl. Slowly, unsteady on his rickety platform, he shifted until his right ear was perpendicular to the outlet. He closed his eyes, listened. Tobias, he could tell, was now at the solo, a rhapsodic dance. Landon could see the notes in front of him, chased them, a cat clawing the green glow of a laser pointer. They were leading him up a staircase, each breath, each cascade of notes, lifting him higher. When the tempo picked up, he leaped three steps at a time, jumping gaps on the downbeat. He could feel himself transitioning out of the darkness, black to green to gray to blue, becoming lighter as he climbed higher. And now he could see light on the water's surface.

"Keep playing, Pop, I'm almost there!" He did not feel the streaming tears of relief, of rescue. "I'm almost there, keep playing, keep playing," he begged. Landon swept up with his arms, aching to break the thin layer between him and the world above. Reached again and again. But nearly at the pinnacle, the tempo of the music slowed, and his momentum slowed with it. And as the music trailed off into silence, he felt himself slipping back, falling back into the blackness of the void.

His fingers gripped the rim of the bowl. He tried to lift himself inside it like an octopus shape-shifting through a tiny hole to freedom. "Come back. Please." His voice childlike, pleading. Then despair sacked him violently from behind, the notion that none of it was real, that madness was finally upon him. Perhaps it was now the only door of escape open to him?

"Pop . . ." Landon whispered into the outlet. "Keep playing. Miles, Clifford Brown, Nick Payne, anything." He could hear his own voice crack.

He pushed the palms of his hands into his eye sockets and rubbed them furiously, sighed, let himself drop back down. He felt dizzy. And then the moment he'd been dreading since he fell through this rabbit hole: the red emergency light that had kept his bubble illuminated flickered once and disappeared. The blackness was no longer just in his head, but all around him.

Landon lay in the dark, clueless about what to do next. Finally he patted the small rivet pocket of his jeans again, and there below the teeth he felt the outline of the small vial that Emmanuel had given him. He wanted to dump the entire thing down his throat and enter the long sleep that would end this misery. His sanctuary had become a prison, and shortly, he was certain, it would become his tomb. Unless he ventured out.

CHAPTER 18

OLVEDA

L andon reached into his sleeping bag, found his phone, and hit the home button: Wednesday, December 19, 6:04 a.m. The start of his fourth day onboard *Philomena*.

He'd finished transmitting at 2:30 a.m. He wasn't sure how he was getting by on less than four hours' sleep a night, but he guessed Emmanuel's powder had something to do with it: quality sleep over quantity. He looked below to the other bunks. The deckhands were still sleeping, since Captain Esteban had promised a later start time after yesterday's strong haul and coma-inducing feast. Chuy slept on top of his sleeping bag in a dirty T-shirt and tighty-whities, Junior on his back naked, blanket kicked to his knees. Landon tried to unsee that, unzipped his bag, and climbed down from the back rails of the bunk.

He dressed in his jeans and gray Kent State hoodie, same as the past two days. He laced up his canvas boots purchased on his trip to Tel Aviv. They were rubber soled, so he figured they would work as well on a ship deck as for their intended purpose in the desert. Go-to gear for the Golani Brigade, he imagined, marching into south Lebanon or on some other ill-fated venture.

Passing through the galley, he saw Emmanuel in his usual spot, a gray wool blanket wrapped around his head and body, only his bare feet sticking out into the aisle from the padded benches around the dining table. The ship had moved again in the night, Lorenzo driving *Philomena* farther out into the deeper waters near the Georgia coast, where they were now anchored. States owned their own shoreline up to three miles out, Landon had learned from his research. This meant that to fish commercially within those waters, you had to have a license from that state; otherwise, you'd have to push out beyond the state boundary waters. That worked fine for blue-water fishing, but since shrimp emerged into the ocean from rivers and estuaries near shore, the conventional wisdom was that the deeper you got, the scarcer they were. Landon had asked Captain Esteban about that.

"During my daddy's time fishing you never had to move north or south of those state fishing lines," she explained. "Water already heavy with shrimp. But nowadays everyone's pushing the envelope." The implication: shrimp didn't recognize arbitrary lines on a map, and sometimes neither did shrimpers.

From above deck the shoreline was no longer visible, due to the haze of sea smoke that clung to the water where the cool air of the night hovered above the warmer ocean. Landon could see that Lorenzo was still in the wheelhouse near the end of his shift, drinking a cup of coffee. But at *Philomena*'s stern, he was surprised to see Olveda, sitting on the hold's hatch, leaning over a notebook. This was likely one of the few moments she had to herself out of the darkness and smell of the hold, not surrounded by thousands of wriggling, shiny shrimp. An unexpected roller under the boat forced Landon to reach out and steady himself against one of the outrigger poles. It creaked loudly. Startled, Olveda looked up.

"Gotta spray that thing with some WD40," Landon said, shaking his head, embarrassed. "Didn't mean to sneak up on you." Olveda laughed; Landon could hear her mother in it.

"Boat's less than a hundred feet long," Olveda said. "No use in fighting over it." She patted the space on the hatch next to her. Landon was happy for the invitation. He hadn't talked to Olveda much during the voyage. She'd been either packing shrimp or resting in her stateroom. This was a rare opportunity, and likely the last before they headed back to Port Royal. He walked over slowly, trying not to lose his balance again as the boat swayed. Olveda shut the hardbound notebook she'd been writing in, first slipping her pen inside to mark her page, and looked up at him, smiling as if he hadn't just interrupted her but was expected. She rubbed a flat disk of metal on a dull chain around her neck with her thumb and forefingers as she studied his face, not trying to hide her curiosity about it. After a while, she smiled, satiated. It made him wish everyone could be so graceful; to see for themselves and be done with it.

"What are you doing up so early?" she asked. "Some scoop I don't know about?"

Landon leaned in. "Yep, here it is," he whispered conspiratorially. "Junior and Chuy both snore and fart in their sleep like elephant seals."

"Disgusting," Olveda said, leaning back as if she were trying to escape it herself.

"You're telling me. The fumes and noise of the engine are like a lullaby in comparison."

Looking past her, Landon pointed out the swatches of deep redness on the horizon, the blue spectrum gradually filtering out past the haze. They sat silent for a while. Landon thought of the mariner's adage "Red sky in the morning, sailors take warning." He knew there was some truth to it; it meant the good weather of a high-pressure system was already past, that what was coming next with the low pressure was likely rain. Still, they watched together as the orb attempted to punch through the weather, diffused by a paper-lantern shade of clouds and haze. Once the spectacle was over, he looked down at her closed notebook.

"You're a writer." He said it as a fact.

Olveda shrugged. "Not like you, Mr. War Correspondent," she said in a deep news-anchor voice. They both dissolved into laughter. "No, seriously, Mom says you been in the shit, same as her."

"Oh 'in the shit'?" Landon teased. "You just get back from 'the Nam'?" She landed a left hook into his shoulder, right below his deltoid. Landon winced, rubbed the dull ache. "Violence is not the answer, Olveda. Didn't they teach you that in school or were you just too busy practicing your pick and rolls in the gym?"

"Pick and roll? Did *you* just get back from 1977, Kareem Abdul Jabbar?"

"If you're so smart, who was he before Kareem?"

"Lew Alcindor," Olveda said, wrinkling her face, the fact so common it was insulting to ask. He looked at her, demanding elaboration. "I read stuff. We can learn from the past. You know, from dinosaurs like you." She laughed again. As the ship's greenhorn, she must enjoy the chance to tease someone else for once, he thought. "So tell me something about your past, Landon. You almost get killed over there? People shoot at you, like with my mom?"

Landon nodded. "Yeah, but they missed by a mile."

"Close calls?"

"A few."

"Any I want to hear about?"

"There's one that still makes me laugh."

Olveda looked at him suspiciously.

"Don't be surprised, there's a lot of stuff in war that makes you laugh. The whole thing is kind of absurd."

"Stop stalling and tell me the story."

"Which one?"

"The close call that still makes you laugh."

He resigned himself to sharing first. Like Emmanuel, she'd outmaneuvered him. He would have to give something to get something.

"Okay, here we go," he said, resigning himself, though he was actually enjoying the windup. "After the Taliban government fell in Afghanistan—"

"When was this?"

"November 2001." She nodded for him to continue. "I had begged my paper to send me in after the 9/11 attacks."

"That time's kinda fuzzy for me," she said, poking again, "because I was, you know, *one*."

"You want to hear this or not?" She shooed him along with both hands to continue. He sighed, began again. "I was working for the *Mi-*

ami Herald at the time. Not exactly an international news publication, but everyone was wide-eyed and freaked out after the Twin Towers came down. I had been on the crime beat for a few years by then and had seen enough bloodshed that my editors pretty much considered that prior combat experience. Also helped that I could shoot my own photos and had a little experience in video, so I got to go. And when I got there, I was like a machine." Landon felt a surge of pride. "Filing dispatches almost every single day for five months. So back to the fall of the Taliban. The Northern Alliance fighters, now followed by a bunch of journalists like me, swarmed into Kabul, the capital, at almost the same time. None of us expected it to happen so quickly. I mean, 9/11 was in September, we were in Afghanistan by October, and by November the Taliban had fled east to the mountains of Tora Bora. None of us knew what would happen next. We figured it would take a while for the new government to organize, so me and some other reporters from medium-sized papers decided to rent a small house in Kabul as our base. We didn't have briefcases full of cash like the TV networks who bought up entire floors of the Intercontinental Hotel. We found something modest in an area known as Karta-i-Seh, midway between the Russian embassy and the Kabul Zoo. It was secure, we thought, and not too far from the city center and government offices."

"You just rented a house in the middle of a war zone? By the zoo? Like it was an Airbnb or something? That's some crazy shit."

Landon nodded; he couldn't really disagree. "There were six of us and three bedrooms, so we each shared a room, but also a kitchen and a shower with hot water. All in all, it wasn't so bad. But not cheap either. Two thousand US dollars a month, split between us. War profiteering at its best, but whatever. Everyone has to make a living. But there was just this one room that had a padlock on the door." Olveda leaned in. "The old Afghani that was our landlord told us it was his food pantry. He was going to stay with relatives nearby while we were renting the place. Said he wanted to keep what was left of his winter food supply safe from looters when we weren't around. Seemed to make sense. None of us really questioned it. We moved in and took showers for the first time in two weeks, and all of us slept the sleep of death that first night. We were exhausted. The next morning I was first up. I went to my laptop, finished a piece I had been writing about the collapse and retreat of the Taliban. When it was done, I needed to transmit. Had an early version of a BGAN then."

"Bee-gan?" Olveda repeated.

"Acronym for broadband global area network. Satellite modem. Like a portable satellite dish that allowed us to file our stories from anywhere. I have one here." He pointed down. "In the crew quarters. They're small and really fast now, but back then it was new technology, really cool shit, but bulky. We had to unfold these gray plastic rectangles and point them at the sky in a specific direction and plug in an Ethernet cable hooked to our laptops. If we got a decent signal, we could access the internet, send text, photos—even video. Although transmission speeds could be glacial in the early days. And pretty often it cut out in the middle of the send. When that happened, you had to start over from scratch, so to file a single story and a few photos it could take hours or even the whole night.

"I wanted to file my stuff ASAP so I could go into Kabul city and see what was happening. Problem was, I couldn't get a signal with the BGAN on the ground. I tried moving the thing around, but there were other buildings and houses that blocked the unit's line of sight. I needed to get higher, so I decided to use the roof, since it was flat and usually secure, made like the rest of the structure out of rebar and plastered cinder blocks."

Landon paused.

"Then what?" Olveda asked.

"I folded up the BGAN, put it under my arm, and climbed up, using an empty fifty-gallon drum as my ladder. So far so good. But when I got to the top, I noticed a spot in the roof that had been covered up with a jagged piece of plywood. When I got closer, I thought it might be a rain patch, but a crappy one, since it wasn't even nailed down. I used the toe of my boot to slide it to the side and saw what it had been covering: a large hole about the size of a manhole cover. I got down on my hands and knees and peered inside, but it was still too dark to see into the room. Then I got down on my stomach and poked my head in farther. In the far corner there was something large and gray. A hot-water heater, maybe? But not any kind that I'd ever seen in Afghanistan, too big, too modern. Besides, it didn't seem to be hooked up to anything, and the top was tapered and ringed with metal flanges."

"So what was it?" Olveda asked.

Landon held up his hand. "I'm getting there. Something in my gut said whatever it was, it wasn't good. Better get a closer look. I found a rusty old ball-peen hammer with some other tools under the kitchen sink. Surprisingly, the padlock on the pantry was stronger than it looked. By my tenth or eleven smack, everyone in the house was up, wondering if I'd finally cracked under the stress of the last few weeks. Then I realized that instead of working on the lock, I should just whack away the U-bolt hinge it was hanging on. That came off with just two solid hits. And then, as I slowly reached for the handle to open the door, I discovered who my friends were. Everyone had backed away from me like I was radioactive. I'm not sure what they thought was inside the pantry: the one-eyed Taliban chief Mullah Omar? Osama bin Laden? Didn't matter, they just wanted distance. Smarter than me, I guess, because I kept going. Slowly, carefully, I pushed the door open, and . . ." Landon paused for effect.

"Don't play games now, Landon," Olveda said. "What the hell was in there?"

Landon nodded. "Turns out they were right for not wanting to be too close . . . because inside, standing there at a jaunty angle with its pointy detonator nose piercing the concrete foundation, was a very big, very unexploded five-hundred-pound bomb." Olveda covered her mouth with one hand. "And a very dumb bomb to be sure, since it didn't go off on impact. But not quite as dumb as the crackerjack war correspondents who had been too tired to press the landlord on what was really behind door number one. So we all had had one of our best night's sleeps of the war cozily and cluelessly curled up in our beds around the instrument of our own potential destruction."

"Damn, Landon! So what did you do after that?"

"We went screaming out of there like a bunch of teenagers who just walked in on their parents having sex."

Olveda laughed.

"Like I told you," Landon said, "absurd, right?"

She shook her head in disbelief.

"We went out to the street," he continued, "everyone in underwear or sweats or whatever they slept in, except me. We stayed there for hours, waiting for an international demining team to arrive with a crane and haul the thing away for a controlled detonation in an empty lot about a mile away. I'm telling you, the mini mushroom cloud that went up from that missile made us look at each other with complete shock and awe. Either the luckiest or unluckiest motherfucking journos in all of Afghanistan. Needless to say, we moved out immediately and found another place. Only got back half our money from the landlord. though. He told us he thought it was an empty fuel tank, discarded by an American plane. No need to get anyone alarmed, since he had it locked safely away."

"Funny, but crazy," Olveda said.

"Definitely not as sexy as the bullet-hole-that-doesn't-kill-you story. Those are the close calls that get you free beers all night," said Landon.

"We need more war stories where we laugh at the end."

"Solid piece of wisdom. Guess I should've written it up as a piece. But I was afraid we all came off dumb as cucumbers." Landon slapped his hands against his thighs. "That's my contribution for the day. What you got for me?"

"Like what?"

"Like what's in the notebook you're trying to hide?"

"Not hiding anything," Olveda said, keeping eye contact with Landon while sliding the notebook farther out of view with her left hand.

"C'mon," Landon pressed. "What are you scribbling up here at the crack of dawn? Is it a diary?"

"Diary? Do I look like Bridget Jones to you, Landon?"

"You're writing romance novels, aren't you? If you are, you're right to hide it. Because that would be, you know, really embarrassing."

She stared at him, shook her head. "Nosy."

"I prefer tenacious."

"I prefer you mind your own business."

"You guys are my business," he said. "Sharing our stories is all we really have to connect us."

"You married, Landon?"

"Was. Divorced."

"Really? She didn't kill herself, having to listen to your sad-ass shit day after day?"

Landon hunched his shoulders. "She probably would have," he conceded, "but I wasn't around a lot. Even when I was." He tilted his hand back, taking an imaginary drink.

Olveda nodded.

"Mom had that for a bit too, after she was wounded. Got on the pills for pain, stayed for the forgetting. Told me later, after she kicked it, that the percs and the beer made her feel like she was in a beautiful hole and never wanted to come out."

Landon let the image sink in. "What got her to crawl out?"

Olveda smiled. "You're looking at it. Said she brought me into the world, didn't want to be a shit example of how to leave it."

"Good mom and good advice. That why you wear her dog tag?" Landon pointed to the disk on the chain around her neck. "I mean, you keep rubbing it like, 'Talk to me, Goose.' How come?"

Olveda clutched the dog tag. "Feeling this around my neck, I don't know, makes me feel safer," she said. "I remember how strong my mom is. How she thinks things through, makes the right decision when it all goes to crap." Landon nodded for her to continue. "Well, we're blood. So this"—she held up the oval disk—"reminds me I got that in me too.

Probably same reason she wears Grandad's old army jacket." Olveda laughed. "She says he was a tough old bird, but takes one to know one. I never met him—he died of some kind of cancer before I was born. Mom thinks it was that stuff they sprayed to kill all the trees back then."

"Agent Orange?" Landon offered.

She nodded. "You're just an encyclopedia of ghoulish war facts, huh, Landon? You get off on that?"

"Nah, it gets off on me," he joked. "So I assume the military and shrimping aren't in your long-term future plans. What is?" Her eyes lit up, and Landon knew he'd found the conversational sweet spot.

"I was going to study writing and comparative lit at UNC," she said. "Still will, once I get some money saved up. But first I need to work my way out of my own beautiful hole." She knocked the hatch on which they were sitting.

"Poetry or prose?" Landon asked.

"What?"

"What you write in your notebook," he said. "I've loved poetry ever since high school."

"Let me guess," Olveda said, rubbing her hands together in faux glee. "You actually consider Bob Dylan and Leonard Cohen to be poets, but you won't say that to me, just to other white guys in a bar. And you've read Ginsberg and some of the other beats, but your number one is Bukowski. Could probably even cough out a couple of stanzas from 'Love Is a Dog from Hell.'" She paused. "I'm right, aren't I?" A mad grin on her face.

"You are absolutely not right, smarty-pants. I would have no problem at all telling you Dylan and Cohen are indeed poets, I think the beats are overrated, and Bukowski is *not* my favorite." Landon looked down, bashful. "He's my second favorite. How do you even know that book?" he asked, genuinely surprised.

"High school English teacher recommended it. Was into him as well. White guy." She pointed her chin at him. "About your age."

"So predictable," Landon griped. "Hard to tell us apart in our Dockers and button-downs."

"Don' be like that," she consoled, patting him on the back, "all sad and stuff, just 'cause I got you figured. So, who's number one?"

"What?"

"You said Bukowski's number two. So, who's number one?"

Landon considered, already feeling he might've shared too much. "Poe," he said, reluctantly.

"You mean like 'The Raven'—that Poe?"

"Yes. But he's written a ton of stuff, much better than that one."

"Wasn't he all obsessed with death, too? Bet you were a Goth back in high school." Olveda raised her eyebrows, teasing. Landon gave her a shooing gesture.

"Please, way before high school. Junior high." Landon laughed. "Kidding. Truth is, I found his poems comforting. He just . . . I don't know . . . seemed like an outsider, like me."

"Wait! You feel you're an outsider?" Olveda asked, convulsed forward in disbelief. "Mainstream, Midwest white man? Outside of what? Little thing going on with your eye there"—she made a circular gesture around his face—"that's just a distinguishing characteristic. Don't make you an outsider. This whole country was made for you, Mr. Landon. You're the center of the Tootsie Pop. You need to read some Black writers if you want to know what it feels like to be on the outside."

"Why are you assuming I haven't?"

Olveda crossed her arms, challenging him.

"Okay," he said, "Baldwin, Morrison, Achebe, more recently Colson Whitehead. Underlined every other passage in Ta-Nehisi Coates's *Between the World and Me*."

Olveda smiled. "Holy crap, Landon—I swear next thing out your mouth is going to be 'Some of my best friends are Black.'" Landon blushed, understanding how ridiculous it all sounded and regretting immediately that he said it. Stayed silent, hoping the moment would pass.

"Just relax, just two people talking," Olveda said. "Just don't go thinking you're all individually persecuted and such. And now . . . I'll make you a deal. You spit out just one little poem by your boy, Edgar Allan

Poe, prove to me what you're saying. You do that, and I let you see what I was working on."

"What you were writing in your notebook?"

Olveda nodded.

"Deal," Landon said. "But no more public shaming."

"Not promising anything," Olveda said. "Go already."

Landon closed his eyes. Found the words in his memory.

> From childhood's hour I have not been
> As others were—I have not seen
> As others saw—I could not bring
> My passion from a common spring—
> From the same source I have not taken
> My sorrow—I could not awaken
> My heart to joy at the same tone—
> And all I lov'd—I loved alone.

When he finished, they were both silent for a few moments, only the sound of the wind passing through *Philomena*'s lashed outriggers.

"All right, guess you've earned this," Olveda said, handing her notebook to him. "But please no more wrist-slashers. I'm 'bout to jump overboard."

Landon ignored her. He flipped open the notebook and saw what her pen had bookmarked. A page with the word PIVOT at the top in all caps, followed by six stanzas, with scratch-outs and erasure markings that bled into three more pages.

"Spoken word," she said.

"Ah, in that case . . . ," Landon said, pulling out his phone.

"Okay, okay." She grimaced, stood up, took the notebook back from him. "As long as you never recite Poe on the ship again."

"Agreed."

Olveda leaned against the stern gunwale as *Philomena* bobbed in the water, shrouded in haze.

BITTER SEAS

In Their Words: Olveda Esteban, Philomena deckhand, 19

—Lukas Landon

[Globe-Democrat digital edition, published 12-19-18.]

Olveda Esteban: This is . . . [*Pauses.*] Landon, do I look at you or into the camera?

Lukas Landon: Whichever. The one you're more comfortable with.

Esteban: It's spoken word. Makes more sense to say it to a human being than a machine. Although with you it's kind of a toss-up. [*Laughs.*]

Landon: Okay, me then.

Esteban, *smiling:* This is a spoken word poem I wrote. It's about what you do after a dream dies. I call it . . . "Pivot."

[*Pauses. Looks down at her notebook.*]

Langston asked, what happens to a dream deferred?
But my dream destroyed is my tragic truth preferred
It's invisible, untraceable in-shall-ah soon forgotten
It won't dry up or fester or stink like something rotten
A dream deferred can still keep hope afloat
But my dream destroyed took me from court to boat
From port to mope, from shorts to nope, from flat to slope
Can't barely cope, sliding down this rope,
Yes, my dream is destroyed. Not deferred.
And yet here is why it's my tragic truth preferred
While I know the past I'm not its slave no more
Others paid that price once stolen from distant shores,
But with their dignity intact still won the wars
So for them, for me, for us . . . I will pivot.
From my dream destroyed
Rise above the noise
Yes, Miss Gwendolyn
I shall create! If not a note, a hole. If not an overture, a desecration
I shall find my way through this confusion and my devastation

I will hurl my words into darkness, and wait for the echo
I'll drink from the cup, Mr. Wright, whether filled with bitters or prosecco
My dream was lost, yes, I admit it died.
But as Maya wrote, we are wired for resilience
So like air I'll rise.
   And pivot.

When Olveda was done, she closed the notebook and looked down, but Landon kept recording her. Wasn't sure why he didn't stop. Had seen the same words on paper, but was shaken as they came out of this young woman's mouth. Fierce and broken-hearted. It rocked him from his stance on the deck as much as the building seas. Reminded him why he'd chosen to become the world's witness. He might've stayed like that forever had the sound of the captain's voice not broken the trance.

"Ollie? Landon! What you up to?"

"Morning, Mom," Olveda said, walking past Landon, kissing the captain on the cheek before heading into the galley for breakfast. "Landon was just getting an early start today. You know, stealing people's souls with his magic box." She looked back at him, giggling.

Captain Esteban looked over at him too. Landon finally stopped recording and lowered the smartphone, but kept a tight hold, as if it were indeed something magic, or had captured as much. The captain said nothing, but burrowed deep into him with her eyes. He lifted the smartphone, handed her one of the earbuds, still plugged into it, and inserted the other in his own ear. Played back the recording. He held up the screen to the captain's face and watched her reaction during the playback. The default hardness rippled in at the edges, a mother's pride, but also a mother's pain and fear. When it finished, she returned the earbud to Landon.

"What are you going to do with it?"

"Whoever that ballplayer was, the one that hurt Olveda . . . we all owe her," Landon said, ignoring the question.

The captain pulled back, confused.

"She may have ruined Olveda's knee, but she clearly helped her discover her voice."

Captain Esteban nodded and headed to the wheelhouse to relieve Lorenzo, but then turned back. "Landon."

"Yes?"

"You're like a wire-guided javelin, homing in on everyone else's pain. Set on convincing them there's some value or other in sharing it. Should ask yourself why, sometime."

CHAPTER 19

PARASITES

That morning's red-sky warning delivered as promised. Thick droplets of water pelted the deck as the ship plugged away in a modestly angry ocean, choppy with whitecaps. The air temperature was sixty-one, but because of the rain and the wind it felt much cooler. Landon positioned himself on deck to capture the action of what everyone was hoping would be *Philomena*'s fourth and final full day at sea.

Despite the weather, Junior worked the nets without a shirt, wearing only jeans and rubber boots, seemingly as comfortable as if he were walking the beach on a summer's day. By contrast, Chuy was dressed in his foul-weather gear, a hooded yellow rain slicker and matching pants. Though they'd only begun working together this season, there was, Landon noticed, an unspoken symbiosis in their movements as they rigged and set the nets, lowered the outriggers for the trawl, then used the rebuilt Stroudsburg winch to haul them back up again, filled with shrimp and the inevitable bycatch from each run. Chuy was built like Lorenzo, stocky, with a low center of gravity that kept him as surefooted on deck as a race car on a circular track. Junior, by contrast, was not more than 145 or 150 wiry pounds, wrapped around a five-ten frame. In between Junior's bony shoulder blades, Landon saw, he sported a fearsome tattoo: a green skull with a black dagger piercing the top and emerging red, like a tongue, between the jawbones. A banner above it read "Crawdaddy" in Old English script. When raindrops struck Junior's bare back, it looked to Landon like the skull was trying to catch them with its dagger tongue.

"Junior," Captain Esteban said, her voice crackly over an old public address speaker lashed to *Philomena's* superstructure. Junior looked up, startled. "You got boiled peanuts for brains? Get something on you right now before catching pneumonia." Her concern came off to everyone in earshot, including Junior, as motherly. Angry, but still motherly.

"Aww, come on now, Cap'n," Junior protested, his lips moving but his words, Landon knew, were soundless to the captain inside the bridge. "I'm sweating up a storm out here. Working twice as fast as Chuy." Chuy sneered as he tied off the net for another drop. But before Junior could continue, Lorenzo came out of the deck with one of the collection of slickers hanging from a high wall hook in the bridge.

"Idiot," he said, handing it to him. "You get sick, and everybody has to pick up your slack. Get this on now." He snapped the slicker in front of Junior like a matador cape. Junior didn't say anything, but he snatched the jacket and pulled it over his bare skin, refusing to button it. He looked at the first mate defiantly, bouncing back and forth from foot to foot, waiting for him to say something more. Lorenzo paused and scanned him more closely, prompting Junior to turn back to his work, breaking from the older Ortiz's gaze. Lorenzo waited a beat longer, but said nothing more before returning to the wheelhouse.

Even with the challenging conditions and occasional deck theatrics, Captain Esteban still seemed to be on a roll. Each location she picked to trawl that day paid off in a net-stretching bounty. After a few hours topside, Landon went belowdecks to watch Olveda work, even though the hold was one of the least desirable places to be in stormy seas. Olveda endured her lowest spot in the ship's pecking order without complaint. It was expected, after all, for new crew members to work their way up from the dark bowels of the ship into the light, proving themselves through both time in service and mastery of one rudimentary and humbling skill set before moving on to another. And despite being the captain's daughter, Olveda had been spared no sharp rebukes for failures, nor praised for doing right the jobs expected of her. Landon asked her about it during her freezing, sorting, and storing routine when the nets topside were being reset.

"My first time in the chute, the boys were shoveling the shrimp down so fast at me, I was up to my eyeballs," said Olveda, taking a sip of water from a pink Hydroflask. "Back then, I didn't know anything. Couldn't move quick enough. I was getting overwhelmed. Next thing I know my mom had jumped down here with me, ripped the buds out of my ears. I had some jams on just to escape the engine noise." She shrugged. "Wish I could've kept them in while she was screaming at me. Her shouting drowned out the engine for sure: 'Don' ever come down here with your ears plugged up. You gotta be ready to hear if we're calling.'" Olveda imitated her mother in tone, register, and cadence. " 'This here ain't no game. This here's a ship in a dangerous sea. You get no free throws on fouls here. Mistakes could end your life, not just your ball career.'"

"She's got a commanding presence," Landon said. "I'd be scared to be on the wrong side of that too."

"No doubt," Olveda agreed. "But then she grabbed another funnel and showed me how it was done. Had five boxes' worth flashed and filled in the time it took me to do one. I think she was secretly glad I screwed up early. That way she could make a show of it." Olveda grinned. "You know, for the rest of the crew she wasn't 'gonna take no slacking from nobody, especially my kin,'" she said, slipping back into her mother's voice. "I got the message. I think she was also showing all of us there was no job beneath her or anybody else onboard the Phil. We all had to plug any hole, including her, even if it meant the captain doing shit work. She stayed working with me until she was sure I could do it right and match the pace of the boys moving it from the top deck. But I think she was also trying to show me she wasn't going to let me fail. That she'd be there for me." Olveda paused, frowning. She focused on filling her bucket for a moment. "It was something she wasn't always able to do in the past. With her deployments and all." Then from above, the sound of the old winch grinding and the nets being hauled up again.

"Already?" Olveda said in disbelief. "See what I mean? Can't rest for a second down here." Landon watched as she took one last swig of water, put her black rubber gloves back on, and positioned herself as a sluice of shrimp began raining down from above. Olveda moved hundreds of pounds of shrimp on her own in just a few hours with machinelike efficiency. But then suddenly she stopped, bothered by something strange in the batch.

"What's wrong?" Landon asked. Olveda ignored him, sorting through everything that had just come down the chute. She rushed into the cold hold to examine the catch from that day that had already been flash-frozen and stored. "Oh, fuck," he heard her say, the sound muffled by the enclosed space. Landon took a closer look at the shrimp on Olveda's sorting table. At first, they looked like everything else he'd seen coming down the chute, but on closer inspection, through the translucence of their bodies, he noticed a white fluff on their undersides.

Olveda used her two-way radio to call her mother down from the helm. Within minutes *Philomena* had come to a full stop, and nearly the entire crew was gathered together in the hold, sorting through both the latest batch and all the boxes already cold stored from the entire day's haul.

"Can't catch a damn break," said Captain Esteban, shaking her head in disgust.

"What is it?" Olveda asked. Lorenzo picked up a handful of shrimp from one of the previously stored boxes. They were larger white shrimp, maybe six to eight inches long, but all had the same tufts of white around their abdomens. One by one he bent the tails back and looked at the undersides. Showed the captain. Landon could see, as everyone else did, that most also had a black band around the tail.

"Cotton disease," Lorenzo said.

Olveda looked confused. "What?"

"Parasites," said her mother.

VIDEO TEXT TRANSCRIPT AND DESCRIPTION: Captain Esteban is at the helm in Philomena's wheelhouse. Her face is set hard against the frustrations of the day, but she's unwilling to dwell on them. She knows she has to complete the mission.

[Globe-Democrat digital edition, published 12-19-18.]

BITTER SEAS

In Their Words: Clarita Esteban, Philomena captain, 40

—Lukas Landon

Lukas Landon: You had a setback.

Clarita Esteban: You could say that. But like we use to say in the army, no plan lasts past first contact.

Landon: So what's the issue? Everything seemed to be going so well. Another day of fishing, and you were talking about heading back to Port Royal, home for the holidays.

Esteban: Cotton disease is what happened. [*Forcefully exhales from her nose and turns back to scan the sea, hands at ten and two, slight dip back and forth to each.*]

Landon: What's that?

Esteban: Parasites.

Landon, *scrunching his face*: That doesn't sound good.

Esteban: Nope. But it's pretty common. More so now that the waters seem to be heating up.

Landon: Global warming?

Esteban, *shrugging*: Ain't no scientist.

Landon: What's it do to the shrimp?

Esteban: You saw it. That white fluff, look like cotton and dark stripe across their bottom.

Landon: People get sick if they eat them?

Esteban, *shaking her head*: Nah, it doesn't transmit to people. But it doesn't taste too good.

Landon: You've eaten 'em like that?

Esteban: Gotta know your product, Landon.

Landon: What's it taste like?

Esteban: Chewy, bitter. Maybe just good for bait after that. Issue is you can't really sell 'em. Wholesalers don't want 'em. Restaurants don't want 'em. Like I said, it's either fish bait or cat food.

Landon: That's some bad luck.

Esteban: Comes with the territory. If this were easy, everybody'd be doing it.

Landon: Crew seems pretty deflated. What will you do?

Esteban: We got lots of clean stock, just this last day's haul is infected. We'll toss 'em and then head a little deeper, little farther out. See if we can strike some more white gold.

Landon: That's longer than you planned. Will you be fishing until Christmas?

Esteban: Hope not. But there won't be a Christmas if none of us get paid. We'll get it done. We have to.

Landon: You hoping for a holiday miracle?

Esteban, *exhaling again, launching her head back*: World's a hard place. You just do what you do to survive . . . or you don't.

Captain Esteban had been clipped in her interview with Landon. He couldn't blame her. It was a bad break that she hadn't fully digested. He decided to cut it short, not push it. He was on his way out of the wheelhouse when she called him back at the door.

He turned around, looked at her, but said nothing. It was clear there was more on her mind, and he didn't want to get in the way of it. She hesitated, looked out over the waves as if she might find the words there.

"We talking here now just as a couple folks. Not for the story."

"You want to go off the record?" Landon asked. "Have a private conversation?"

"Call it whatever you want," the captain said, a sliver of impatience in her tone. "Just want to say something without you reporting every word." She turned to look him in the eyes.

Landon nodded his assent and as further confirmation tucked his reporter's notebook in his waistband and slipped his smartphone in the back pocket of his jeans.

"Had some bad luck here today," she said. Landon nodded supportively.

"And most likely will have some more before all said and done. So I'm not telling you how to do your job." She paused, took a deep breath. "But I am asking you to be kind here."

Landon looked at her, slightly puzzled. She sighed, knowing it hadn't come out quite right, or he hadn't heard it in the way she intended. "I'm asking you to see the big picture. Couple setbacks doesn't mean the whole thing's a disaster and that we're running around like a three-legged dog not knowing whether to sit or stand. 'Cause that's what the folks back there are hoping for. That's what they're expecting from us." She turned her gaze from the ocean to him again to emphasize the point. "Our fate is partly in your hands, how you tell it."

Landon nodded. "Since we're off the record"—Landon paused, considered his words—"you know Junior's doing meth. Looked like a circus on deck when I was watching. Him shirtless, pupils as wide as a solar eclipse."

It was a bloodless move, Landon knew, but he didn't flinch from delivering it. Sharp reporters often used moments of vulnerability to probe deeper. But this one landed on Captain Esteban like a slap.

But what he'd said turned her expression blank. It had caught her so off guard, he deduced, that she wasn't sure she heard him right. He could see her gathering her thoughts, trying to resist her anger, but failing. "Tell me something I don't know," she finally said. "You test six out of ten of every crew in the Atlantic fishing fleet, you'll find they're pissing hot." Her body convulsed with an involuntary shudder. Words flowed unchecked. "This here ain't working for a living, it's getting waterboarded for one. You've seen it with your eyes now. Body can't hardly pick themselves up the next day after fourteen, sixteen hours working nets on a shifting surface in sun, wind, and rain. Man needs something stronger than a cuppa coffee to get him through a week of that. I'm not gonna stop him as long as he's doing his job and not hurting nobody else."

She turned away from him, but Landon could still see her face had purpled with anger at his betrayal. "Understood," he said, attempting to dial down what he'd initiated, "and of course I'll keep everything in context. From what I've seen from you and the crew so far, I'm really impressed."

She held out her hand to stop him, no longer solicitous but on another track now, a new objective. "I was trying to tell you something honest here, Landon." Her voice was deeper now, all control. "But you come at me with your knife out, like you're exposing some crooked cop or a pedophile priest."

"Captain . . . ," Landon interrupted, feeling dread now, realizing how badly he'd miscalculated.

She ignored him, continuing with an eerie calm. "You're a drinking man, right, Landon?" Statement, not a question. "Don't look so surprised. Reporter with your international experience bounced down to a regional rag. Knew there had to be some story. Guy like you seen some ugly shit." She shook her head in mock consideration of all the terrible things. "I think the only way you're sleeping at night is to get yourself halfway or more down a bottle. From the looks of it you've been doing it awhile too. Thrown you off your game, but good. But you still think there's a little candle of redemption at the end of the tunnel for you. Couple big stories like this one will get you your land legs back and maybe even your old job in Miami or something better." She shrugged. "Book, even? But first you gotta deliver, and to do that you gotta get clean. Dry out long enough to be that reporter you once were." Landon listened, frozen by her words. "Yeah, I saw it in your desperate emails, heard it in your calls, trying to make this thing happen. And I saw it in your eyes when you came onboard *Philomena*. Maybe you hadn't been drinking for a couple months, readying yourself. But the drinking man was still in there. Saw it in you. Still thirsty, looking to hustle somebody to get what you want."

Landon stayed silent, felt her words peel away his spirit from his body. Holding himself present yet apart. Saw in himself, perhaps clearly for the first time, not his father, Tobias, but the Old Man. Maybe that's the way it had always been. The way he always was. *The glory that was Greece, and the grandeur that was Rome, the glory that was Greece, and the grandeur that was Rome* . . .

"Don't ghost on me, Landon. Not calling you out to embarrass you. That would be mighty hypocritical of me. I got to drinking after my second deployment too. Seemed like that one just took the lid off everything for me. You know, not just the war, but everything." She paused, continued to look into the distance. "Being away from my girl when she needed me most, almost getting raped by my DI in boot camp when I was just starting out. Oh yeah, I left that one out in our little chats. Gotta keep something for yourself, right, Landon? And there was a lot of pain from my injury too. They never tell you how long it takes to heal. Takes a damn long time, and the shit that seeps outa that hole in you, dark like Texas crude. They say it's the dirt and pieces of your uniform the shrapnel pulls inside you. All I can say"—she shuddered dramatically—"something nasty."

She gauged Landon again for his reaction, but he stayed mannequin still. "Yes, a clever omission on the part of the army, not telling us that." She chuckled. "So I turned to the booze to help wean me off the painkillers, but found out they were even better together. It was affecting my work—got so bad I had a talking-to about a dishonorable discharge. Decided then it was time to pull the pin. But wasn't going to go out empty-handed. Used the army to get me sober first, put me into rehab. Get me on the right track again. Figured if I was leaving, going to rehab wasn't gonna hurt my career any. And that's how I ended up back here. Long story. Hope I'm not boring you." She let out a dry little laugh. "All that to say I feel you, Landon."

Landon stayed motionless. *The glory that was Greece* . . . Waiting for her to make her point, one still in the distance.

"For me the worst was how the drink took me further and deeper into my own shame. Noth'n can make you feel more unlovable, more distant from the rest of humanity than shame. And that keeps you from letting others see what you're fighting and letting them help shoulder your burden."

Landon finally exhaled, sensing she was about to bring it home.

"I know you got your own burden, Landon. And it's more than the drink. I might just be an ol' wrecker driver and now a dumb shrimper, but I do my research. 'Specially with so much at stake." She gestured with an open hand to the ship and surroundings.

"When you said you were at Blue Diamond couple years before me, I started asking around. Seems there was a pretty big story happened at that time and got buried in the sand, like so much else in that forsaken war. Couple errant mortar rounds end up killing an innocent haji." Landon stepped forward. "Yep, thought that'd wake you up. He wasn't just anybody, either, kind of a pillar of the community. Whole place was buzzing like a hornet's nest after. But surprise, surprise—nothing ever got in the news about it. And then, well, I guess Fallujah happened, and all that was just in the rearview mirror. No one thinking about anything else once Fallujah kicked off." She paused, rolled her shoulders. "Know anything about that, Landon?"

He looked at her, stayed silent.

"Noncom grapevine is pretty reliable. Said the reporter was a white dude. Goofy eye. Worked for a big paper. And here's the really interesting part: seemed he was there when the whole thing happened. Story that big and fucked up—a reporter would be bound to get on. But nothing." She paused. "Crickets."

Captain Esteban clucked her tongue. "Some truths just never get told. Me being female and Black, well, we get used to that, 'cause it's not really our world, now is it?" She looked at him. "But for you, getting to the bottom of those messes, that's your very job. Thing you live for. You know, like the astounding revelation"—she feigned a shocked tone—"that one of my deckhands uses some illegal stimulants to keep at his job.

"But here's the thing, Landon—accidents happen in war all the time. You know that. So common we even got a name for it, right? Collateral damage. Better than saying dead civilians, right? Still, that don't make the guilt go away. Could make somebody take up some serious drinking, holding on to a secret like that. Also makes me think this person, with all his guilt, might also be a practical individual. Knows what kind of thing ends a career for good. Could make someone more flexible in ideas of what's news and what's not. You feel me, Landon?"

Landon blinked, stared ahead vacantly as if he were still translating the captain's words from a foreign tongue back to his own. Finally he took a deep breath, nodded, turned, and silently left the wheelhouse, knowing all the goodwill, all the trust he'd worked so hard to obtain, had been forever lost.

PART THREE

LIGHT

We had pierced the veneer of outside things. . . .
We had reached the naked soul of men.

—Sir Ernest Shackleton, *South*

CHAPTER 20

TURNING POINT

Under the Sea: Day 3

With the loss of the red emergency light and the darkness that now enveloped him, Landon's ears began to compensate for what his eyes couldn't see. Trickling. He lifted up from his hammock, placed his palm against the wall, could feel the sheath of water sliding over it. He stirred to a seated position and discovered that the lowest part of his makeshift hammock, what held the mass of his weight, now touched the surface of the water. Fear spiked his adrenaline again. Paradoxically, the unbidden energy offset his paralyzing fatigue. The cold and pulsing anxiety had worn him down; the nausea of swallowing blood had been replaced with gnawing hunger; the thirst was even worse. He'd drunk one of the two cans of Junior's malt liquor stash, but the high alcohol content had nearly knocked him out while making him urinate, dehydrating his precious body fluids while further degrading his survival bubble into a stagnant cesspool of vomit, shit, piss, and desperation.

All of that, along with the rising water and concern about his dwindling air supply, forced Landon to accept that sitting back and waiting for a rescue might be the same as waiting for death. Option 1—leaving his space—hadn't filled him with confidence, but now he had to try. He recovered his phone from the zip bags that kept it dry, touched the screen, and used the light to look around. His eyes now confirmed what his ears had heard. The phone's light reflected a steady sheen of water sliding down the bathroom's walls to the water's surface. It was too consistent, too dense, to just be condensation. Besides, Landon could see that the water level had risen. It had been about three inches below the bathroom door handle, but now it had climbed the same distance above it. He couldn't tell how fast the water was rising; it might have taken hours, or minutes. He looked above, shone the light on the toilet and then for the first time considered the mechanical pump handle next to it. When the ship was right side up, the pump suctioned in seawater when raised and flushed away waste solids when plunged back down. There was some value to him in that assembly, but in his current mental state he couldn't quite see what it was. Even at full capacity he was no engineer. He resigned himself to put a pin in it. Replacing his phone in its plastic bags, he slid to the edge of the hammock so that his feet and calves were in the water. He reached into his sweater and removed all the balls of paper, pushing them high onto the blanket so they would stay dry. He would need their insulation again once he was finished with what he needed to do. Then he took a breath, preparing for the cold immersion, and slipped off his perch.

"Batman's balls!" Landon cursed, his lisping yell muffled by the confined space. It had been some time since he'd heard his own voice, or anything beyond the ship's hull groaning under the surrounding water pressure. Beyond the thin doorway of the head lay a harsh underwater world in which he would not survive long. It would be dark, cold, possibly stocked with menacing sea creatures—sharks, eels, and crabs ready to feast on the pale, clammy flesh of his face, his jaw detached and frittered away by a toothy parrot fish, his skull the mobile home of a coconut octopus newly emboldened to cross the open seafloor wearing the fearsome totenkopf of Lukas Landon.

He'd become physically weaker, but his mind was also fraying. He felt muddled, dissociated, the way he used to feel after a twenty-four-hour coke and booze binge with his dealer Cole, a former minor league pitcher who was generous with his personal stash.

His brain cells were becoming oxygen-deprived; the CO_2 buildup was taking its toll. Landon thought it might cut through his fog if he could hear himself say out loud what he was going to do. He picked up his phone. The stopwatch read fifty-one hours, twenty-two minutes. No wonder he was losing it. He swiped it away, brought up the camera icon, flipped the view screen to selfie mode. He pressed record, looked into the lens, and began to speak.

"The red emergency light has been out for a while now. I'm surrounded by water, darkness, and sounds. *Scary* sounds, like the creaking of the ship's steel as it settles, or maybe the pressure at whatever depth I'm at is starting to crush *Philomena*'s hull like an aluminum can. Also I hear scuttling, some kind of marine life moving around, exploring this new 'reef' that suddenly showed up on the ocean's bottom. Probably a good hiding place for the smaller fish and a good hunting ground for the larger ones. But fact is, the water level here is rising and my air bubble is getting smaller—must be leaking out slowly somewhere.

"I need to do something more than just sit here and wait to die. I just want people to know what happened to me if I don't make it. Maybe this phone will somehow survive. Kind of doubt it. Apple makes them purposely fragile as Fabergé eggs. Okay, I gotta stop, burning through my battery." Still recording, Landon pulled the screen close to his face. "Only fifty-five percent now, no more playing Candy Crush for a while. Okay, to the point: the only real option I have is to open that door, and if I don't drown right away, I'll take a few deep breaths and swim out. That's going to be trippy because everything is upside down. I'm used to it in here—toilet on the ceiling—because I had some time to adjust. Out there, on the other side of the door, it's going to be a different story. And it's going to be dark, so I probably won't be able to see anything anyway. Just as well, since I don't have a mask or goggles. I'll just feel my way around. Now what's got me really freaked is finding out what's on the other side of the door. A giant squid waiting to wrap me in its arms? Or maybe sharks already munching on the bodies of the rest of the crew.

"Maybe they'll all just be floating in some kind of nightmarish suspended animation, waiting for me to bump into them. But even if none of that happens, I'm worried I'm going to get turned around and not be able to find my way back to my bubble. This is just a recon mission, so I need to come back, replenish my air. But if I panic, make a wrong turn, this will be the last recording I make."

Landon looked down at his smartphone, snapped his fingers. "Unless I have a beacon. My own little lighthouse! Fifty-five percent is enough to keep the lights on for a few minutes."

Landon stopped recording. Spent the next few minutes propping the phone on his blanket sling, wedging it between the orange life vests, the last can of Junior's malt liquor. Made a safety net from the crumpled magazine pages to keep it from the wet blanket below.

And, in a final calculated risk, he removed the plastic bags from around the phone; he didn't want the light diffused. He'd need every lumen it could offer to get him back to safety. After it was all set up to his satisfaction, he knew it was time. An involuntary shudder rippled through his body, a first-time skydiver hearing the wind rush when the plane door opens.

CHAPTER 21

RECONNAISSANCE: STATEROOMS

I f he didn't go now, he'd lose his nerve. The water level, he noted, was just below his bottom ribs. There would be resistance when he pulled the door back against the mass of water within his sanctuary, but he was uncertain whether the door was a barrier or just a divider between compartments. The difference was significant; one might mean his expedited death, one just a pause on his already long march toward it. His mother, Annabel, would be ashamed that he couldn't figure out the physics, a simple calculation based on the resting angle of the ship. After so many hours under the sea, he just didn't have the computing power left.

Landon reached for the door handle, a simple U of galvanized steel, identical top and bottom. Below it was the half-inch-wide latch that held the door shut. He flipped it down and slowly slid it back, then inhaled deeply through his nose and began to pull. As he'd anticipated, the inside water pressure worked against him. He grabbed with both hands and positioned his right foot against the frame as leverage. Slowly, the door began to move. He pulled harder but paused when his muscle contraction sent a ripping pain across his torso. He took another breath, started again. It felt like he was hoisting a bucket from a well, sucking pressure pulling back against him until the door cleared the frame, opened. He exhaled with relief. Just a divider. He pushed the door back against the inside wall and used the spring clip to latch it to a metal eyelet he found feeling beneath the waterline. There would be no reason to shut it again, since the air inside, not the door itself, was the real barrier against water filling the space. And besides being less claustrophobic this way, the opening offered a glimpse into the otherworldly.

The elliptical of his air bubble extended out beyond the door about two feet, like a science fiction portal to another dimension. Beyond that, he could make out the steps where he'd broken his rib, now forming a new ceiling. He fought back his fear, told himself it was just a reconnaissance. He'd look around and come back. Plus the staterooms were only a few feet away—though he'd found out how perilous those few feet could be on his way here.

Before anything else, he needed to reorient himself. On the surface, the two staterooms were across from each other and just above the head. Now they were below it. And when they were upright, the captain and Olveda's stateroom had been on the left, the rest of the crew's on the right. Now that would be reversed. He was already getting flustered and confused. He rehearsed the choreography in his head. Step 1: Poke face forward into the water like a turtle, look around, and retract head. This would also help to lower the shock when he physically left the bubble. Step 2: Hyperventilate to lower the CO_2 level in his lungs. Landon knew this was dangerous and could cause a blackout, but he'd read that it was how free divers were able to trick their bodies into going longer without breathing, descending hundreds of feet and then returning all that distance with only the air in their lungs. The involuntary reflex to breathe was caused not by a lack of oxygen, Landon had learned, but the buildup of CO_2 levels. Hyperventilating lowered the CO_2 levels and would theoretically allow him to remain underwater longer, if the fear and adrenaline didn't negate it completely. Step 3: Swim into the captain's stateroom first, see if anyone was alive. If so, Step 4, he'd join them. Maybe they had an air bubble too, and they could make a plan to escape together from *Philomena*, or at least have some company while they waited. If not, Step 5: Landon would swim back to the head and regroup. He felt this was a logical and solid "go-no-go" decision tree, but taking the first step made his asshole pucker. He would be nearly blind in an upside-down ship, and it would be only him and him alone, someone who sometimes got lost on marked hiking trails. His confidence was dropping as quickly as his body temperature. He needed to execute Step 1.

He took one last breath and poked his head through the wall of water to the other side. The change in medium was bracing, frightening, transformative. Irrefutable proof of the underwater world in which he now existed. For a time, anyway.

He forced his eyes open through the sting of the salty sea and looked around. With the beam of his smartphone light, he could just see down to the stateroom doors, which shimmered in green and dropped off into the murky horizon. He let himself adjust to the temperature, the viscous blur, and rotated his head to look up. At first he saw nothing. Blackness. But as he held his gaze, the darkness above seemed to take shape: small shafts of light working their way around opaque edges forming an outline. Landon felt pressure in his chest, the need to breathe already. Yet he held himself there as the blackness receded, coming into focus like a black-and-white print in the developing tray of a photographic darkroom: a human figure, the face itself the shade of an eggshell, drained of all color, warmth, or life. Was it . . . Chuy? He was wearing exactly what Landon had seen him wearing last, asleep on his bunk, a dirty T-shirt and his tighty-whities. Suddenly the figure's eyes opened, and a grin spread across his deathly pale face. Reaching down toward Landon, he squeezed his left palm twice in a brief wave of acknowledgment. Landon pulled back into his bubble so quickly he scraped his head on the metal doorframe. He cursed and ground his fist into his eye sockets, blinked a few times to clear the remaining salt water. He felt the crown of his skull; a lump was already forming there, fresh drops of blood falling into the pool of water around him. He shivered uncontrollably, felt a warmness around his crotch, pleasant at first, distracting in its comfort until he realized he was pissing himself, emptying his bladder in an involuntary fluid dump initiated by his body's fight-or-flight response.

Vivid hallucinations, Landon knew, meant he was running out of time even faster than anticipated. He needed to move on to Step 2. What was Step 2 again? He raised his hands out of the water and patted his cheeks as if trying to rouse himself to stay awake on a long nighttime drive.

"Think!" He vacillated between being angry at himself and filled with despair, then fear. The slaps became more violent. Pain brought focus. Finally, it came to him: Step 2, hyperventilate to lower CO_2 levels so he could begin Step 3, swimming to the captain's quarters. Landon began gulping down deep breaths. He did this for nearly a minute until he was slightly dizzy, then lowered himself into the darkness and pulled himself forward with an underwater breast stroke. He did not look up, did not think about Chuy floating above him, only thought about Steps 3, 4, and 5.

He could see the blurry outline of the captain's door on the left. He had been submerged for only thirty seconds; he should have at least another minute before his lungs started to plead for oxygen and his brain began to panic. He found the handle of the door and tried to turn it, but it wouldn't give. Locked. Captain Esteban kept her quarters locked whether she was inside or not, even on her own boat—something she'd learned in the army? More likely something she'd learned as a woman. Trust no one.

About to return to his bubble, Landon found himself looking at his own stateroom door, on the right. He felt for the handle and tried to push it open, but could find no purchase floating in the hallway. He braced his feet against the opposite wall and pushed forward, and the door gave way with only slight resistance. The exertion taxed his already dwindling air supply, and he exhaled into the water to alleviate some of the pressure to breathe. One stroke, and he was inside the room. It was so dark, he had to feel his way around. He started to the right, but then remembered everything would be opposite and so swam to the left first, toward the steel bunks. He felt for a break in the water, an air bubble, but found only a lumpy, floating mass, the fabric soft in his fingers, but containing solid objects within. Junior's Crown Velvet bag, Landon realized. He stuffed it down the front of his jeans. The burn in his lungs was getting stronger. Not much time left. He turned right toward where his own bunk would be, remembering it would now be at the bottom. He'd been in the water for a minute-fifteen, minute-thirty. Trying to remain calm, he swam down, waving his hands in front as if he were trying to stop traffic, and found what he was looking for. His fingertips, though puckered like raisins, could still make out the coarse waxed cotton exterior of his duffel bag.

Now his brain was screaming for air. He found the shoulder strap, looped it over his head, and swam up toward what he believed was the open door. But when he got there, he felt nothing but smooth, solid steel. He'd gotten turned around. He swam in the other direction. Same thing. He couldn't see anything, not even the beacon light of his smartphone. The stateroom was like a cave, he thought. What did cave divers do? His mind raced while he tried to push back his growing dread. Cave divers followed their spool lines back out. But he didn't have a line. Stupid—he should've improvised something. *The glory that was Greece, and the grandeur that was Rome.* What else? What did you do when you were lost on a hike? he asked himself. Retrace your steps. But there was nothing to retrace; he was floating in an upside-down ship. A few moments more, and he wouldn't make it out. He pushed into the wall again and began feeling his way around it. If he moved clockwise from the room's center he'd eventually find the door opening again—if he didn't drown first. His fingers moved across the room, spanning the length of his arms each time. *The glory that was Greece . . .* He tried to think about why he needed to survive. Why not just let it all end here? But if he did . . . he'd never finish what he started: telling the story of the ship and crew. Each of them was so strange and wonderful and complicated—all deserving of some kind of legacy that only he could provide. Especially if they had not lived through the ordeal. If he was the only one left alive, he needed to survive long enough to write the ending. And maybe he needed to live for another reason as well: himself. There was so much that he'd done wrong in his life. Burying the truth about Ramadi, never sharing with Vanessa the reasons for his insistent path of self-destruction during their marriage. These were things he couldn't fix, but he could finally acknowledge them, own up to them, tell the truth about them. That was all still in his control . . . if he could stay alive. His brain whirred, but he wanted to laugh. Was he getting narc'd? Nitrogen narcosis was a drunken state divers sometimes felt at depth that, if severe enough, could prompt them to make mistakes that cost them their lives. He had to get back to the bubble. He had to tell their stories, otherwise all of it, all their time, his time, this time would be wasted. As he felt his way around the wall, at last his fingers found the edges of the doorframe.

Maniacally he pulled himself into the hallway. The light of his phone showed him the way back to his bubble, to the left, just a few yards away. He stroked hard toward the light, swimming with all his might, forcing himself to keep his mouth closed, though he wanted to open wide and suck in the entire sea.

Finally he breached the waterline. He flopped and stretched, chased air, mouth as wide as a whale shark gulping plankton, but found no relief. He was a blood-covered newborn that needed to be held by the feet and struck between the shoulder blades. Where was the violent blow that would knock the liquid natal ectoplasm from his lungs and make way for the new ruling gas? Seconds ticked by like hours. Desperate, he bent at his waist and launched himself back like a trebuchet, his spine slamming against the wall of the head, transforming the silent spasm of his lungs into a medieval scream of pain and protest, but also new life enabling him, finally, to fill his lungs to capacity. But in doing so, he pulled stray water droplets into his trachea, forcing him to cough and sputter and finally vomit a small stream of bile before he could gasp and cry and try to breathe again. Once he'd done it several more times, he began to laugh. When would death stop toying and just take him?

CHAPTER 22

SUNKEN
TREASURE

When Landon had recovered enough to get to his feet, he felt the pressure of the duffel bag's shoulder strap against his body. He pulled it over his head, unlatched the clip and hook closure, and began digging inside. He removed his soaked sleeping bag first, still taco-wrapped around the waterproof black polypropylene shoulder bag containing his laptop.

He shook the bag. No water sloshing around. He was glad he'd taken the time to roll the seals and click the snap-lock binders before rushing to get topside. He placed it on his hammock, continued to feel inside the bag. His clothes were all waterlogged, as he'd suspected. But when he dug deep on one side, his fingers located what he was looking for. His own sunken treasure, a gallon-size ziplock freezer bag.

The discovery unearthed uncomfortable memories of how his pre-trip prepping had bothered Vanessa when they were married. "You'd rather spend your last two days at home doing this," she had said, waving her hand dismissively at the assortment of ballistic nylon and electronics that seemed to indicate a camping trip to the apocalypse, "than spending time with me?"

The truth was, Landon didn't believe he had a choice. He would not be comfortable deploying overseas or even going on a day trip without methodically planning, packing, repacking, and imagining all the scenarios he might encounter and what equipment he'd need to cover them.

He didn't trust himself to remember everything. Landon knew that even at his peak proficiency he was a fallible, far from exceptional specimen, prone to and often reaping the dubious rewards of a lifetime of mistakes. He had to do all this—the prep, the obsessing over the details, the endless treading of water—just to keep himself afloat in life. Far from guaranteeing success, he knew, this was his meager hedge to not fail from the start.

And here for once was the irrefutable proof of the validity of that caution. He pulled the plastic bag from the duffel and looked at its glorious contents: three peanut butter and chocolate granola bars, a bag of trail mix, and two dried beef sticks. He'd squeezed the air out when he packed it prior to the trip to make it smaller, more compact, but the vacuum had also kept the seal secure and the snacks dry. He slid back the plastic zipper, and the bag slowly filled with air. He pulled out a beef stick, greedily peeled back the wrapper, stuck it in his mouth, and bit down. Too late to remember his incisors were gone. That force—his tender gums against the hard, dry jerky stick—triggered spasms across his entire body as if he'd been tased. The suction of the water surrounding him was the only thing that kept him from smacking his head on the overhanging toilet rim. He reached a hand to his lips and felt the ruptured gum flap, blood pooling in his outstretched palm, diluted by droplets of salt water falling from his soaked hair. The pain, however, was only a minor obstacle against his hunger. He reached inside the waistband of his jeans, where he'd stuffed Junior's Crown Royal whittling bag, opened it, and amid the burls of wood located Junior's pocketknife. Folding the beef stick, he pulled the knife blade through the middle, cutting it in two. He fed one of the pieces into his back molars and began gnawing it like an openmouthed raccoon chewing on garbage scraps. Still, the savory flavor tasted more like ribeye steak than salty beef byproducts. He cut up a second and ate it the same way after just barely finishing the first. He kept himself from racing through the rest of his food when he realized he had little to wash it down with. He dug out the last of Junior's two malt liquors from under the life jacket, pulled the top, and took a long draw. It was warm and flat, but felt to him like part of a champagne brunch. His energy level instantly increased along with the unintended benefit, or consequences, of a small, comfortable buzz.

He wanted to take another long slug, but it was already a third empty, the only liquid he had left to drink. Finding the duffel bag had been a boost to his flagging spirits, but not finding the captain or Olveda had sharpened his own sense of isolation. He hoped that, like Junior and Chuy, they had been above deck when the storm hit, and possibly escaped before the ship had capsized and settled on the ocean floor.

He had been sound asleep when the storm hit, and now he considered whether Emmanuel's white powder had saved him or sealed his fate. The extra calories he'd just eaten helped to stoke energy and body heat, but his core temperature was still dropping from the swim. He reached into the duffel bag again, pulled out his gray Kent State hoodie. He twisted it to wring out the excess water, then tossed it on his makeshift hammock. Next he pulled out a pair of thick gray sweatpants. He smiled, remembering how Vanessa used to make fun of him when he wore the now-threadbare set on his Sundays off. If he only had a curly black mustache and a fake five-hundred-pound barbell, she'd teased, he could pass for an old-time strongman.

Also stuffed in the bag was a black beanie, a Gore-Tex parka shell, and lots of extra socks. All things he thought he might need during his prep stage, if the weather turned colder on the trip. Finally, at the very bottom of the bag was his leather-bound copy of *Walden*, sealed and dry in its own plastic freezer bag. It was where the book always lived on his journeys, often never even cracked open. Landon simply took comfort in the knowledge it was there. He went back to work squeezing the water out of each piece of clothing, the exertion elevating his body temperature and mood. The twisting removed the sopping water, but everything was still soaked. Even so, he wanted to put it all on to escape the cold. But he knew he still had another reconnaissance mission left, the one that would take him to what was once the very top of *Philomena* but now rested against the ocean floor: the wheelhouse.

He didn't want to go back outside his sanctuary again. He wanted to . . . what did Vanessa call it when they stayed home and watched movies? Cocoon. Yes! They used to do that so often early in their marriage, soaking up each other's warmth, building their vocabulary of insider jokes, moments that only they would understand. Sometimes he would bury his face in the nape of her neck, breathe in her scent of sandalwood and vanilla. She would swat him away to stop his tickling, while reassuring him with her soft laugh. Landon closed his eyes, inhaled deeply, willed himself into that time and place, that smell, again. It would not come, just the rank staleness of oxygen-depleted air, tainted with sweat, diesel fumes, and excrement. He wanted to lie on his hammock, chew on granola bars, and drink the last of his beer. Maybe even take a nap. He wanted to cocoon, if only with himself. But if rescue divers did find the ship, he'd never see or hear them, and he'd suffocate or drown in his sleep, no one ever knowing what had happened to him and the rest of the crew.

As much as he hated the thought of leaving his metal womb, he knew he had to. He owed it to Captain Esteban, Olveda, all of them. And, as he'd come to realize, himself too, if only to set things right. To be the man he always should've been. He believed others would see, in the stories of the crew, fragments of their own lives. That it would motivate them to go—somewhere, anywhere. Maybe not on a shrimp boat, but a motorcycle instead, or stilts or a snow machine, wooden shoes, it didn't matter—anything to lift them out of the inertia of their lives and into a new orbit. Landon's own effort had richly rewarded him with new supplies and food, but best of all the jump-start of his metabolism made him believe he was finally thinking clearly again—the most potent survival tool in his kit.

CHAPTER 23

RECONNAISSANCE: THE WHEELHOUSE

Landon decided to use his recovered laptop in place of his phone as his new "lighthouse" beacon on the second recon swim. He figured the MacBook Air's screen had a wider spread that would be easier to see underwater, even if it wasn't as bright as the phone's flashlight app.

Losing his way and nearly drowning in the bunkhouse made him realize he needed a greater margin for safety. So he'd unraveled the yarn on both sleeves of his green sweater and tied them together in one line he estimated, by counting ten lengths from shoulder to fist, to be about thirty feet long. He wound the length like a kite string around a travel-size shampoo bottle that had been in his dopp kit, another treasure from his duffel bag. He unscrewed the top of the shampoo bottle and used Junior's knife to poke a hole through the bottom. He then threaded a doubled-up length of dental floss, also scavenged from his dopp kit, through the bottom hole and the lid opening, making a roller, which he tied loosely to the side belt loop of his jeans.

He tied the trailing end of yarn to the handle of the bathroom door, where it would gently unspool with slight tension as he moved forward, leaving a safety line that he could follow back, just like cave divers did. This was critical, considering the infinitely more complicated route to the wheelhouse and the ship's total darkness. And in that shroud of dark he'd have to navigate a confusing underwater maze: first down and past the staterooms to the ladder, climb down the ladder into the galley, exit the galley side door into the open ocean itself, then descend deeper still, cross over to the stern-facing wheelhouse door, and make a quick sweep to get inside. After, he'd have to do it all in reverse to make it back to his bubble. Landon figured he might be able to hold his breath for three minutes—maybe three and a half at most—which meant he couldn't dawdle, and there would be no room for error. If he was fortunate enough to find a second air bubble in the galley or wheelhouse, he could catch another sustaining breath. But if his bathroom bubble was the only remaining one onboard, he had to give himself another breathing safety option. Landon remembered watching a nature documentary that featured a species of arachnid found in the lakes and rivers of northern Europe. The so-called diving bell spider spent nearly its entire life underwater, living inside a web inflated with air from the surface. The spider also carried an air bubble around its body, like a scuba tank, to breathe while it moved through the water. Landon couldn't spin a bubble web, but he did have another option: the toilet pump. The pump, depending on whether it was switched to wet or dry, used either water or air pressure to flush waste into the ship's waste holding tank. He needed to dislodge the pipe fitted to the underside of the bowl without breaking it. Lying on his back on his hammock, it took five or six upward stomps before the pipe separated from the bowl. He twisted the pipe outward from the toilet and wrapped the airtight polypropylene bag around the pump opening. Then he switched the setting near the handle to "dry," pulled the handle down, then pushed back up. The bag ballooned with air, but quickly went flat again as it seeped out from the opening's edges. Landon wrapped the bag tighter, squeezed around it with all his might, then pumped again and again and again—until the air pressure in the bag prevented him from pushing up any more on the handle. He let go of the handle and choked up on the bag below where it was fitted to the opening. Satisfied he'd gotten a good seal, he pulled the bag away and rolled up its edges until he was sure it would hold, then clicked the lock tabs in place. He smiled to himself, proud of what he'd done. Like the diving bell spider he'd made his own web bubble. On the trip out it would act like a fish swim bladder, helping him to stay neutrally buoyant. At his destination, the air would sustain him, the ten-liter bag maybe providing one lungful for the return trip. After that he'd use it to stash the first-aid kit he knew was mounted on brackets at the rear wall of the wheelhouse, and whatever else he might find.

With all his preparations and precautions complete, it was go time. His stomach fluttered in nervous anticipation, especially after the close call on his last swim. But he knew there was no other choice. He could no longer sit in his hole and wait to die. He had to be proactive if he was going to save himself. He also still harbored some hope, though fleeting, that he might yet find some of the other crew members alive. His might not be the only air bubble left on *Philomena*. And if that was the case, there was even more reason not to delay.

As he had done previously, Landon knew he had to expel as much carbon dioxide from his system as possible, since a high CO_2 level, not a low oxygen level, was the primary trigger of the need to breathe. He needed to hyperventilate to change the gas balance in his lungs, but overdoing it could lead to blacking out midway through his underwater swim. That would mean game over.

Landon had often been frustrated by the balance that life demanded from him, though he rarely if ever acceded to its wishes, even while Vanessa continued to warn him that the way he lived was unsustainable. He recalled how, during his darkest days at the end of their marriage, she had quoted a passage from Kahlil Gibran's *The Prophet* to him while he lay in his usual spot, in his usual state: on the couch in his study, drunk. He looked numbly at her dark eyes, swollen from crying, as she sat beside him and read. "Verily you are suspended like scales between your sorrow and your joy. Only when you're empty you're at standstill and balance." At the time he'd dismissed it as so much namaste yoga-brain claptrap. But how right she'd been. If he lived through this, he vowed to go back and read the entire book. Maybe quote it back to her in a friendly email, admitting he'd been wrong—or maybe even a phone call, if she didn't reject it after seeing the caller ID.

He took deep breaths in rapid succession, visualized what he was about to do, and then once again pushed out of his bubble into the water. He shuddered for a moment as the water wrapped him in an icy chill, but flutter-kicked through it down the short hallway and to the ladder leading to the galley below. He used the rungs to pull himself down, feeling a little woozy from his hyperventilation, but not enough to abort and return to his bubble.

Once finally inside the galley, Landon was feeling marginally confident. His sweater-yarn safety reel was releasing itself properly, and his polypro bag, nearly full of air though compressed at depth, kept him evenly suspended in the water. Still, the way the floating detritus in the galley brushed against his arms unsettled him. At one point he nearly panicked when he swam into a shroud of material that wrapped around his face. When he grabbed it away, he felt the outline of small bottles. Emmanuel's spice vest! The find both comforted and disturbed him. It was something familiar from one of the crew members, but its meaning was uncertain. Had Emmanuel fled without his vest to escape the sinking ship, or had the violence of the event ripped it from his body? Regardless, he wasn't leaving it behind. He looped one of the arm openings over his head, the rest now trailing behind like a flowing cape.

As he ventured deeper into the ship, the blackness that surrounded him, the lack of visual stimuli, conjured more disturbing images in his mind, of fish and crabs nibbling away, sampling his puckered white flesh. And still ahead was the most difficult and frightening part: going out the galley door into the open sea. Plenty of potential for things to go wrong there. Landon felt the yarn spool at his waist and was reassured by the tennis-ball-size lump still wound around the shampoo bottle. Enough, he assumed, to get him the last ten or twelve feet into the wheelhouse. Feeling the first pangs of the urge to breathe build within his chest, he wondered if he should abort and go back. But if anyone was still alive, he couldn't delay in reaching them. They'd be exposed in the wheelhouse, and would have a better chance nested with him in the protective shell of the overturned hull.

He turned the handle and pushed out the door, feeling the resistance of the water pressure on the other side, but also the pushback of a turbulent ocean current. Anything too strong, he reasoned, would sweep him away from *Philomena* and out to sea like an untethered astronaut. He pushed harder and slipped out the door, careful to pull the handle up and expose the locking flange so it stuck out beyond the doorframe, keeping it from closing in the current and from severing the connection of his flimsy safety yarn.

The current tugged Emmanuel's vest, tightening the ring against his windpipe. And when he pulled the fabric up, closer to his chin, the water current pushed the air bladder out from under him, rotating it to his back, pinioned only by the nylon strap that now vibrated in the flow, mirroring the terrified beat of his own heart. His lungs were already aching, and he still had to let go of the doorframe to climb down to the back of the wheelhouse. There he'd be shielded from the current, but he'd need to get inside as quickly as possible. He felt as if he were jumping between two buildings, and if he missed, he was finished. *The glory that was Greece, and the grandeur that was Rome.* From the frame, he reached one hand below and felt around for the rail he knew surrounded the wheelhouse. Once he had a grip on that, he hesitated, thinking through the maneuver, then pulled himself down and crabbed around to the back.

The current ceased immediately. But now the need to breathe was overwhelming. A heat flash across his body, his heart throbbing against his chest wall, his brain screaming for oxygen. His eyes were burning from the salt water, but he didn't dare close them now. Should he just try and shoot for the surface? Let his air bag pull him up? He'd get bent for sure. But what other options did he have? If there was an air pocket in the wheelhouse, it would be at its highest point, farthest away from where he was now. There was no time left; a few seconds more, and his primitive brain stem would be in charge, overriding all higher functions and inducing him to open his mouth and lungs. He'd drink in the dark, green sea, and that would be all.

LANDON FELT FOR the wheelhouse door handle, surprised to find it was already open and pinned back against the rear wall. He stroked hard to pull himself inside, felt along the ceiling with his hand, desperate now, moving forward, searching for a slight change in temperature. Nothing. He was about to pull up his air bladder when . . . his fingers broke through. He pushed his mouth up to join them, lips breaking through the water's surface and pulling in a lungful of air, along with some water. He pushed his face back under, coughed it out and then back up again, gasping, pleading, sucking it in—momentarily, temporarily replenished. He steadied and calmed himself. *The glory that was Greece, and the grandeur that was Rome.* There wasn't much air left in the pocket, not more than a few balloons' worth, and he was sucking them down rapidly. As he took them in, a profound emptiness took hold: there was no one left but him.

The reality of his isolation swept aside all the little victories it had taken to get this far, filling him with an aching sadness. And once again he considered whether he too should draw his last breath and exit into the open ocean. Head for the surface. That way they might at least find his body there. Wasn't that preferable to this tomb at the bottom of the sea? But as he breathed in his tiny air pocket, he noticed a silver disk wrapped in a black plastic band floating at his eyeline. He reached up and felt the raised lettering between his thumb and forefinger. Captain Esteban's dog tag! The one Olveda had been wearing. Again the dual feelings of comfort and concern—had Olveda escaped the ship or been swept away to drown?

Landon put the disk in his pocket. All these reminders that his job was not done yet. And as he thought, he remembered another. He took a breath and dove down and to his left, feeling the wall above what had been the area above the starboard window, but now was low port. His fingers felt the raised edges of what was taped there, already beginning to peel away.

Carefully he removed the holy card, put it in his pocket with the dog tag, and surfaced back inside the shrinking air pocket. As he took in what little air was left, he was no longer ambivalent about his purpose here. He'd suffered too much, worked too hard; he needed to carry whatever it was inside him now to the end. He felt pride in what he'd done to keep himself alive, especially his problem-solving creativity. Something he'd never been confident in doing when faced with the challenges of his own life above. And maybe because of what he'd learned here, all that would change when he did make it out. He would not end up like the American soldiers who drowned in a desert irrigation ditch. He would be Jonah. Yes. He would be Lastman's crazy-eyed Jonah, burped back onto dry land and the realm of the living after three days and three nights in the belly of the whale. That would be enough, he was certain, to make any reluctant prophet like himself change his tune.

Landon took one last full breath from the air pocket, then felt around to find *Philomena*'s wheel below him. When he had a grasp on it, he pulled out a rectangle of white cardboard from his jeans pocket, the back of one of his reporters' notebooks. Back in the head he'd used a black Sharpie to print a message in big block letters, punched a hole in the cardboard, and threaded it with the coiled wire of the notebook's bindings, which he now wrapped around one of the spindles of the ship's wheel.

When finished, the cardboard sign floated above the wheel. Then Landon swam to the back of the wheelhouse and found the first aid kit, still in its mounting brackets. Before removing the kit, Landon pulled the air bladder around in front of him, raised it above his head, unclicked its snap-locks, and rolled down the fold. The air inside forced the bag fully open, his own mini diving bell. Landon pulled its edges down toward his mouth until his lips cleared the waterline and found the air. He breathed in hard, two or three times, before collapsing the bag flat. The diving bell spider had nothing on him, although its air bubble probably did not reek of shit.

With one more breath, he burped the bag and dived down to retrieve the first aid kit from its wall mount. It clicked as it came free, trailing the old gas mask that had been in the engine room behind it on its rubber retention strap. With everything that had happened, Landon forgot he had taken the mask from the engine room and placed it with the first aid kit after his interview with Lorenzo, feeling, in his meticulous mind, that it belonged with the emergency supplies. He stuffed both kit and mask in his black bag and was about to close it when his arm brushed against another floating mass of material suspended in the water. He flinched, but then felt that it was just clothing of some type. He packed it inside the bag too; maybe it was something that would be useful later. He resealed the bag and then reached around for his yarn spool, ready to follow it back to safety. His lungs were already beginning to rebel, his last breath at least forty seconds earlier.

But when he patted his homemade diver's reel, he found only a frayed end still tied to its center. Landon realized it had probably snapped against the tension during his desperate dash into the wheelhouse for air. He swept away the panic before it could paralyze him, focusing instead on his physical pain—being deprived of oxygen and the only place left to get it. He just needed to replicate all his moves in reverse to return safely to his bubble. No time to overthink it. He swam out the open wheelhouse door, reached around to find the railing, and slid up until his fingers probed the crack of the galley door. The metal flange had held, and he worked against the current, pried the door open, and got inside.

Now his chest was inflamed, his adrenaline surging, and he was getting dizzy. *Fast is slow, slow is smooth.* Couldn't remember where he'd heard that, sounded like military jargon, but it applied now. He had maybe another minute, he reasoned, before blacking out. He felt around, found the hatch and ladder that led back up to the staterooms, threaded the needle without banging his head or limbs on the opening. Immersed in the dark salt water for so long, his eyes stung, but still he peered into the darkness looking for his beacon home. Nothing! Where was the glow of his laptop screen? Dread as he realized his stupid mistake.

Without being plugged in—the machine had probably gone into

sleep mode to conserve the battery. He, Lukas Landon, not Chuy, had been the real chucklehead on the ship. This was the error that would probably kill him, drowned in the passageway so close to home. His body would never be found, and others' thoughts and memories of him would decompose just as quickly. A life that was supposed to help bring understanding through stories, but whose own narrative was one of halting missteps, an inability to love, accidental destruction. A legacy as empty and black as the place he would now die.

But the negative thoughts angered him. Algernon in an endless maze. Tired of the puzzle. He would not give up. He'd hurl himself against the ship's walls until they toppled. He gathered all the energy he had left, pointed himself toward where he believed his air pocket was, and stroked. He pulled, hands scraping against both sides of the narrow hallway. He flutter-kicked until his feet cramped, his lungs about to burst, his sanctuary dangled in front of him but forever out of reach. He pulled and kicked with all he had left, vest pulling back against his neck, bag trailing behind. But wait! Why wasn't he moving? He wanted to scream, felt his mouth yawning open to breathe in this liquid world—marshaled everything to fight against it. What was holding him back?

He snapped and writhed, reaching forward, wondering how he could die when air was only a body's length away. As he twisted he felt a tug against his shoulders, turned, and reached behind him. The shoulder strap of his black bag had snagged on the handle to the captain's bunkroom. He was convulsive now, in a frenzy. Finally, a snap of his entire body pulled the strap free. Landon breached the waterline into his bubble like a flying fish, heaving, gasping, dizzy, frightened, and still alone in the darkness—but alive.

CHAPTER 24

SOLITARY ANIMAL

O nce the adrenaline of the experience drained away, Landon felt
hollow. His reconnaissance had been successful in that he'd ex-
plored the ship, solved life-threatening problems on the fly, and gotten
back alive. But what it ultimately confirmed was that he was the sole
survivor on *Philomena*. He'd been a loner all his life, but this was a new
paradigm. The bubble above was self-imposed isolation, conscious separation, refusal to connect. It sheltered him from the ridicule of others,
shielded him against rejection, protected his vulnerabilities.

Here, Landon conceded, the boundaries of isolation were not self-
imposed and imaginary; they were steel, water, surface pressure, things
that could never be breached without significant effort. The separation
from others that he'd sought on land was now irrevocable underwater.
He no longer even breathed the same air, but his own dense, compressed
gas. It was as if he were living on a different planet.

He pulled into himself; the cold was getting worse. By the light of his
phone he eyed the clothes and duffel on his hammock. There was also the
bag still draped over his shoulder, he remembered; he could finally give
in to what small comforts it might provide. He climbed out of the water
and onto the wool-blanket hammock, thankfully still holding taut. As
cold as he was, he forced himself to take off the clothes he was wearing:
his jeans, underwear, and his now-sleeveless green sweater and white
T-shirt. He removed and took stock of all that was in his pockets: the

dog tag, the soggy Santa Philomena holy card, the vial of white powder from Emmanuel, and finally, his two front teeth. Placed them on the shelves inside one of the cupboards, where they'd stay dry. And then he went to work. He squeezed the water out of each piece of clothing and put it back on, even reinserting Junior's dry porn-mag insulation as a base layer. But first repocketing his teeth and the powder, wanting them both close. The former having become, strangely, comforting talismans, the latter, insurance. Then he began to don the extra clothes from his duffel.

He started with the socks first—one, two, three pairs, until his feet looked more like clubs than human extremities. His feet had been bare since *Philomena* capsized, and he could see, as he pulled on the socks, that his toes were a waxy yellow from lack of circulation. His fingers were the same. Next, he lifted both legs and pulled on the sweatpants, baggy enough to get over his jeans with little struggle, but when he tried the same with the sweatshirt, he really had to tug to get it over his sweater's bulk, reminding him how much he'd always disliked that sweater. Everything about it had been slightly wrong for him: the green color, its coarse bulk, and most of all, the transactional nature of the way Vanessa had given it to him, as if their growing estrangement from each other had been knitted and purled into the yarn itself. Its roughness scratched at him, but he felt he deserved that discomfort—a penitent in a sheep-hair coat in his waning moments. Next he topped it all with the Gore-Tex shell, beginning to look as he had as a child in winter, when Annabel had layered him like the Michelin Man before letting him outside. Last, he found his black beanie, pushed his wet hair back, closed his eyes, and pulled it over his head. He kept them closed, savoring the warmth building from the heat of his own body, captured in what seemed like a thousand layers.

Next, from the black waterproof bag he removed the first aid kit, gas mask, and the dripping wet mass of . . . the captain's M-65 field jacket. Finding it, like the other crew items, was like throwing back a shot of Maker's Mark—a happy, warming reminder of its owner, coupled with the tingling burn of their absence. He wrung it out, laid it over one of the ropes holding up his hammock, where he'd already placed Emmanuel's spice vest, and turned his attention to the first aid kit. It was an industrial version, with a waterproof hard case about the size of an attaché, green, with a red cross on a white circle at its center.

Landon unlatched it and opened the lid. After helping treat Chuy's ankle injury, he already knew most of what was inside. There were bleed bandages, gauze bandages, elastic wraps, a tourniquet pack, burn dressings, occlusive dressings, a clear box filled with airways of all sizes, a roll of duct tape, a pack of six Cyalume chemical light sticks, and even a foot-long M6 oxygen cylinder and yoke regulator, with a button pressure gauge attached. He'd already checked its fill level previously. It was built to hold over 160 liters of compressed medical-grade oxygen, but the needle gauge had pegged to the midpoint between 1000 psi and Red/Refill. Probably just a few liters left, and toxic at depth. He'd use it, he thought, for a few last breaths, if or when the time came.

But then he found what he was really looking for. He held a tube closer to the glow of the MacBook Air's screen and read the label: "Lidocaine gel." The anesthetic was normally prescription but could be bought over the counter if the active ingredient content was 4 percent or less. Landon knew this, having procured multiple tubes of his own prior to heading off to war, and he'd been fairly certain he'd find some in *Philomena*'s kit, considering all the potential for bodily harm onboard a shrimping trawler. He opened the tube, squeezed a generous amount on his fingers, and packed it into the gap where his two incisors had been. He winced, and the chemicals generated an instant pool of saliva under his tongue, leaking out in a stream of clear drool. He ignored it and instead enjoyed the immediate numbing sensation. Next he found a bottle of aspirin, shook out four, popped them in his mouth, and washed them down with a slug from his last remaining can of Cobra malt liquor. This also washed some of the lidocaine down his throat, anesthetizing the area of contact around his mouth and epiglottis. It was a price he'd gladly pay to get the aspirin down, desperate to ease the stabbing pain of his broken rib, now a seven or eight out of ten on the pain scale after the physical demands of his mission outside the bubble.

As he waited for the medication to kick in, Landon reached for the pack of chem lights from the first aid kit, shook one, and cracked it. The yellow glow filled the space with such brightness it hurt his eyes. He'd made a mental note to use the lights sparingly, since they only lasted a few hours each, and he'd have to rely on them once the batteries drained out of both his laptop and phone. He used the illumination to examine the clothing he'd found during his recon. First he patted down Emmanuel's vest and found waterlogged spice bottles and little else of note until he examined the back flap pocket, which held the cook's prized black book, now soaked through with seawater. He couldn't imagine Emmanuel without it, but he remembered the cook's answer when asked why he was always studying it: "Someday the book may be lost, or taken, like has happened once on board this ship." Landon placed it aside on his hammock, hoping he could find a way to dry it out and return it to Emmanuel.

Next, he turned his attention to the captain's jacket. He touched the sleeve, thinking of her wearing it, fierce at the helm. Wondered again whether finding it was evidence that she'd been lost to the storm or escaped, shedding heavy outerwear that might weigh her down before donning a life vest. Maybe that was why he'd found the wheelhouse door open during his recon swim: the crew had bailed out before it was too late.

Landon reached into the hip pockets of the field jacket. He felt nothing on the right, but noticed a tiny hard lump in the left. He opened the flap and retrieved the object: a wooden shark, no bigger than a thumb. A bull shark, he knew for certain from its front-loaded muscular bulk—and also because Junior had told him as much.

Maybe it was the meth, but the deckhand couldn't keep his hands still when he wasn't working the nets or doing other chores on deck. Even under the stimulant's influence, the carvings were still a marvel. For nearly the entire voyage, Landon had watched Junior sitting on deck in his downtime, frenetically whittling away at an undersea menagerie from the remaining basswood burls in his Crown Royal bag, like some ancient whaling mariner working scrimshaw. By the end he'd made one for the captain and every other member of the crew, representing what he saw as their ocean-living counterparts.

Junior had told Landon earlier it had nothing to do with physical similarities. "It's what I see in their nature that they got in common with whatever I chose for them."

"Okay—so why a bull shark for the captain?" Landon had asked while Junior was working on the shark one night, early in the voyage. "Because she's the alpha, the apex predator?"

Junior laughed, wiped the sweat from his face. "For a college man"— Junior used his knife to point at the "Kent State" on the chest of Landon's hoodie—"you ain't working to see much beneath the surface."

Smarting from the dig, Landon stopped writing in his notebook. "Go on, educate me."

"Cap'n's a bull shark, because she can't never stop moving, constantly swimming. Never stopping, or she'll die." Landon raised his eyebrows. "Same reason Olveda's an Atlantic manta," Junior continued. "She has a kind of—whatya call it—fluidity."

"Grace?" Landon offered.

"Yeah, like that!" Junior emphasized with the knife point in the air again. "Emmanuel got a puffer, 'cause you think he's all one thing, and then he can change shape in an instant, all sorts of tricks up his sleeve."

Landon nodded, continued writing.

"Ol' Lorenzo got a tarpon, because he's our man of the night, and tarpon, as you know, is the night hunter. And Chuy, well, ain't no going real deep on that one—a green turtle, 'cause that little peckerwood is slow and lazy." Junior laughed at his own cleverness. "But he gets there eventually," he added generously.

"And me," Landon said. "The octopus. You said before, when you made it for me, it was because I juggle a lot of things, but I'm not sure I buy that. Feels like you intended something else."

Junior stopped carving, gave Landon an approving nod of the head, raised his eyebrows in surprised affirmation.

"So why the octopus?" Landon asked.

Junior broke eye contact, went back to carving. "Simple. Octopus a solitary animal. Lives nearly its whole life alone. Most everyone could see that's you, Lukas Landon, just walking down the jetty, 'fore you even came aboard."

Landon placed the wooden shark back in the pocket of the captain's jacket, folded it up, and placed it under his head as a pillow as he lay back in the hammock. Couldn't remember ever being this tired in his entire life.

CHAPTER 25

CHUY

Wednesday, December 19, 2018
One day before the storm.

The cotton shrimp disease had cost *Philomena* nearly a quarter of their haul, and the thought of having to stay out longer had put everyone in a thoroughly foul mood. While it was clearly bad luck for the captain and crew, Landon knew the setback added drama, spiced the larger story with a new and overwhelming obstacle. These microscopic parasites, presenting as tiny, cotton fluffs, had the power to change the course of a 110-ton vessel and all seven people onboard. Instead of west, they would go east; instead of returning to port, they would stay out at sea.

Landon was relieved to have a few more days out. His talk with Captain Esteban had shaken him. Not just that she knew about his past, but her deliberate unshrouding of his own opportunism and—he hated to admit it—duplicity. It was something he'd compartmentalized since the events of Ramadi. And he understood that by revealing what she knew, Captain Esteban was simply doing what was in her nature: protecting her own. She exhibited a clear sense of purpose, devoid of moral ambiguity. Landon envied that about her. He felt shame that he was the thing against which protection was needed.

Regardless of these disturbing thoughts, he needed to file an update to the series, revealing this sudden change in fortune. He went above deck with his BGAN and laptop to transmit, so focused on his preparations that he didn't notice that Chuy had come on deck with an uncharacteristic feline grace and perched just behind him until he heard the deckhand slap a packet of Marlboro Reds and slip one into his mouth.

Silently Chuy tapped out another Marlboro and offered it to Landon, who took it, grateful for both the interruption of his thoughts and the cigarette. Chuy pulled a lighter out of his pocket. Landon took note of the thick calluses on Chuy's hands, illuminated by the small flame raised to his own cigarette and then to Landon's. He nodded his thanks, inhaled deeply, discharging the smoke moments later through both nostrils. Chuy breathed in his own smoke, exhaled from his mouth, inhaled the gray plume back up through his nose.

"What's that?" Chuy asked, chin pointing to Landon's setup. Landon realized he'd never been out on the deck with Chuy alone before, never transmitted his work in front of him, even after three days together on the water.

"Satellite modem," Landon said as he exhaled another plume. He tapped his keyboard a few times to bring it out of sleep mode and dragged his updated story icon from the blue folder on his desktop to the BGAN's transmit folder. They both watched as the long blue status bar filled the screen, ticking off the progress of the transmission: 1% . . . 3% . . . 5%—then falling back to 3%.

"Why is it doing that," Chuy asked, "going higher, then lower?"

Landon had not seen this curiosity or attentiveness from the deckhand previously. Chuy usually didn't ask questions; he reacted, lashed out, instigated, keeping everything and everyone, even Lorenzo, at arm's distance. He did his job, was actually good at it, a methodical and hard worker. Yet little of it seemed to bring him any happiness. Nothing apparently pleased him but teasing the cook or sleeping. Just worked, ate, shit, and slept. Landon had seen this before. In himself, in the weeks after he returned from Iraq and Afghanistan. After the excitement of being home faded, the days and nights of indulgence in booze and drugs wore off. He would crash. Sleep for what seemed like weeks. When he finally emerged, there was nothing—no desire, no emotions, just a deep emptiness that called him back to his bed. He fed that emptiness with benzos and sleeping pills. Lorazepam during the day, prescribed for anxiety, but it really just kicked his legs out from under him, kept him in a dreamlike state, staring at the vast wasteland of daytime television. And Ambien at night, enough to push him over the edge into sleep again, even though he'd done almost nothing—no work, no exercise—to warrant more rest.

These stretches could go on for so long he'd even given the condition a name: his ZF state, for zero fucks. Sometimes it lasted until he had a new departure date scheduled, a return to the places where nothing and everything mattered, all at once. Each time, especially after Ramadi, he hoped it would be his last. A life for a life, and then he might be remembered fondly, before he burned everyone out of the last reserve of goodwill they had for him. He wanted this most for Vanessa. It would be a win-win for her: no longer having to watch him waste away, and a modest life insurance payout.

"It's just like this run on the Phil," Landon said, responding to Chuy's earlier question. "One step forward, two steps back." They both laughed. "Signal ebbs and flows, especially out here."

"So that's how you get all that stuff you write about us and all the videos to your paper?"

Landon nodded. "Four of the main stories already ran in the print edition—and all of the rest online. You might be famous when we get back. Never know."

Chuy chortled, with a tinge of vulnerability that surprised Landon. "Hope not. Better some people don't know where I am."

"Is that why you haven't done a video interview with me yet?" Landon asked. "Everyone else has."

Chuy took another drag from his cigarette, turned his face away to blow out the smoke. "Nah. Just don't have anything to say. Nothing to write about, anyway."

Landon considered pressing the point, but Chuy was already talking—only rookie reporters got in the way of that.

"You been a lot of weird places, right?" Chuy asked. "Middle East and stuff, Afghanistan?"

Landon nodded. He saw what was coming; he'd seen it, heard it, so many times before, usually prompted by alcohol, weed, the things that took away inhibition, allowed natural curiosity to bubble up into actual words.

But Chuy, for the moment anyway, was guileless. "You ever kill anybody over there?"

The BGAN started clicking, indicating a stronger signal, and the transmission progress bar on Landon's laptop showed only another ten minutes until completion. He took time to consider the question.

"Not on purpose," Landon said finally. Then disguised it with a grin. "Journalists are supposed to be noncombatants. We're there to watch and report what happens, not to fight. Technically, we're not even supposed to be armed, because that could give one side or the other the wrong impression."

"Wait, wait, wait," Chuy said, hitting the air brakes with his right hand and simultaneously snubbing out his cigarette on the outrigger pole behind him, flicking the butt overboard. "You go to all these places where they're shooting at you, trying to kill you, and you don't even have a piece to protect yourself?" He laughed at the insanity of it. "Junior was right. You are a crazy motherfucker, Landon."

Landon considered what Chuy had said and Junior's take on him. Maybe everyone else thought the same, or worse. "If we're not embedded with the military," Landon continued, "sometimes we hire private security to watch our backs. They carry weapons so we can do our job—observe, report, shoot video, take pix."

"You ever see someone get killed, though?"

Landon looked back at the BGAN transmission progress bar. It was dropping back down to half, now showing fifteen to twenty minutes until completion. The signal had gotten worse. He looked up at the darkening sky, then out at the waves, an insistent chop turning rough.

"Storm coming in," Chuy said.

Landon nodded. "Seen people die too many times," he said grimly. He scrolled through the memories, trying to decide which to choose: Karbala? Fallujah? Maybe Dasht-e Qal'eh. There was currency in all, but he didn't have the time or patience for a long, slow dip into details.

Decided on a story that was compelling and personal even when abbreviated.

"The one that stays with me," Landon lied, because they all did, "was when I first crossed into northern Afghanistan. This was shortly after 9/11, and the US was using air strikes against the Taliban, and supporting Tajik and Uzbek warlords who called themselves the Northern Alliance. The air strikes were having an impact, and the Taliban started retreating south, toward Kabul." Chuy nodded impatiently—not the details he wanted. Landon expedited the narrative. "We got cocky, was the thing," he said. "A handful of us had attached ourselves to one of the warlords, a Tajik, Commander Kamal Daoud. The commander had set up his forces, about five hundred men and a few dozen APCs—armored personnel carriers," Landon explained, "in a valley north of the Taliban lines, ready to chase after them as they retreated. Three of us—me, René Dilliard, a French radio reporter, and Paloma Lopez Munoz, a Spanish journalist from *El Diario*—asked Daoud if we could ride inside one of the APCs. But they were already filled with his men and had no room for us. Then Paloma, all five-foot-nothing, one hundred ten pounds of her, asked if we could ride on the outside."

Chuy looked at Landon, incredulous. "That's ballsy."

"Very," Landon said. "Dilliard and I were both hesitant, but we weren't about to be left behind—especially when Paloma had already scampered up the thing and sat on top of it like she was at an outdoor concert."

Chuy smiled at the image, and Landon continued. "So we climbed up too, but when Commander Daoud gave the order to advance, we hadn't gone more than a hundred yards when two Taliban fighters popped up. One was armed with an RPG, a rocket-propelled grenade. He pointed it at our vehicle and fired." Chuy jutted his jaw, impressed. Landon went on. "The grenade hit but didn't explode. Maybe it didn't arm, since they were so close. But Daoud still gave his men the order to retreat back to their starting point and regroup."

"What a wimp!" Chuy said. "Running away at the first shot."

Landon held up his hand to stop him, the most important details to come. "So when our APC swung around without any warning and headed in the other direction, Paloma was thrown off. René and I were next to the gun turret, had something to hold on to. We screamed at the driver to stop, pounded on the turret plating, but they couldn't hear anything over the noise of the engine. Or maybe didn't want to hear anything. We were ready to jump off ourselves and help, but when we looked back . . ." Landon paused, closed his eyes, remembering. "We saw her trying to stand up. She'd barely gotten to her legs when we saw the second Taliban. He was aiming down on her with a PKM—mounted on a bipod."

"PKM?"

"A Russian-made light machine gun. We saw the rounds stitch across her tiny body." Landon grimaced at the recall from twenty years earlier. For the ten thousandth time he wished it had been him rather than her.

"That's hard-core, man," Chuy said, shaking Landon out of his momentary trance.

"Yeah," Landon said. He paused for a beat. "She was dead before she hit the ground. What really sucked was we had to leave her there until nightfall, until Commander Daoud was certain the Taliban had finally fled."

"What did you do?"

"He ordered one of his APCs to take René and I back to recover her body. We found her facedown, right where she fell. The rounds had nearly cut her in half. I didn't want to look at her face. Felt like I'd failed her. We both did." Landon sighed. "One of Daoud's guys gave us a blanket. We wrapped her in it and lifted her onto the outside of the APC again." There was disgust in Landon's voice. "Fucking NA didn't want her inside. Her body was already beginning to smell. But I think it was more that they were ashamed, like us, that they had turned and run away while Paloma had actually stood up and faced the Taliban. She had a heart bigger than all of us. Was so much braver than we could hope to be."

"What happened after that?"

"We rode on the outside again. Held on to her body, like—like a funeral procession, almost." Landon still marveled at the memory. "It was a clear, cool night, and the sky was filled with so many stars—only the way an Afghan night can be. And I remember being angry that Paloma would never see anything like it again." Landon paused, looked down. "It wasn't just that she was dead, but that her death felt so meaningless, an inconsequential skirmish on an inconsequential ridge that no one would remember but us."

"Hard-core," Chuy said again, shaking his head.

"And she had the sweetest smile," Landon said, caught in the current of the past. "It was authentic and innocent, despite all of her experiences and the terrible things she'd seen in her career. That fucked me up for a while." It was as if he was talking to himself now. "That smile she gave me right before we got on the outside of the APC. She wasn't upset that they wouldn't make room for us inside, she was almost gleeful. How lucky we were to be there, like we were getting away with something, not about to ride into a battle." Landon paused again, for what seemed like minutes. Finally he spoke again. "Seeing her smile like that, I was less scared. I think René was too."

Chuy bowed his head in solidarity. Was quiet for a time, giving Landon a chance to drift back to the present again. Chuy lit up another Marlboro, but instead of offering one to Landon, he looked over at the reporter's laptop. The BGAN transmission had fallen back again, to just 50 percent complete.

"Looks like you got a ways to go on that thing. Weather can be a bitch." He shook his head, exhaled a long stream of smoke, then flicked the barely smoked cigarette into the choppy sea. "Gotta go. Up early tomorrow so we can fish out the hold. Finally get back to Port Royal." Chuy looked restless, but he covered with a smile that was as close to charming as Landon had seen from him. "Thanks for the stories, Landon."

Landon acknowledged him with a raised hand and watched him go belowdecks. It had taken him nearly the whole voyage, but he felt he knew everyone onboard now, all their stories and some of their secrets. And Captain Esteban knew his. Another hour passed before the BGAN was finished transmitting. Landon closed up his gear and went to bed, exhausted. Tomorrow, he was certain, he would know how this story ended.

CHAPTER 26

LOST AND UNFORGIVEN

Thursday, December 20, 2018
Sixteen hours before the storm

The next morning, the pitch and roll of *Philomena* threw Landon against the metal wall behind his bunk. He bolted upright, trying to orient himself, remember where he was. Looked down and saw Chuy's and Junior's bunks both empty. Already on deck, he thought, slipping off his own top bunk onto a surface that seemed to roll under his feet.

Once he was dressed, Landon climbed the ladder that led from *Philomena*'s sleeping quarters to the galley. Emmanuel was seated on the built-in bench around the galley table, the same place he slept at night, thumbing through his black book. He shifted his eyes from it, blinking acknowledgment of Landon, and then toward the two industrial-size battleship-gray thermoses bungeed to his food prep counter, opposite where he sat. Coffee and hot water—the only two things Emmanuel would be making for breakfast in this weather. Landon nodded his thanks, but headed out the galley door and looked to *Philomena*'s stern. This time the deckhands were both dressed from head to toe in their foul-weather gear, a couple rubber ducks sliding around on the deck. The seas were too rough to fish, but the port boom arm had come loose and was slamming against the gunwales. Chuy was gathering up the unspooled trailing net while Junior stood ready at the electronic winch to hoist it back into place, where it would be secured until the storm passed or for the journey back to Port Royal. Whatever Captain Esteban decided.

Chuy was still stowing the lines when Junior set the winch in motion. The trailing end of the net caught Chuy's right heel and heaved it skyward, flipping him into the air. He landed hard just as *Philomena* dipped to port. Landon watched in disbelief as Chuy rolled toward the ship's metal gunwale, stopping only when his ankle and elbows made contact, the wind and water dampening the sound of everything but his cursing.

Junior looked panicked but regained enough composure to lower the boom arm again and attempt to reset the process before things got any worse. All the movement captured the attention of Lorenzo and the captain, inside the wheelhouse. Lorenzo dashed out and over to Chuy, where Landon was already helping him to his feet. Together they brought him inside the galley, propping him on the bench Emmanuel had vacated, wet slickers and boots puddling water on the floor. Soon everyone but the captain and Olveda had crowded inside. Lorenzo looked at Junior, who was trying to hide his face in one of his hands, but said nothing.

Chuy, however, let loose. "You simple fuck, Junior! Why didn't you wait for me to clear before you started up the winch?" Junior, squatting, said nothing, just rocked back and forth on his haunches, rubbing his forehead.

Lorenzo gently pulled off Chuy's right boot and peeled off his woolen sock. His ankle was already the size of a plump grapefruit. "Cabron!" Chuy shouted when Lorenzo tried to rotate it.

Landon moved in, nodding for Lorenzo to let him try. "Got a little training," he said, taking Chuy's foot in his hand, wrinkling up his nose. "Smell like ass."

"Eat shit, paperboy," Chuy said, stretching his neck back, trying to distance himself from the pain.

"Now, there's the Chuy we all know and love," Landon said, examining the ankle. "At least it's not black and blue. Can you push your toes against the pad of my hand?"

"Can you lick my balls?" Chuy replied, but he pushed down and then yelled, so loudly everyone took a step back.

Olveda poked her head up from the deck below. "Must be something amazing for breakfast with all this noise."

"Chuy just had his first wet dream," Landon said, then motioned toward Chuy's ankle. "Just needs a wrap."

Olveda nodded, went up to the wheelhouse, and returned with a green Pelican case. She set it on the floor of the galley, opened it, and found a beige elastic bandage held in a tight roll by a metal clip. She handed it to Landon, who began expertly wrapping Chuy's ankle in a figure-eight, snapping it taut under the pad of his foot then up and over the ankle, repeating this until it was fully braced and mostly immobile. He used the metal clip to secure the end of the bandage.

Everyone, including Chuy, seemed impressed.

"Nice work, Landon. Maybe you can find some work as an athletic trainer if this reporter thing doesn't work out," Olveda quipped.

Landon chuckled. "That's seventy-three hours' worth of prime Florida EMT Basic school you're seeing there, folks." Then he lowered Chuy's ankle to the cushion to rummage inside the first aid kit himself, emerging with a bottle of aspirin. He was about to shake out two when Emmanuel touched his arm, stopping him. Landon understood. He recapped the aspirin bottle and placed it back inside, then clicked the first aid case shut again and handed it back to Olveda. Lorenzo turned his gaze to Junior, still rocking back and forth silently.

"Help him down to his bunk," Lorenzo said. "He's going to be even more useless today than usual." Junior jumped at the chance to escape Lorenzo's focus, but Chuy pulled away. "Not the tweaker. He's likely to break my other ankle on the way down."

Chuy looked up to Emmanuel, who stood against the wall, saying nothing as usual. He reached a hand to him, like a child, asking to be helped up. Surprisingly, Emmanuel responded. He took him under the arm and helped him to the ladder, then climbed down before him, a human safety net while Chuy hopped down on his good leg.

In the crew's bunkroom, Emmanuel helped Chuy out of his foul-weather gear and settled him into the bottom bunk. The cook stared at him for a moment, decided something was not right.

"Which is Junior's?" he asked. Chuy pointed to the middle. Emmanuel grabbed the pillow off Junior's bunk and stuffed it under Chuy's swollen ankle. They both laughed, enjoying the small payback. "Thanks," Chuy called out as Emmanuel turned to leave.

The cook nodded, then stopped but did not turn around. "I'll bring you some tea."

"I don't need tea," Chuy said. "I need Oxy."

"This is special tea," Emmanuel said. "It will help take away the pain and lessen the swelling."

"More recipes from your little black book? No thanks, *maricon*." Chuy grimaced at the memory.

"This one is different," said Emmanuel. "No side effects." He grinned as he pulled the oval door shut behind him and climbed the ladder back to the galley.

WHEN EMMANUEL RETURNED to the galley, Lorenzo told everyone to start locking down the boat. The weather was going to make fishing impossible, and they were likely headed back to Port Royal by the afternoon.

"Is that what my mom said?" Olveda asked.

"That's what we need to do," Lorenzo replied, but with less certainty in his eyes than his voice. "This isn't going to let up, and we're not accomplishing anything out here but bobbing around like surface trash."

Olveda nodded, but it was clear she wasn't convinced. Lorenzo doubled down. "You and Junior secure the hold." He looked around at the galley, then at Emmanuel. "Looks like you're already packed away here."

"Anything I can do?" Landon asked.

"Yeah," Lorenzo said, on his way to the wheelhouse, "stay out of everybody's way."

Landon pulled back. He wondered if the captain had mentioned their talk to Lorenzo, or if maybe Lorenzo had just felt challenged by Olveda's remarks and needed to reassert himself.

Emmanuel moved to the cupboards and removed the ingredients he needed for Chuy's tea. Junior followed Olveda back into the hold at the ship's stern. Only Landon was left standing there, unsure of what to do or where to go.

THE BOAT WAS moving forward slowly, Captain Esteban searching for smoother water, but in the pitch and yaw Olveda stumbled back like she'd been thrown from a mechanical bull. Junior held out his hand, steadied her. Even when flustered, his footing was more confident than the greenhorn's. Once he felt she'd found her balance, he let go and they got to work ratcheting down the plate freezer to prevent any shifts that might upset the balance of the ship.

"What happened up there, Junior?" Olveda finally asked. Junior shook his head. Something building inside him. Anger? Despair? His heart was beating so hard, he could almost hear its thumping in his chest. Despite the damp, chilly air, he was sweating. He wanted her to just forget it. He was too wired already. Didn't need somebody else chipping away at his already fragmented concentration.

"Things just got fucked up," he said, not looking at her, mechanically attending to his tasks—securing tools, shovels, pails, deck squeegees, empty crates. But his hands were as jittery as his heart. "I lost him for a second. Thought he was aft. He shoulda been watching too," he said, becoming defiant now, like he was a boy again, being interrogated by cops. The questions, the meth, and the rocking of the ship had tipped him far back into ugly memories. The police had visited him plenty, coming around asking where his Pa had gone after his various dustups at the local bar.

Senior had done it all—brawls, stabbings—and afterward he would head out to the Lowcountry for a few days or months, depending on how bad the situation. There, he'd bed down with a Gullah woman he'd been on with for years just because—or maybe because he actually loved her. Junior didn't know. There'd been rumors his father had a whole other family there. Maybe that was part of the reason his mother had left them both when Junior was twelve. That and the beatings her drunken husband doled out like penny candy. Junior wished Senior would just stay down there, and sometimes it seemed he would, especially in the winters, when there wasn't any crewing work. Those were times of hardship, but also of peace. No angry rantings or violence, just the sound of hard rain on the leaky roof. Watching the stream of water droplets coming off *Philomena*'s hatch took him back there. His game, as a boy alone, catching as many of the drips as he could, until there were so many pots and pans on the floor, it looked like a banquet table.

Junior would sit in the living room, smoking from an old pack of Senior's Kools. Always Kools, 'cause that's what the Gullah woman smoked. Those times, hard as they were, were also his calmest. He'd still go to school every day, even if just for the company, to not be alone in the old house during the dark days of winter. And he would have to fend for himself, scrounging for food, money. Sometimes even selling off car parts, fishing nets, other things that accumulated in the informal scrapyard that had been encircling their run-down clapboard-and-tarpaper house for years, a growing moat of junk and debris from projects Senior started but never finished.

Junior would get whipped good when Senior finally did return from his extended stays, hungover and burning with the anger of perpetual poverty and failure. Especially when he learned what Junior had sold just to keep himself fed and warm for the winter.

These days his Pa was all but useless, welcome nowhere, not at the bar, not in Gullah Lowcountry, his credit run dry all over the state. Junior had to feed and clothe him, haul a case of beer and a quart or two of local moonshine to Floyd Senior's damp, decaying bedroom each week just to keep him from shaking to death. Junior knew he wouldn't last another year. Crewing on the Phil was Junior's only respite—hard, peaceful days just like when his father was in the Lowcountry, a feeling of self-sufficiency, purpose. But he knew now, as he worked in silence with Olveda, that the job might no longer be his once they got back to Port Royal and the shares were paid out, if there were any. Lorenzo knew what he'd been doing; Lorenzo knew everything, could see through everyone. He knew Junior had probably been a good deckhand once, could see the remnants of it, experience demonstrated in his economy of movement, the all-in work ethic. Never complaining. Even his off-time whittling fortified the crew on their down days, talismans to rub in their pockets, summon the strengths of their animal guardians in the periodic droughts of hope.

But something was off with him. Every season, he lost a step or two. Just like Senior had, with his drinking. He didn't want to end up like that, one of the lost and unforgiven. That's why he'd started using crank in the first place—to work harder, longer. It helped at first, but then the fatigue would hit and the black, black moods. Days would turn into nights and nights into days, with utter exhaustion but no sleep. And there would be stretches when, like his father, he'd never get out of bed. Times his brain felt like it was being fed into a paper shredder, his thoughts torn and scattered. Times when he just didn't want to live anymore, but the only thing capable of chasing those dark thoughts away was the smoke he could conjure from a glass pipe. That's not where he'd been when he started the voyage, but that's where he was now. And why this thing happened with Chuy. He hadn't expected to be out so long. He thought for sure he'd be home after just three or four days of good fishing, flush with his share of the money, able to lay off the pipe and put himself down with some Valium he had stashed away. Sleep for a week. Now it seemed like they'd be out here forever. Maybe never come home again.

CHAPTER 27

"AIN'T GOOD ENOUGH"

Captain Esteban was concentrating on the next wave, sliding down the backside of one peak and steering *Philomena*'s bow head into the rising crest of the next. She shook her head when Lorenzo asked her if she wanted a break, kept looking ahead. He said nothing, waiting for her thoughts, preparing his own arguments.

"If we can find one more good spot, get some calmer water, we'll pack the rest of that hold. One and done, and then we can head back in," she said, forcing optimism into her voice. Lorenzo said nothing, watching the waves, steering the boat with his mind, all the moves Clarita would make just seconds later. They were so much alike. So stubborn, so broken and angry at the world, so unwilling to yield. He supposed they shouldn't be. Each of them had been given rich gifts during their lifetime—deep and abiding familial love, adventures, purpose, and now, at this point in their lives, maybe each other. It was new and tenuous. And both had seen the hazards of giving yourself over to something too completely, he to his now-dead wife, she to service to a nation that put her in harm's way in unnecessary wars and rewarded her with a lifetime of residual physical pain and emotional mistrust.

Still, they were working something together that might take care of them for the rest of their lives. Lorenzo didn't believe in destiny, but it sure felt like it. The very ship that brought him to the shores of America might get him through his final tours at sea.

But that was only if they saw things the same way. Clarita was captain; he was just a hired hand. He liked it that way. He wanted to be indispensable to her and the ship, but not be in charge. He'd run things long enough in his life, was willing to defer to her, eager for it. Still, if she didn't listen to him, accept his collective wisdom from years working the water, there would be no trust, and Clarita was not good at trust. How could she be? As a Black woman in a white man's world, she'd been betrayed, overlooked, discounted nearly every moment of her life. All she ever got, she had to scrap for, fight it out until bloody and off balance, just to get the same chance as anyone else. He felt the same perpetual vigilance. He would always be an immigrant in America, even though he'd spent most of his life here. Even though English came off his tongue as easy as Spanish. Some would stare at him with contempt when he'd speak it. He'd look back at them, dare them to say something. Even though he was not large, he was solid from years of physical labor.

White people struggled to place him; was he Greek? Spanish? Mexican? Dark hair and eyes, but white skin. Still, they knew he was not one of them, and with that unknown came a certain fear, an understanding not to push it too far. Though he knew for a fact that Clarita was much more dangerous than he. Always standing her ground, casual defiance the threat of mutual assured destruction between her and those who would consider trying to take what she had, what she had earned with sweat and actual blood. She would fight and kill to protect her family, her ship, her livelihood, her sense of self, from those who would attempt to take them from her and leave her with nothing. Clarita was always rightfully suspicious, even with him, but he knew, especially now, she had to listen and trust him, or they all would lose.

"What?" She looked back over her shoulder at him, knowing his silence did not signal his agreement. "You wanna call it now. Go in before we're full up?" There was a hint of accusation in her tone, nearly a dare.

"Didn't say a thing."

"Yeah, but you thinking it. Go on then. Talk."

"Rough out here," he said, finally.

"Ya think?" Sarcasm in her voice.

"It's not going to get any better. It's going to deteriorate."

"Says who?"

"Marine forecast. C'mon, Clarita," he pleaded. "You know we're done here. We had a pretty good run. We're a little short, but we might break even for the season."

"Break even ain't good enough." Her tone was flat. Final. "Break even means starting behind next season. We already up against it, Enzo. Still got loans out on this boat, the plate freezer, people to pay . . ."

"It's all family here," he countered. "We're good, even Junior."

"Yeah." She sighed. "Especially Junior, 'cause no other ship gonna take him anyway, tweaking like he is."

"I can fix that," said Lorenzo.

"Yeah? How you gonna do that?" She spoke impatiently, turning over her shoulder to glare for a second. "Send him to rehab on our employee assistance program? We're out of money, Enzo. You saw the books before we came out. We're leveraged to our teeth right now. Missed payment or two, bank will take this boat, and then we're all done. Just like they said we would be. You can already hear 'em in Port Royal: 'Uppity bitch, thinking she a cap'n 'n all.'"

"Not going to be like that."

"No, and why not?"

"I got some money saved up. We can get through the winter, start early in spring, maybe even charter some sport fishing or other stuff. It's always tight like this, starting out."

The captain was silent at the wheel. Lorenzo thought maybe he'd convinced her.

"So you're gonna come in and use your money to save me, huh? Damsel in distress can't figure this shit out, so the gallant Lorenzo Ortiz come to the rescue? Don't work like that with me."

"I know that."

She held up a hand over her shoulder to stop him. "I make my own way, always have. Help me like I hired you to, but don't try to save me.

There ain't no saving that needs to be done. Only fixing, only getting things right when things go to shit. God knows I've seen it, got the scars to prove it. We need to head into this one. Take the risk or hang it up for good. That's my choice. Rather have you with me than not," she said, then turned over her shoulder to look at him and smiled. All it took.

SINCE THE WEATHER was bearing down from the north, Captain Esteban decided to look for calmer seas farther south, piloting *Philomena* away from their home berth at Port Royal. It was late enough in the season and the weather correspondingly poor; the captain didn't expect to see a lot of local boats. Probably already put in, where she wished they could be right now too. But the late season also meant they could fish their last pass closer to the shoreline, one last day of dragging the waters nearer where the rivers and estuaries flowed into the Atlantic. It would be a much better potential source for the white shrimp that would make or break them. She and Lorenzo decided they would take *Philomena* as far south as Tybee Island, anchor in calmer waters, then begin a slow push back home to Port Royal. If the seas cooperated, they'd drop the nets at dawn, work five or six solid hours, pack the holds, and maybe be back by the next morning. They would be burning extra fuel staying out, pushing everyone to their limits. It would be all-out, but everyone knew what was at stake.

ON THE DECK, Landon was looking out over the water, the roughest waves he'd ever seen. Strangely he felt no fear, only growing isolation. He normally didn't get seasick, but *Philomena*'s rolling and heaving left him irritated. He moved to the galley, looking for Emmanuel, some non-confrontational company. There the cook was still busy, finishing the preparations for Chuy's tea. Something elaborate, Landon figured, considering the time it took to prepare.

"Got anything that will put me in a better mood?" he asked. Emmanuel gave him a sly smile. "Actually, I'd settle for something to just keep me from puking."

Emmanuel nodded, began to reach for something in one of the cupboards, but Landon held out a hand in the air. "Not now, maybe later. Just do what you were doing. Mind if I sit here though?" He pointed to the built-in bench at the galley table.

Emmanuel shook his head. "Excuse me," he said, moving past Landon with a steaming mug of tea in his hand that smelled of licorice, fennel, and turmeric. Landon marveled at the cook's climb down the ladder to the staterooms, not spilling a single drop of the tea in transit. He sat down and opened his laptop to file another piece with the latest updates. He was surprised by his ability to concentrate, to go with the movements of the vessel and shut out the noise that surrounded him inside and out. By the time he'd finished writing and proofed the piece twice, the seas were calming and *Philomena* was slowing. Captain Esteban was looking for a place to anchor for the night. Perhaps she'd been right to push it, to stay one more night. Bold or reckless? It was hard to tell. The outcome itself would decide. He went above deck with his BGAN and laptop, transmitted the story with one clear uninterrupted signal, then went to his stateroom.

He was dog-tired, but his mind was buzzing. He looked down and saw Chuy, bum leg propped up, already asleep in his bunk, no doubt with a little help from Emmanuel. He remembered his own sleep aid. Taking out the baggie of white powder that the cook had given him, he sprinkled a bit in his palm, then licked it. It tasted bitter, reminiscent of the anesthetizing coke he'd rub on his gums after doing a line. He shook out another bump, this time tasting the salty sweat of his palm. If two was good, three would be better.

CHAPTER 28

UNDERDOGS

Fifth in a Globe-Democrat series on South Carolina's beleaguered commercial shrimping industry.

Our senior features writer Lukas Landon is filing dispatches all this week while aboard the trawler Philomena as her captain and crew make one last run in an attempt to stay solvent at the end of a brutal season. [Globe-Democrat print and digital editions, published 12-20-18.]

BITTER SEAS
Holiday Blues

A spate of bad luck forces Captain Esteban to make a risky choice. If she's wrong, it could mean the end of the line for Philomena and her underdog crew.

—*Lukas Landon*

Captain Clarita Esteban and the crew of her 110-foot shrimping trawler Philomena have been called plenty of things in their short time working together, many of them so ugly and disparaging that putting them in print is offensive. But one description is undeniably accurate and proper for individuals who have faced such daunting challenges: underdogs.

Esteban, as you've learned in this series, is a decorated U.S. Army combat veteran wounded in action in Iraq. And after retiring from the service, she decided to replace the arid desert of her wars with the vastness of the sea. Using the same determination and focus she possessed as a wrecker driver supporting combat operations in both Afghanistan and Iraq, she worked, studied, and tested to become the only Black, female captain in the 750-boat South Carolina shrimping fleet. But the insidious racism that has been an unfortunate part of South Carolina's heritage revealed itself again even before Philomena set out on her maiden voyage with a racial epithet (see the photograph below) painted on the ship's bow, shortly after its restoration at the start of this season. Undeterred, Esteban and her crew now compete with local established shrimpers as well as overseas farmed shrimp from Asia, which continues to capture the country's majority market share. This has forced some local fishing fleets to resort to niche operations focusing primarily on the highly prized and higher-priced white shrimp, usually more active in the cooler waters of the late season. Esteban has decided to go all in for the whites, with sales agreements with wholesalers working on behalf of high-end South Carolina restaurants, mostly in Charleston, to purchase at $5 per pound all the whites Philomena can catch. But the early season was dismal for nearly the entire South Carolina shrimping fleet, with a huge reduction in recorded tons even into late August, the worst early reporting in five years. Some blame climate change and rising water temperatures that inhibit shrimp spawning cycles. For many of the smaller operations, this has meant either bankruptcy or desperate changes in their seafaring operations. Some have traded in their shrimping nets for good, retrofitting boats for long-line fishing or sport fishing charters. Some have given up fishing altogether and turned to other options, like shuttling scuba divers to nearby under-water wreck sites or even running sunset booze cruises for romantic couples. Captain Esteban is not one of them. At least not yet.

"I'm not somebody to give up with the first sign of hardship," she said while preparing to take her ship and crew out for one last trip of the season, provisioning with enough food and fuel to stay out at least a week to ten days. "I'm also not real popular with my crew right now, this being so close to Christmas. But it's do or die for us. Got a balloon payment coming up on my boat first of the year. If we don't get what we need, it won't just be my crew who won't get paid, but also my creditors. Could lose the Phil, and our first season might be our last."

But Esteban's got a plan, more like a mission, and the mission, in her army parlance, has a "main objective."

"We need to put away ten thousand pounds of whites," she said as the crew loaded in the final provisions the night before. "That's the magic number. Sounds like a lot, but this late in the season we're not going to have a lot of competition out there. Everybody's done, made their bones or gave up trying. We have to do eight hundred to one thousand pounds a day. We do that, and it'll be a good Christmas for everybody."

And things started out well enough. For nearly three days straight Captain Esteban's plan was working; each location had Philomena's nets full to bursting with "white gold."

But near the end of day four, the captain's daughter and green-horn deckhand Olveda Esteban was packing the shrimp in the ship's hold when she noticed something odd about the color. A closer in-spection determined that some of the catch was infected with cotton disease, a parasite harmless if ingested by humans, but which turns the shrimp milky white or translucent gray and makes them nearly unmarketable for anything but animal feed. Instead of coming back to their berth at Port Royal, the captain had the crew dump the in-fected shrimp and head farther south for better fishing spots.

In just the space of a few hours, what seemed like a voyage to a "pink" Christmas and prosperous new year turned into the holiday blues. Philomena and crew forced to continue on a journey without an end date.

"Yeah, it was kind of a kick in the you-know-what," said Floyd Swain, also known as Junior, the only deckhand to carry over after

Captain Esteban bought Philomena. "But so is another year without any money. We'll get through it. The captain knows what she's doing. She'll do right by us, and we'll do right by her."

But not everyone is on board with Captain Esteban's plans. Even her engineer and first mate Lorenzo Ortiz believes that it's time to pack it in now that the seas have grown rough and Philomena is nearing the end of both food and fuel supplies. Ortiz, as noted earlier in the series, has a deep connection with Philomena, the ship that brought him and his family as well as hundreds of other Cuban refugees to Miami during the Mariel boatlift in 1980. Discovering that the ship was going back into service in South Carolina under Captain Esteban, he took his current position as a way to bookend a long and mostly successful career at sea. But at this moment Ortiz has his concerns, though he expresses them diplomatically.

"Of course we have differences of opinions on some things," he said on his way belowdecks to relay the new orders to the rest of the crew. "It's my job to point out the alternatives to the captain, but it's her job to make the choices. Something she's proven very adept at doing, whatever the environment. She's a bold mariner and we'll all follow her lead, wherever it takes us."

And where it's taking them at this moment is farther out to sea and closer to the Georgia state line. The plan, Captain Esteban says, is to anchor overnight off Tybee Island, then begin early in the morning the sixty-nautical-mile-plus journey back to their home port of Port Royal, dropping nets where the Savannah River flows into the Atlantic and every other estuary along the way until Philomena's cold storage is full. Ten thousand pounds.

This isn't some arbitrary number. To Captain Esteban it's the over/under line between making it to another season or failing as a groundbreaking shrimping captain. But don't mistake her intentions, she warns. She's not trying to be a role model; she just wants to do the job she loves well enough to make a living at it.

"I don't point to this and say this is the way to go for young Black girls out there thinking what they want to do with their lives," she said. "I'm not even sure this will be anything more than a summer job for Ollie [her daughter Olveda]. But I sure as hell don't want anyone to think this door is closed to them. If they love it, if they want it, there's no waiting for permission from anyone. Go on and take it."

As a diesel mechanic and wrecker driver trained by the army, Captain Esteban has multiple and maybe easier career options if the shrimping doesn't work out. But she says that's a scenario she doesn't even want to consider right now.

She loves the sea and the challenges of maneuvering through an unforgiving environment and casting her nets to pull up the ocean's bounty, making a living with her brain and brawn, managing a crew of "misfits" (her words) through an intricately choreographed dance on the ocean, where everyone must do their work in the middle of Mother Nature's wrath on a tiny strip of slippery deck that shifts under their feet. Sometimes that choreography is flawless. Other times . . . it's like today.

Late in the morning, deckhand Jesus "Chuy" Ortiz, Lorenzo's cousin, was preparing to stow the nets when an outrigger arm was winched prematurely, hoisting him into the air. He landed on his back and slid into the port gunwale, suffering a severe ankle sprain.

"It's the kind of thing that happens when the crew gets tired," Lorenzo Ortiz concedes. "People start to lose their focus, perception narrows, and stuff happens."

But with Chuy Ortiz confined to his bunk for now, his responsibilities will have to be picked up by his older cousin—not an ideal situation, considering Lorenzo Ortiz typically works the night shift at the helm in the wheelhouse, making sure the ship is safe while others sleep. Now he'll have to sacrifice his own sleep to work the deck during the day. Chuy will stay in the "box" on deck, where he can help sort out the bycatch from the shrimp without having to move around too much on his bad ankle. Emmanuel Etienne, the Haitian cook, will go belowdecks with Olveda, helping to freeze, crate and store the shrimp in the "cold hold" while Captain Esteban is once again in the driver's seat.

In a ship this size, larger than your average thirty- or forty-five-foot day-tripper but nowhere near the size of a factory ship with overlapping crew, everyone feels the loss of a single crew member, whose duties must be absorbed by everyone else. And—as everyone knows but won't say aloud—that extra burden, that tension, can lead to other even more serious mistakes, possibly deadly ones.

While the crew stows the gear and Captain Esteban sets a heading southeast, the mood on the ship has shifted dramatically from guarded hopefulness to melancholy. Aboard Philomena the spirit of the holidays is elusive, as much as the precious white shrimp that must be netted and stored to ensure her future.

IMAGE: Philomena in dry dock, undergoing repairs and restoration, at her home port of Port Royal, South Carolina, earlier this year.

CUTLINE: Even before she put to sea for the first time under new owner and captain, Clarita Esteban, the shrimping trawler Philomena was defaced by a racial slur painted across the bow in dry dock. To date, no arrests have been made in what Port Royal police concede was likely a hate crime.

CHAPTER 29

SEND UP
A FLARE

Landon's reconnaissance to the wheelhouse had nearly killed him. But exhausted as he was, sleep would not come. He'd been insane to go out there a second time, blindly feeling his way around an upside-down ship at the bottom of the ocean. The experience frightened him to a cellular level, and he wondered where he'd found the balls to do it. War reporting was a church bake sale compared to an untethered, unoxygenated swim through a black metal maze.

But somehow he'd pulled it off. And now lying here, waiting for something to happen, though relatively comfortable by comparison, felt wrong. He'd been rewarded when he'd taken calculated risks; he'd recovered his duffel bag with food, clothing, and his laptop, and found evidence of the crew's possible escape, first aid supplies, and medicine, even a tiny O_2 cylinder and the forgotten gas mask. He sat up in his hammock. All this would help keep him alive in his bubble. But how were rescuers going to find him, if they didn't know where to look?

Even if the captain or Lorenzo had time to radio out their last coordinates in a Mayday call, that was just a small starting point in a very large ocean. Landon needed to give them some help. Send up a flare to the ocean's surface. But how, and with what? He'd read that flotsam from sunken ships could help searchers chart drift patterns back to where a ship might have gone down. So what could he send topside? Landon reactivated his laptop light to look around, but then remembered what he was leaning against—the ancient orange life vests. Even with their dry-rotted foam, he knew they would still float. But that wouldn't be enough to connect them to *Philomena*. He could write on them with one of his Sharpies, but the seawater would bleed the letters out, making them unreadable. Landon looked toward his feet, where the gas mask and green Pelican case still shared the hammock with him. The first aid case was perfect. Foam-lined and waterproof, it would float straight up when sealed, like it was made out of cork. But he couldn't send it up empty. He needed to fill it with items that would identify it as coming from *Philomena*. Landon opened the kit, dumped the contents on his hammock, and knew exactly what he'd replace them with.

Once it was filled, he'd secure four of the old life vests to the Pelican box, using their own straps, swim it all to the galley, open the door, and release it all like a bundle of balloons. When rescuers found it, they'd know to stop looking on the water and start looking underneath it— motivated to work even faster, knowing someone down there was still alive.

Only one hitch in the plan: Landon didn't want to go back out. Not now, not ever. He'd been lucky twice, and he didn't like his odds on getting away with it a third time. He felt an involuntary shudder reliving the nearly fatal close calls of the earlier incidents. He thought about what frightened him the most. It wasn't the cold, or even having to hold his breath. It was the vast blackness—the inability to see where he was, where he needed to go, and, critically, how to find his way back. If he could remove that obstacle, he'd be confident enough to venture out at least one more time to do what he needed to do to save himself.

Landon looked at the mess in front of him, the first aid supplies and gas mask. He picked up the mask, examining it from different angles. It was a Panorama Nova made by the German company Dräger and was not dissimilar to full-face masks used by some scuba divers, usually those in salvage or public safety who needed to communicate with each other. The mask had the same five-point strap connections that kept an airtight seal around the face. It had a wide plexiglass viewport sealed in a metal frame, providing a 180-degree field of vision. But it was built to keep out smoke and gas. Would it do the same for water? Among Landon's dozens of digital magazine subscriptions was *Scuba Diving*. He vaguely remembered reading an article from a year earlier about poor but enterprising salvage divers in Myanmar who still scavenged World War II shipwrecks in the highly polluted Yangon River. From the photographs accompanying the article, Landon recalled the divers wearing DIY gear with heavy chains across their bodies as diving weights and gas masks, identical to his, hacked with tubing that provided surface-supplied air from either tire pumps or homemade compressors. Landon had a potential pump with the toilet, but no hoses or anyone to operate it. He was tempted to try using the medical oxygen cylinder, carrying it with him on the swim, but he knew the pure oxygen content would be toxic at his current depth, whatever it was. Instead, he decided he'd release the O_2 into his bubble on his return, chancing that it would diffuse and be breathable without sending him into convulsions. He was still reluctant to go out again, but this time he would have an advantage he didn't have on the first two trips: he'd be able to see exactly where he was going. That was enough. Would have to be.

AFTER LANDON HAD filled the green Pelican case with the identifying items from *Philomena*, he secured the life vests to it with their straps and then wrapped them tight with duct tape. It took him twenty minutes more to create his improvised dive mask, reinforcing the viewport's seal with more duct tape and sealing off completely the mesh opening over the mask's mouth area, where the filter was normally fitted by a screw mount, as well as the exhale ports. He was hoping air pressure inside the mask from small exhalations might keep water leaks to a minimum. So much of it was educated guesswork, but he had to try.

He stripped out of his multiple layers of warm clothing, knowing how much he'd need them on his return, and prepared for the swim in just his now-sleeveless green sweater and boxer shorts. Then he activated four chem lights, securing two to the "package" and using dental floss to tie one more each to the top of both hands, allowing him to see wherever he reached without losing any dexterity. Next Landon donned the mask, which he'd defogged with his own saliva, brushed away his hair, and secured all five attachment points. Once he was confident he could get a good seal, he lifted the mask from below and began hyperventilating again to lower his carbon dioxide levels, then resecured it.

Landon picked up the package from the hammock and entered the water portal leading to his destination. Once immersed, he was amazed at the new clarity with which he could see and navigate the narrow passageways of the overturned ship, excited that the mask did not flood, though its tight squeeze around his face combined with his hyperventilation had made him lightheaded. He proceeded anyway, dropping a fifth activated chem light at the head's entrance to mark his return.

But while the mask performed well, Landon struggled with another element of his plan. The Pelican case wrapped with life vests was so buoyant now, he struggled to hold it down underwater, forced instead to pull it along the low ceiling. When he reached the ladder entryway to the galley, a deck below him, the effort to pull the case down taxed his reserves, forcing him to exhale into the mask and breathe back in his own carbon dioxide waste, making him feel even dizzier. He resolved not to do that again. It could make him lose consciousness and drown. He'd come too far for that kind of silly mistake.

He had to hurry now; he was already fighting his instinct to breathe. With one arm on the lowest rung of the ladder, he used the other to pull the buoyant case below the threshold and into the galley, where he safely released it to float up against the ceiling, then followed inside. But the exertion left him panicky; he felt spots forming behind his eyes, and the buoyant air-filled mask was yanking up against his face. He wasn't going to make it on one breath. He'd have to return to the bubble. He went back up the ladder, looked left for the glow of the chem light at the entrance, and swam for his air pocket. Frames of black pulled across his vision. Disoriented, he turned around, stroked in the wrong direction, then turned again and saw the light. When he did reach the bubble, he was sucking in so hard he had difficulty removing the mask. Even after leaving the water, he thought he might die. When he finally succeeded in pulling the mask off his face, he chased the air with his entire body, unable to get enough, starting down a dead-end path of short, shallow breaths: still—not—enough.

Desperate, he lunged for the small oxygen cylinder on the hammock, thankful that he'd already threaded its tiny regulator. He twisted the dial to maximum flow and waved it underneath his face, trying not to breathe in its full density. Eventually his lungs responded, relaxing as he allowed the cylinder to run dry, emptying the last lifegiving contents from its tiny aluminum nipple—the final pure air, he realized, *Philomena* would ever have inside her.

He gave himself time to recover—thirty, forty minutes, who knew? But he had to finish the mission he'd started. Donning the mask again, he quickly swam back to the galley and located the Pelican case where he'd left it, pressed against the hard deck above him. He opened the galley's side door and used the dangling waist cinch of one of the life vests as a tether to pull his orange and green sea "balloons" through the passageway and out the doorframe. Once outside the ship, the current tugged on the package as it had on Landon during his earlier recon. He fought against the force that pulled him into the opening, as if he were about to be swept out of a plane. At the threshold, he wondered why he was letting the life vests go, wondered why he wasn't holding on to them for a rocket ride to the surface, wondered why his hand suddenly opened, and he watched the package race upward away from him. It took a moment to realize the significance of what he'd done. He'd chosen life—or rather, the slim hope of it—over near-certain death. After killing himself slowly nearly every day since that moment in Ramadi, he'd found himself finally at the threshold. All that lay between him and completing the task was the open galley door leading out into the darkness of the open sea. But he'd chosen not to go; he'd conceded that he'd been wrong all those years. That even after that terrible turning point, he still had purpose, a reason to live, but would not or could not see it through his perpetual haze of self-medication. Instantly he felt the guilt and dread of all that wasted time, that voluntary estrangement from everyone who'd ever mattered in his life. And with that rush of emotion, an even greater fear: that to live meant he would have to change. For Landon, as for so much of humankind, change might be more terrifying than death.

CHAPTER 30

IMMORAL INJURY

Back inside his bubble, Landon didn't have the energy to do anything but lie down. This time he'd made it back without any issues, but he knew the slowly souring air of his bell jar, even infused with the oxygen that had been left in the M6 cylinder, was poisoning him. Dressed again in his layers, he rolled onto his side in his makeshift hammock. By the waning glow of his last chem light, he discovered another with him in the space. He wasn't startled. He'd half expected him near the end like this.

Landon could see the left side of the man's face. Same as when he first saw it: a strong distinguished chin and high cheekbones, covered by a neatly trimmed silver beard.

"Is this what happens when you're near death?" Landon asked. "You experience all of your greatest regrets?"

The man said nothing, just shifted, exposing the right side of his face. His skin was peeled away, revealing a few strands of muscle clinging to gray bone. His skull was mostly hollowed out, as if someone had scraped clean the inside of a soft-boiled egg. Exactly what the mortar shrapnel had done, slicing through his head at supersonic speed after the detonation of its high-explosive core.

"I'm sorry, Abu Abid." Landon turned away. "I still see your face in my nightmares. Your wife and children, too."

Landon looked back, but Abu Abid was gone. Now seated across from him on his hammock, where Abu Abid had been, was the figure of a woman, her legs folded in front of her, back straight, hands on knees, eyes closed. The perfect yoga sukhasana. "V?" Landon squinted, trying to focus his own eyes. An impossible light began to radiate behind the image of the woman who had once been his wife, Vanessa. It washed out the gloom of the space, illuminated the taut, flawless texture of her skin, the ringlet waves of her auburn mane, playfully swept to the left. She was wearing a neon-yellow bikini top and blue board shorts, the same as in the favorite photograph he'd taken of her at Virginia Key Beach. He had snapped it on his phone in the golden light of dusk as she sat motionless in the sand, striking the exact same pose of peaceful meditation. Tears welled in gratitude and relief, as if his long trial was now nearly ended.

"V, you look beautiful," he said, reaching for her, then checking himself.

Opening one eye, then the other, smiling to soften her words, she said, "I wish I could say the same for you."

Landon nodded. "Been under a lot of pressure. About sixty, seventy pounds per square inch." He chuckled. "Depending how deep we are."

"Still with the corny jokes that no one gets."

"Thought that was how I won you over," Landon said. "I know it wasn't my looks."

Vanessa scowled. "For a man so knowledgeable about the world, you were always an idiot about us."

"And still champion." Landon pumped both fists in pretend celebration.

She peered at him closely. "Finally found a use for that sweater, I see."

"Was saving it for a special occasion." He gestured to the space. "But it's perfect for my new surroundings." They sat in silence. Nothing but the groaning of the ship.

"I'm so desperately happy to see you," he finally said.

She tipped one ear, as if she hadn't heard right. "You're *desperately* happy to see me? After years of pushing me away and making me feel meaningless?"

"I was trying to protect you," Landon said. "I didn't think you'd understand what happened over there. What I did." He hung his head. "And if I did tell you—I was certain there was no way you could still love me."

Landon had barely gotten the words out when he felt both her hands push against his chest, forcing him to grunt out what little air was left in his lungs and reigniting a fire of pain from his broken rib.

"Don't you hear yourself? Every one of those fears is about you—not me. I didn't need your protection from the unjust realities of the world." She took a breath, calmed herself. "You drop in on a few wars, and you're an expert? Most women are fighting every day of their lives. If we're lucky, it's just fending off the crude comments, insults, and sexual leering. If we're not so lucky, we're slapping away the ass grabbers, breast brushers, and mouth breathers rubbing their crotches while they stare. And if we're really unlucky, we might end up with our faces being pushed to the floor and our underwear pulled down around our knees."

Landon struggled to sit back up. To catch his breath in the ever-thinning air of his bubble. To steady himself against the sting of her words.

"You want to believe your pain is special, and that no one else can understand. Well, you're wrong. We all suffer. It's the universal human language."

"Yes," he said, hoping she would finally stop.

"And how dare you make the assumption that I couldn't love you if you told me the truth. I'm an elementary school teacher, Doctor Dimwit! Patience and understanding are our two greatest superpowers." He wanted to smile, hearing the pet name she'd used for him when he annoyed her, which he knew to be often during their marriage, but she held up her hand to indicate she had more to say. "I know the world is slippery, and sometimes we make the wrong choices."

"Unforgivable ones," he said, still short of breath.

"Unforgivable ones," she repeated, as if sounding the words out. Gave herself a moment to consider this. "There was only one unforgivable thing you did."

"What was that?"

"You had an obligation to try and fix yourself. I was right there, ready to help. But instead you decided on a slow-motion suicide, pulling anyone near you into your vortex of hopelessness and surrender."

"I'm sorry."

She ignored the apology. "With every bottle you opened, with every line you snorted . . . lying alone on that fucking couch, in that fucking room." She balled her fist. "You drifted farther and farther away from me until I couldn't see you anymore, us anymore." Vanessa rubbed her temples. "I'm not saying your despair wasn't real. It was profound and debilitating. But you were wrong to decide to live there the rest of your life. It cost us—"

"Everything," Landon finished for her. He sighed deeply. "I should've never doubted you. I've been surrounded by unbreakable women all my life. Even here."

"Go on, then," Vanessa prompted. "Tell me about them. How they reached you when I couldn't."

Landon winced, but continued. "Captain Esteban is granite-hard, but gentle too. Has this sense of deep obligation to every one of her crew. And Olveda, her daughter, she's only nineteen but lightning in a jar, resilient and graceful. A full-blooded poet. I could learn a few things from her."

"How about the others?"

"Well, there's Lorenzo, so connected to this ship it's like they're the same entity. And his younger cousin, Chuy. Deckhand. He's got a lot of demons to work through, but I think he can do it if he tries. He makes me want to try, too. Junior's the other deckhand. He's an artist— whittles little knots of wood into sea creatures. I'm pretty sure he's self-medicating, though."

"Something you know nothing about."

Landon ignored the sarcasm. "Emmanuel is the cook." Landon smiled broadly. "For most of the trip he didn't say more than two words to anyone. But then I discovered he's as deep as he is silent. Now we're like best buds." Landon reconsidered. "*Were* best buds. I wish I knew what happened to everybody."

His face pinched with uncertainty. "I'm hoping they all made it off *Philomena* and were rescued." He looked at her pleadingly. "I'm the least deserving of all of them, V. So why am I still breathing?"

Vanessa considered the question. "Because for some reason you've decided that you want to be. After years of slowly killing yourself, suddenly you're down here at the bottom of the ocean and you're fighting to live. But I think that's only going to work if you accept that you deserve it. Forgive yourself for whatever it is you think you've done. Start by telling me."

Landon's body began to shake. He was exhausted, hypothermic. His grip on reality was slipping away as fast as the oxygen levels in the room. Why wouldn't this insistent hallucination simply disappear and let him suffocate or drown in peace? But real or not, he owed Vanessa an answer, and so he began. It was the story he had also promised to Emmanuel but never had the chance to tell. The day he was most frightened.

He nodded, took a deep breath. "Fourteen years ago in Ramadi, Iraq—I killed a man." He squared up to look her in the eyes. "And then I betrayed myself and my profession by never reporting it." He exhaled.

"Thank you for telling me." Vanessa immediately steadied him. "What happened, exactly? I'm listening with an open heart and an open mind."

Landon closed his eyes, returned to the nightmare. "I was at Camp Blue Diamond for a few days, waiting for a chopper to take me to Fallujah. Operation Phantom Fury was about to kick off. There wasn't much going on in the interim, so I asked to go out with an army mortar squad from an artillery unit assigned to brigade headquarters. They were just preregistering around the camp. They call it 'dialing in,' so they can be ready to shoot fast if something happens.

"I think the squad was bored. Said they had already done some targeting with sixties earlier in the week and now were going to step it up to the eighty-one-millimeters, so this was just to keep them fresh. Also it was important, they said, because of the spread. The eighty-ones had twice the kill radius of the sixties—up to thirty feet.

"They put a few smoke rounds on target. Everything looked good, and then . . ." Landon hesitated. "Then they decided to do a rapid-load, high-explosive three-round burst. You know, shove them down the barrel one right after another, fire for effect, since they were already locked in. That's when Sergeant Reyes looked at me." Landon stopped.

"You can tell me, Lukas."

Landon chewed the inside of his cheek, wanted to bite hard enough to draw blood.

"He asked me if I wanted to drop the first one. He told me it was easy, like 'dropping a water balloon from a window.' I think they just wanted to fuck with me," he said. "They were pissed that I was headed to Fallujah while they were stuck in Ramadi. They all wanted their combat action badges."

Landon gritted his teeth. "I never would've done it during actual contact, but I rationalized—I should see what it feels like, so I could write about it better."

He sighed. "So Reyes looked through the sighting system, and then one of the other guys handed me the round. It was smooth and tapered at both ends, felt like a little torpedo. They fitted three propellant charges above the tail so it would fly only the distance they'd already ranged. Then Reyes gave the order to fire. We launched all three in maybe six seconds.

"One of Reyes's guys called me out after the cycle. Said something like, 'Dude, your hands were shaking so much I thought you were going to miss the hole.' Other one said, 'Give him a damn break, bro. How you gonna see the muzzle right when you got one eyeball going all sideways?' Reyes hammer-fisted the soldier's helmet. But even he was trying to stifle his own laugh. I didn't care. The fact that they were making fun meant they accepted me. Saw me the same as anyone else in the squad."

"Band of frat brothers," Vanessa dismissed.

"That was the last time we all laughed that day. Reyes's radio crackled with a call from the spotter downstream, and I'll never forget what I heard."

Landon mimed speaking into a field radio: " 'Roundhouse Three, this is Roundhouse One, we got an unidentified pax on the ground just outside the power grid fence.' That's when Sergeant Reyes's face went white. Took him a few seconds to respond.

" 'Roundhouse One, this is Roundhouse Three Actual. Say again?'

" 'Copy, Roundhouse Three Actual, there's a U-I pax down. Looks like an older male. Over.'

" 'Roundhouse One, is the pax moving? Over.'

" 'Negative, Roundhouse Actual, and . . . looks like he's bleeding.' " Landon sat on the memory for a beat, then continued.

"His name was Ibrahim Salem Farhad. But everyone called him Abu Abid. He was an engineer, in charge of the city's electrical grid, and had been inspecting it near the fence line." Landon's voice choked. "The spotter had missed him, and the eighty-one's spread had been wider than Reyes had anticipated.

"After we dismounted from the Humvee, we saw he was still alive." Landon shivered. "His chest was rising and falling. Agonal breaths, they call it. And he held up one hand"—Landon imitated with his own—"like he was waving to someone. Surreal. It wasn't until we got right over him that we discovered what a frag of eighty-one-millimeter mortar can do to a human head. The entire right side had been sliced away. My heart dropped straight into my stomach." Landon peered silently into the darkness. "One of Reyes's guys pulled up on the M4 slung across his chest, asked if he should finish it. But Reyes just shook his head while looking directly at me. Like I might report it. Like I wasn't already fully complicit, for fuck's sake."

They both sat quiet, respecting the story's gravity.

"So what happened to him?" Vanessa eventually asked.

"He bled out in just a few minutes."

"And after that?"

Landon swallowed. "There was a brief investigation, and it was ruled an accidental death. The whole story was buried."

Vanessa took his hand, a reassuring gesture.

"But here's the thing," Landon said. "Reyes was right to look at me, because I *was* going to write it up. Did write it up! Every detail. Came clean, just like I told you now. Probably a career ender for me, and at least an Article 15 for Reyes and his squad."

Vanessa stared at him, waited for clarification.

"So I did a tight fifteen hundred words on it, told the truth about Abu Abid's death, and even some details about his life. The Ramadi electric grid was shit, but he had been a hero for holding it all together with worn-out 1970s Soviet-era spare parts. After the American embargo he was making local kill switches with broomsticks and empty mackerel cans."

"Resourceful," Vanessa said.

"The piece provided acknowledgment for him and accountability for us. All the things good journalism is supposed to do—or would have—if I had actually transmitted it."

"You never sent it."

"No. Got cold feet. I was about to head off to cover the biggest battle of the Iraq War. Felt I couldn't shit the bed before something that important. Thought maybe I'd circle back to it after." Landon shook his head, disgusted with himself. "Yeah, that didn't happen. And here's how Abu Abid was actually acknowledged: the camp commander sent his XO—his executive officer—to the family with a solatia payment of two thousand dollars."

Landon bowed his head. "It was ludicrous. I did some research later, found out that the three mortars we fired cost $3,600. Abu Abid's life was worth $1,600 less than the ammo used to kill him. The Pentagon was spending more than that each week on hot sauce and maple syrup for a single forward operating base."

Landon willed the relief of tears, but still they would not come. "His twenty-year-old son, Abid, as the eldest child and only male, was the one who received the payment. The XO, impressed with Abid's English and feeling guilty for the pittance given to the family, offered him a job as a translator with the headquarters company at five hundred a week. It seemed the least he could do, considering that Abu Abid's death had left Abid as the sole provider for his mother and three sisters."

"At least something decent came from it," Vanessa offered, feebly enough to be a question.

"No. Not in this story," Landon said bitterly. "Later I reached out to the XO to find out how Abid was doing in his job as translator. Found out he lasted just two months before one of Zarqawi's death squads grabbed him on his way home from the camp. A recon patrol from Blue Diamond found him in an abandoned warehouse. You know how many holes they drilled in him? Thirteen. One for each joint and finally—in the head."

Landon felt depleted, reached for anger to rouse him. "This is what happens when we go to war arrogantly and ignorantly. When we don't even speak the language, so we're nothing but imbeciles with machines guns, toppling governments and upturning economies—creating such chaos and disorder that those we invade have no choice but to either fight against us or help us to kill their own countrymen."

He banged the wall with his fist. "And if they do join us, then they have to translate our silly thoughts and incomplete sentences into their precise tongue while we call them ragheads or camel fuckers behind their backs, remaining stubbornly ignorant of the fact that their ancestors gave the world science and medicine. Yet our 'advanced' civilization with our billion-dollar weapons can't or won't differentiate who is for us or against us and can do nothing to protect one innocent man from our own mortars, or his innocent son from the indescribable pain of a cheap power drill."

Landon sank into himself, out of breath, whispering now: "And do you know how much the XO paid Abu Abid's wife for the life of their son?"

A long pause. "Two thousand dollars?"

Landon released a deep, primal sob. "I killed a good and innocent man, V!" The blood in his veins felt heavy as lead. "I set off a chain of events that led to the torture and murder of his son."

"Yes," Vanessa said. "It's heartbreaking."

"Then because I was a coward, I never gave them the dignity of reporting the value of their lives and the grotesque tragedy of their deaths. I betrayed them, their family, my own humanity, and my entire belief system."

Slowly he raised his face to hers. "And you're telling me I should forgive myself?

"I've been rudderless for so long. And then I came aboard *Philomena*, met these incredible people. Wanted to tell their stories so badly. It doesn't make up for what I did. It won't bring Abu Abid or his son back to life, it doesn't erase my most shameful deeds. And I can't do what you say—I can't forgive myself. I never will. But here's the thing—I also don't want to give up on myself. Not yet. No matter how much bad I've done, I still, for some reason—maybe the captain and crew—feel I have some good left in me too. I don't know if they're alive or dead, but I don't want to give up on them either."

"Like you did with us?" Vanessa asked.

"I can't forgive myself for that either, V. And I know, you being here with me now, this is not real. Just my air-starved brain going into electrical overload."

"What would you say to me if I actually were here? If you did have one last chance to talk with me?"

"I would say I'm sorry for shutting you out, for not trusting you with my dark secrets, for not doing all I could to make it back to you, whole." He paused. "I would say I love you, and I wish I could have made you a koi pond."

"A koi pond?"

Landon exhaled, relieved to recall a happier moment. "My father built one for my mother. It was the single most perfect act of love I've ever seen. The moment that every person dreams about; to be surrounded by trickling water, birdsong, and gold-and-white-speckled fish swimming at your feet." Landon smiled. "And knowing that someone had done it all, transformed the very earth, just for you."

"You never told me about that."

"I regret that I never did anything so fearlessly romantic for you."

"Fearlessly romantic would've been nice," she conceded, "but I would've settled for you just being present—well, present and sober—every once in a while."

"Please forgive me," Landon said.

"Oh, Lukas, I forgave you years ago. That was never the issue."

She looked at him with growing concern. "But there definitely is one now. Your skin color. You look like a Smurf. Maybe we should fix that with some calm breathing meditation. Watch me, Lukas," she directed, indicating her perfect lotus position. "Do what I'm doing."

Landon watched as Vanessa breathed in for four, held for four, then exhaled for four, and repeated. As she closed her eyes, he did too, only the sound of her breaths guiding him just as she had years before, calming him from his night terrors.

When he could no longer hear her breathing, he opened his eyes. He was once again alone.

AND NOW THAT Vanessa was gone, he remembered, there was so much more that he wanted to tell her. He wanted to explain that he'd never imagined he would be such a flimsy straw man in the wake of his first real moral tempest. That he had been studying and working to decipher exactly how to be good, years before they were even together. Prior to going to war, he had felt he was close. An obvious delusion. But he *had* tried. He had flirted with the Greek and Roman Stoics, read Seneca, Epictetus, and Marcus Aurelius, all in an attempt to discipline his emotions and dedicate himself to living a virtuous life. In the innocence of high school, he'd embraced the hopeful, individualistic, and eco-moralizing of American transcendentalists like Ralph Waldo Emerson and Henry David Thoreau.

Maybe, he now considered in the ache of lost opportunity, he shouldn't have been looking for answers on how to be a good man in just the writings of long-dead men, but also in the lives of all the good people who had always surrounded him.

He gazed into the darkness. The ocean above him. So much had happened here already before. All the ships that had passed overhead, from the poorly navigated expeditions of Columbus to the pirates who prowled its waters to the slavers that dumped their human cargo in it to the modern-day adventurers who sailed or rowed across it to those through history who, like himself, became lost on it or under it or, eventually, both. Was this the way the world hid its shame, under an angry sea?

Perhaps he was exactly where he should be. Perhaps he should never leave. He stopped himself. That was the kind of thinking, the self-pity and surrender, that had led to all those wasted years, all that inertia. More than ever, now, he needed his resolve. He hadn't made this tremendous effort just to collapse before the finish line. He needed to stretch things out until help arrived. The way to achieve that was, paradoxically, by doing less, not more; by slowing down, by being still. It was the lesson that Vanessa had been desperately trying to teach him in their time together.

He reached through his layers to pat his jeans pocket and found the little vial Emmanuel had given him, the vial he had protected and watched over like a fragile robin's egg. It might slow his breathing, extend his life, just long enough for him to be rescued. He unscrewed the cap and shook what was left of the white powder into his mouth, working hard to gather enough saliva to swallow it down. He looked at his phone: 30 percent charge. Looked at the stopwatch app: 71 hours, 25 minutes, 4 seconds. Time enough for one final video before saying good night. This would be it. He would wake up, or he wouldn't. Either way, he had a few things left he had to say. He hoped with all his heart that it was not too late to still be heard.

CHAPTER 31

XANADU

Emmanuel's powder had been sedating in pill-size taps. With a mouthful it had put Landon in a narco-doze from which he'd been surprised to ever wake. Yet even under its paralyzing influence he could not sleep through this: a sunrise of pale yellow light moving just beyond the head's open door, like the glowing light of traffic below his apartment window on a rainy night.

After his visit from Abu Abid and Vanessa, he was having trouble determining what was real. He expected CO_2-induced hallucinations as he continued to pollute his bubble with his own breath. Yet this seemed impossibly real, a vast, expanding sphere of illumination, pushing back the darkness in which he had mostly existed since the bathroom's red emergency light succumbed to the salt water one day earlier. The light, thousands of lumens at least, perforated the darkness with amoeba edges before transmuting into two distinct tubes, sweeping like Hollywood arc lamps. The metronome of their movements pulled tighter and tracked forward. The beams bent left, toward the captain's cabin, stopping at the door, unsure where to go or what to do next.

"It's locked," Landon said, as if he were coaching them on their journey. But the lights held on the door, and Landon could see it slowly give way as it was pried open. Both lights disappeared into the stateroom and quickly reemerged. Empty, Landon thought. Next they moved across the hall into the stateroom he'd shared with Junior and Chuy.

"That one's empty too," he said, turning himself on his hammock so that his feet were pushing against the back wall and his face was just inches from the lip of the waterline. After only minutes the light beams streamed out of the bunkroom and turned right again. "Told ya," he said.

But this time they were headed directly toward him. His open door was their target now, small, steady sweeps, diffused but delineated, purposeful. His pulse quickened, a small adrenaline surge; this was the outcome that he'd been awaiting. The reason he chose to stay rather than risk a desperate swim to the surface, a reckless maneuver that would've resulted with him first bent and dead or blacked out and dead, either way adrift in the darkness of the winter waves, bobbing among whitecaps until his body sank. Nothing more than feckless shark bait.

But Landon knew he had not confined himself to his bubble because he feared those sorry outcomes. He'd chosen to stay because it was his best chance to stay alive. And he extended those odds with his survival improvisations, like the hammock and his porn magazine insulation. He extended it further with his daring recon missions, which netted him the food and clothing in his duffel bag as well as the first aid supplies in the green Pelican case from the wheelhouse, which he'd wisely turned into an underwater flare—a marker buoy sent to the surface, so these guys could find him. For once, he believed, the choices he'd made were good ones. He'd thought through his physical trauma and mental anguish and not given in to the pain and the moments of despair. He had blown the conch shell loud and long from his island at the bottom of the ocean. And now, finally, here were his long-awaited rescue divers, his saviors from the world above. What was strange to him, though, was that he seemed to be watching the events unfold from two perspectives. A first-person point of view, in which he was himself, and then a dissociated one in which he was watching from across the action.

He shook these thoughts off as the lingering effects of Emmanuel's concoction and turned his attention back to his rescuers. He grinned widely. They jockeyed ahead of him, their bright yellow dive helmets reminding him of gold-speckled koi, the koi that swam in the pond his father had made for his mother a lifetime earlier. They were getting closer and closer, and eventually they would break the surface, the same way the fish did at feeding time. He'd waited so long for them. They were almost too late, maybe only minutes to spare, but still he wasn't angry with them. The love he felt for these individuals welled inside his chest, felt impossible to contain; they who had risked their own lives to make sure he was not left behind, not left alone in the dark at the bottom of the ocean to die in pitiable, heartrending, legendary isolation. His love simply grew larger, fuller and brighter, just like the lights they carried, coming slowly, cautiously, but expertly toward him.

They painted the once-magnificent *Philomena* with their light, exalted her every crack and crevice, left nothing hidden on their way to him. He was the prize, he knew, for which they had come. Obviously, since he had given them everything but a map: the balloon of life vests tied to the waterproof Pelican first aid case and jettisoned to the surface; the laconic note he'd left in the wheelhouse, the lowest part of the ship, and their first point of penetration, which pinpointed his exact location. With his black Sharpie marker, he'd written simply, "In the head. LL," on the cardboard cover from his reporter's notebook, with an arrow pointing up to the bow. That's why they'd come for him. He was sure of it. And now they would find him and bear him to the surface. Never again would these lucky divers have such a complete and unambiguous sense of purpose than in this underwater rescue.

He could wait no longer. He crawled to the outer edge of his hammock, inhaled deeply, three, two, one. He plunged his face and outstretched arms into the water, and swam toward the lights.

CHAPTER 32

A NEW WOMB

Landon had ventured out of the head three times before, and without breathing gas. Now the divers were pulling him through the passageways, floating, effortlessly. Small fish swam by his light. Pots, pans and eating utensils littered the ceiling, now the floor of the galley, as they passed through and out the hatch door. They didn't need to enter the wheelhouse as he had, but bypassed it and descended an extra ten feet to clear any possible entanglements.

Once they'd swum out of the ship and into the open water, Landon could finally see where *Philomena* had settled. She lay on the bottom of a sandy seabed, her bow propped up by the double-stacked pilothouse, her stern resting on the seafloor. For all the violence that she had endured, *Philomena* was finally at rest, anchored to the bottom of the sea like the child saint for whom she was named. He thought about the fact that this had almost been his grave too. There he would've dissolved into the salt of the seawater and into the mouths of crabs and sea urchins until he disappeared. His bones scattered on the floor of the head, turning into fine powder no different from the sandy muck on the bottom. It was something he'd probably deserved and earned, yet somehow escaped. He finally understood that there was no fate, only random chance that could change with the sputter of a diesel engine, the location of a rogue wave, and the trajectory of a mortar shell.

He remembered a soldier he'd written about for the *Herald* after one of his early deployments. One who suffered a brain injury from a roadside blast in Iraq. When he was flown back to the States, his wife and two-year-old daughter came to meet him at the veterans' hospital in San Antonio. While they clung to him like a life raft, the soldier told Landon, he just looked at them blankly, felt nothing. Like the explosion had burned away that part of his brain that allowed him to love. He hadn't forgotten them; he knew who they were—but he felt for them no more than one might in brushing past fellow shoppers at Walmart. Landon had once wished he'd suffered that kind of brain injury. At least then he would've had an excuse for living so disconnected, so aloof from others. He wasn't like the soldier, unable to feel and give love. He could, but he feared others would not be able to love him equally—a self-fulfilling prophecy. He shuddered as momentary regret swept through him, the realization of what might've been lost had he perished there below.

What about the others, though? Had they been saved too, abandoning the ship before it sank? He'd hoped so. Had he died there, so many stories might've been lost. Whole lifetimes of experiences and wisdom, disappeared. Realizing all of this now was good, but for what purpose, if it could be lost again? What if, Landon considered, instead of dying and turning to dust, we reentered a new womb at the end of our lives, a placenta that shrank and preserved our thoughts, memories, selves, stored somewhere for someone else to access. Or what if, at some appropriate time, we could be reborn, carrying what we knew forward? Learning from the past, building on it, rather than starting from scratch? That might make the whole thing worthwhile. In a world like that, he could see his place.

Landon looked over his shoulder one final time. Maybe that's exactly what had happened to him. His bubble had preserved the lessons and memories of his life, but also renewed his ability to value them. What was it that Olveda had said her mom had called it? A beautiful hole? Maybe that wasn't the warm gauze of alcohol and percs or the melancholy notes of a trumpet on a winter's morning or a pocket of air in a ship's head, or even a place at all. Maybe the beautiful hole was a stage in your life. A pupal period when you are most isolated, lonely, and vulnerable, yet finally open to others, precisely because they are absent. And in that moment you find either transcendence or death. The possibility to emerge, a shimmering orb of light, better than you were before—or not at all. Causa sui.

Now free of the ship, one of the divers signaled for Landon to let go of her harness ring, which he'd been tethered to. The two divers grasped him and gently swam upward toward their diving bell. Landon closed his eyes and felt himself ascend. As they neared the mouth of the bell, its beam of bright yellow light enveloped them all, turning their figures into silhouettes.

CHAPTER 33

WAKING MOMENT

(Globe-Democrat print and digital editions, published 12/26/18)

SPECIAL TO THE GLOBE-DEMOCRAT:
The Loss of Our Colleague
—*Rhona Kipley-Parsons, City Editor*

While reporting the series Bitter Seas on the South Carolina shrimping industry, Globe-Democrat features editor Lukas Landon was aboard the Port Royal–based shrimping trawler Philomena when it capsized and sank in 150 feet of water off Tybee Island, Georgia, during a sudden winter storm early Saturday morning.

(See additional Globe-Democrat news reports on the incident **here**. See earlier pieces in the Globe-Democrat Bitter Seas series **here**.)

Five of the seven people originally onboard Philomena escaped with their lives when ordered by Captain Clarita Esteban to abandon ship immediately after the engine stalled, but before it was capsized by a rogue wave that crashed against the ship's exposed starboard flank.

According to Captain Esteban, deckhand Jesus "Chuy" Ortiz died in a heroic attempt to save our colleague Lukas Landon, thought to be asleep belowdecks.

Emergency beacons attached to some of the survivors helped Coast Guard Search and Rescue personnel out of Charleston locate them in stormy seas late Saturday afternoon. Ortiz's body was found a short time later, less than a mile from the others.

Landon, however, was trapped below when the ship went down. Remarkably, he survived for three days in an air pocket in the bow of the ship. During that time he attempted to help searchers locate Philomena by sending up a makeshift marker buoy filled with some crew belongings and his own (earlier) proof of life.

Until the marker was found, Landon was presumed lost or dead. It wasn't until late Sunday afternoon that U.S. Navy salvage divers penetrated the wreck and discovered his body. They reported that Landon had showed creative ingenuity and fierce determination in protecting himself from hypothermia by building a platform to raise himself out of the water. A Navy spokesperson reported that there was also evidence that Landon had even swum through the bowels of the ship, scavenging food and medical supplies, using a repurposed gas mask to see underwater. Despite his mobility throughout the ship, they praised his insight and discipline for not attempting to swim to the surface after so long below, a decision that likely would've led to a painful death from decompression illness (DCI).

Ultimately, as his breathable air was reduced over time, Landon finally succumbed to hypoxia and elevated levels of carbon dioxide, according to the Charleston County coroner, with the time of death estimated only a short time before the divers found him. One interesting fact that the divers noted on their discovery of his body was its positioning: perhaps to conserve air and remain calm, Landon had assumed and ultimately expired in what yoga practitioners refer to as the lotus position.

Before that, he did, however, file one final report for us via his recovered smartphone. In a heartrending last video recording, our colleague Lukas Landon provides both footage and commentary of the challenges he faced as he fought to stay alive.

We at the Globe-Democrat debated whether to release the actual footage as opposed to just the transcript, but while it is disturbing to watch, we believe it is valuable and instructive, a study in grace as Lukas Landon came to terms with the end of his life and the lessons he was able to distill from it in those, his final hours.

We're providing both the actual video recording **(link for print edition)** as well as its transcription here.

Sixth and final story in a Globe-Democrat series on South Carolina's beleaguered commercial shrimping industry.
(Globe-Democrat print and digital editions, published 12/26/18.)

BITTER SEAS
Waking Moment
—Lukas Landon

[*Looking into his smartphone.*] It looks like this is about to go. Not sure how long I got, maybe another five minutes—but it lasted a lot longer than I thought. [*Smiles, scoots back on his homemade platform above the water.*] I lasted longer than I thought too, but I can tell my little bubble here is just about out of oxygen. Don't feel sorry for me. It's not altogether unpleasant. The CO_2 kind of gives you the giggles.

The situation is obviously not great, but it still beats drowning. What will likely happen is that I'll just get more and more sleepy, probably nod off. Then I'm going to just lie down in my hammock and pass out. Normally, I wouldn't be this calm, but my friend Emmanuel Etienne gave me a powder when I was having trouble sleeping because of the stormy seas. A little goes a long way, but I figured when I was running out of air I might as well take what was left. Better to sleep through this than wake up gasping, right? [*Nervous laugh.*]

Anyway, I guess this is my final report. Don't want to be all morbid or anything, but I have had some time to think down here, and I've realized, with the help of some friends, that I've had a lot of regrets in my life, and it's time to acknowledge them and let them go. Whether we know it or not, we are in each other's care, indebted to each other for our happiness and survival. It's not something we can do alone. That's a pretty big realization for someone who's spent his life keeping people at arm's distance. But I had the perfect disguise.

As a reporter, people just assume you're an extrovert, happiest within the crowd. In my case, that couldn't be more untrue. But I was deeply curious about people, because maybe I found myself so lacking in every way. So, what could I offer them?

I could tell their stories. At first it seems like an imposition, that people are giving you a gift by sharing things with you, but quickly you realize that they also need you and want you to listen to them. Not just their heroics but their shame as well, because even in that, people have a little hidden, guilty pride. They want to tell their story and for you to listen because it gives them a tiny sense of security that maybe, just maybe, they won't die in complete obscurity. That the record won't be fully erased where they're concerned. That there was, in between all the mistakes and selfishness, indolence, lies and violence, something of value, fleeting or unflattering as it might be.

That's something I should've applied to my own life too, and that I need to correct now. I sent my laptop to the surface along with some other things. Tell you about those in a second, but first—I put them all in the waterproof hard case that held the first aid supplies on the ship. If it's found and survives, on my laptop there's a folder named "Iraq 2003–04" and a file titled "Abu Abid." It is as much a wound as a story, and it has lain festering in my heart for more than a dozen years. It finally needs to be told. I hope this will help to explain, at least in part, my retreat in the past few years from those who once mattered most to me. But being down here forced me to look at all the facets of my life more deeply, not just the endless feedback of self-hatred for my terrible mistakes. The truth, as I've come to understand it now, is that I wasn't a phantom in my own life. My actions, questions, curiosity, shyness, existence, impacted others more than I knew. [*Looks down at the smartphone, shakes his head.*] It's red now.

Jesus—always a deadline. Need to speed this up. I was aboard Philomena just five days, and everyone was able to see who I really was, wouldn't let me disappear into their stories. And when they shared their stories, it wasn't transactional. There was nothing desperate. They were actually giving me a gift, and they knew it. Captain Esteban had been through much worse than me in war and in civilian life, never got a fair shake as a Black woman in the army or on the sea. But the story she told me was not one of the long and bitter taste of injustice, bigotry, and violence, but of refusal to be defined by it. By changing the landscape, finding new path-ways, scrapping hard and honest and building a life where others follow you because they want to have what you have inside of you. She is tough in a way I never was. Pushed her crew and protected them with the same fierceness. [*Shakes his head.*] Called me out too, held me accountable when I hadn't even done that myself. Captain Esteban, if you do recover my care package, you'll find inside your M-65 field jacket, which Olveda informed me was once your father's from his time in Vietnam. That jacket made you look like more of a badass than seems humanly possible. There's also something you left in the pocket.

From Lorenzo I learned that even if you only love once, the pain of that loss is worth it every day because you have known love, and that ember never burns out completely. It's always there smoldering, threatening to catch fire, the possibility of passion goading you forward rather than its absence hollowing you out. He also showed me that when someone helps you over the wall, you repay that debt not by climbing the next one, but reaching back over the one you just cleared. Lorenzo, I tried to dry out your Santa Philomena holy card that had been taped to the wall in the wheelhouse. I know that neither of us has much religion anymore, but some things contain power from what they symbolize and the places they've been. This has both. That's why I've sent it back to you. I hope it will adorn the next ship lucky enough to have you as a leader.

In Emmanuel I began to understand that the serenity of your own mind is beautiful company, that loneliness is not a disease or an affliction but a heightened state of openness, both to yourself and others. And in that openness, you can often be the first to see and heal the pain of others. Emmanuel, I found your vest with my face when I swam into it. But while I didn't think you'd need that back, I know you want the black book I found inside it. It's a good thing you memorized it, because it is soaked through and probably unreadable now. Maybe you can fill it back in once it dries, because the knowledge that was once inside needs to be passed forward somehow. I think your grandma would agree.

Olveda showed me that when dreams are destroyed, there is more than just loss, but opportunity to be your most graceful and creative self. Ollie. Don't know how you lost your mom's dog tag, but I found it floating in the wheelhouse. I was at a very desperate point in my journey down here, and I remembered you saying it gave you strength when you needed it; it did the same for me. I put it in the kit for you, but fact is, I don't think you need it anymore. All that strength was already inside you. Couldn't write the way you do if it wasn't.

Junior [*laughs*] . . . Junior showed me that hurt does not have to transform itself into hate, that absorbing the pain and venting it off with private little vices and wondrous moments of small creation is almost like shielding someone from the blow of an abuser, dissipating their violence with your own body until they are spent and harmless. Junior, you'll find your whittling bag and your dad's old pocketknife inside the case. I have to tell you, finding that and a few other items of your stash probably saved my life, so thank you. When I used your knife down here, I began to think that you must have an artist's soul, because they often take the bad stuff in their lives and use it to make beautiful things.

Finally, Chuy showed me—and maybe I showed him—that we are

not ugly, dissolute creatures, deserving the hatred of others, but are worthy of love, respect, and the right to share the air of humanity, and despite our imperfections, can transcend our worst mistakes. Chuy, brother [*laughs again*], I couldn't find anything of yours down here—so I sent you something of mine. Something I lost in the storm. My two front teeth. I won't bore you with the long and ignoble story how it happened, but it was dramatic and involved the rim of a toilet. I was thinking you could make a necklace with them the way they do with old shark's teeth, and when people ask, tell them they're from a reporter you caught near Port Royal, an ugly old bastard, but still with a little fight left in him.

All those things [*shakes his head*], they were hard to give up because they reminded me of all of you. But they also reminded you of someone else in your life. And for that, they had to be returned, since, as I've discovered down here, those connections are priceless, and we never forgive ourselves when we squander them.

So that's what I learned, a lifetime of lessons in a handful of people. Often we're so anxious, so restless asking over and over again what is in store for me? What is my life supposed to mean? [*Pauses, takes a deep breath.*] I've often wondered: If people knew the story of their lives in advance, how many would elect to live them? We are all collateral damage; victims of the unintended consequences of our own decisions. We all suffer desperately and in our own way. But we shouldn't let our own suffering make others suffer more. [*Pauses, thinks for a moment.*] Maybe our suffering should motivate us to make others suffer less. [*Nods.*] Yeah.

[*Closes eyes, fatigued.*] I think I'm out of words here—and time. Getting tired. But I know I had one last thought—well, not really my thought, but an important one anyway. [*Reaches into his bag and pulls out a leather-bound book inside.*] I know this isn't something you'd normally bring to sea for a few days. [*Holds up the title in front of the camera, embossed in gold leafing: "Walden."*] My father, Tobias, gave me this book on my fifteenth birthday.

I took it with me the first time I went to war, and when I came home alive, I figured it was a good-luck charm. It's gone pretty much everywhere with me since. Including here onboard Philomena. There's so much in here—I mean, some self-righteous, navel-gazing crap, but also some bull's-eyes.

Stuff that makes it all worthwhile, especially when Thoreau is trying to make meaning of his self-imposed self-isolation. The living deliberately thing. There's this one line at the end [*opens the book, flips to the back*]. I've highlighted, underlined, and starred it because, well, it spoke to me. [*Laughs.*] I know I have had an unhealthy reliance on the spiritual guidance of long-dead white men, but this seemed good, like this was the key I had been looking for my entire life. And it made me want to do exactly what he was saying. But I never really did. Until now.

[*Reads:*] "I desire to speak somewhere without bounds; like a man in a waking moment, to men in their waking moments."

Full fathom five thy father lies:

Of his bones are coral made:

Those are pearls that were his eyes:

Nothing of him that doth fade

But doth suffer a sea-change

Into something rich and strange.

—WILLIAM SHAKESPEARE, *THE TEMPEST*

Acknowledgments

From the point of inception to publication, the story of *The Ocean Above Me* took five years, hundreds of hours of research, thousands of hours of writing, and dozens of drafts shaped with the thoughtful guidance and encouragement of a handful of dear and trusted readers.

These include my patient wife, Anita Sites; my brilliant "bonus" daughter, Cameron Paul; and my sisters, Kathleen Dempsey and Shawn Sites.

At a pivotal point in the evolution of the manuscript, I turned it over to my longtime friend Richard Murphy, novelist and screenwriter, who coached me through a significant rewrite and then generously shared the work with his own professional contacts.

This landed it on the desk of agent Michael Signorelli of Aevitas Creative Management, who had coincidentally worked as an editor on my second nonfiction book, *The Things They Cannot Say*, at Harper Perennial, and agreed to represent me.

Michael connected me to talented story editor Celia Johnson, whose insightful notes helped to reshape the work into a more cohesive narrative, at which point it was shared with Harper Perennial associate publisher Amy Baker, the editor of all three of my nonfiction works. Amy's faith in me and the material gave the novel its final home, back under the Harper umbrella.

There rising star and literary wunderkind David Howe gently guided me through rounds of major and minor revisions that transformed the novel into what you see today, a work of which I am individually proud, but also enormously grateful to the very many who were so kind and gracious toward my fiction debut effort.

To thank Miranda Ottewell for simply copyediting the work of this first-time novelist would be a gross underestimation of the thorough service she provided here. With her remarkable breadth and depth of knowledge, she found and corrected not only my errors in language and usage, but also of fact and intention, providing essential clarity in places it was desperately needed.

Thanks are also due to James Hynes and James Scott Bell, whose publications I carefully studied in the efforts to understand and make my transition from nonfiction to fiction. I'm also grateful for the many news articles, studies, and technical manuals (too numerous to cite individually) that helped to buffer my understanding of fishing trawlers, the shrimping industry and those who work in it, and the physics and physiology of diving and decompression. In that arena, Joma Dix, a friend, diving professional, and founder of Project Laut, an ocean conservation organization, provided key insights that helped to shape and provide authenticity to Landon's experience underwater. Additionally, Joma and his multitalented partner, Sita Angela Jaekel, are responsible for the novel's dramatic cover image, which they captured during stormy conditions off the island of Nusa Penida, Indonesia—Joma as model and Sita as photographer.

Special thanks to Kimmie Jackson, Sonya Springer, and her DC-area book club, who helped me to understand and more accurately reflect the cultural and racial dynamics depicted in the novel. Sydnee Thompson gave a near final read to the manuscript, guiding my efforts to ensure that the characters here reflected with accuracy and nuance the way language, institutions, and history would've shaped them.

There are many anecdotes in this novel that refer to the wars in Iraq and Afghanistan. All are fully fictional, but some are inspired, at least in part, by my own journalistic reporting experiences or those of colleagues. I'd like to specifically credit my longtime friend and colleague Levon Sevunts, whose eyewitness account of the deaths of three journalists (Joanne Sutton, Pierre Billaud, and Volker Handloik) in Afghanistan in 2001 helped provide realistic detail and emotional veracity to the depiction of correspondents in war.

And finally I would like to acknowledge the sources of this story's overall inspiration, whose strength of character, innovation, improvisation, and resilience speak to us in that darkest moment when there is little to recommend fighting on, and only the tiny flame of purpose convinces us to do so.

These include capsized tugboat survivor Harrison Okene; Wild Boars football coach Ekkapol Chantawong, and the rest of the young team members and their rescuers; commercial saturation diver Chris Lemons, whose remarkable story was depicted in the documentary *Last Breath*; and Holocaust survivor, author, and psychiatrist Victor Frankl, whose experience and identification of our "will to meaning" is truly our last best hope in the vacuum of despair.

About the Author

KEVIN SITES is an award-winning journalist and author. He has worked as a reporter for more than thirty years, half of that covering war and disaster for ABC, NBC, CNN, Yahoo News, and Vice News. He was a 2010 Nieman Journalism Fellow at Harvard University and a 2012 Dart Fellow in Journalism and Trauma at Columbia University. For a decade he lived and taught in Hong Kong as an associate professor of practice in journalism at the University of Hong Kong. He's the author of three books on war, *In the Hot Zone*, *The Things They Cannot Say*, and *Swimming with Warlords*. He lives in Oregon.

READ MORE BY KEVIN SITES

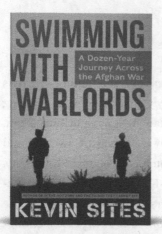

SWIMMING WITH WARLORDS

"Kevin Sites is one of our national treasures—a fearless correspondent who has devoted himself to documenting not just the facts of war, but also its deepest emotional textures." —Hampton Sides, *New York Times* bestselling author of *Ghost Soldiers* and *In the Kingdom of Ice*

THE THINGS THEY CANNOT SAY

"The harrowing accounts detail the experiences of 11 US soldiers and Marines who have been ravaged by modern warfare and its psychological aftermath. What makes Kevin's reporting unique and essential is that it didn't stop on the battlefield—he followed his subjects home." — *Vice*

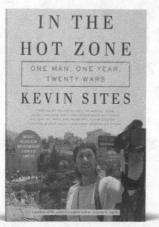

IN THE HOT ZONE

"These images and dispatches form the numberless rooms of hell have an undeniable cumulative power." —*Kirkus Reviews*